lawhoma hills

A YEAR BEHIND THE PINK DOOR

ELLIS MCHALE

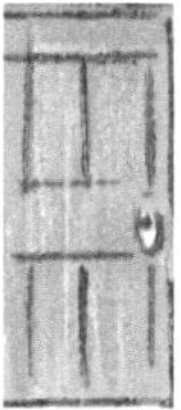

Cover Design: Get Covers

Illustration layout: P. Michener Graphics

Published by Pink Door Publishing

Printed in the United States of America

Paperback ISBN (Black & White Edition): 979-8-9948740-0-4

Hardback ISBN (Full Color Edition): 979-8-9948740-1-1

 Formatted with Vellum

For my chairman and goat roper, I love you to the Milky Way—and to their Momma, my tiny dancer and Gran's toad; YMP. Here is to all the days of running amuck together.

contents

N

Nature Cent.

BIRCH CREEK Sports

HILL H.

BIRCH →

Power & Light

KSW7

MoVA

CHESTNUT →

Law...

W

TOWN

Sweetshires   CAFE   Florist   Corner Birds   Rep Petals

SYCAMORE →

BLUE CREEK LAKE

Foxgloves

PINE →

Chicken Turtle

Boat Stop Jetty

163 ACRES

Clam

Prairie Dogs

Cinnamon

SW County RD 40

S

assistant living

Hospital

AIR PRORT

← **OAK**

Lanes restaurant

BARBER

Post Office

← MAPLE

Sidewalks

Frank Rights

Northeast Central

Theater

Wirder

E

CONCERT STAGE
XXXXXXX

FARMERS Market
XXXXXXX

← PECAN

Rockfall

landscape

Construction

School

Bus Barn

← WILLOW

employees

SE CTY RD 40

RANGER STATION

GOATS

FEED

PRESTON MAIN

PARKS

CAMP RUN AMUCK

Branded Adeline Branch

the practice of noticing

Lawhoma Hills saved my life.

Maybe it was my Annie, or her boys. Lawhoma is them. Lawhoma is more.

The summer Annie carried those babies, two gulf fritillary butterflies settled in my garden and held their ground through the heat. Bright, copper wings opening and closing in the zinnia bloom-heads, they waited each morning when I stepped onto the grass with my coffee sweating in the cup. I spoke to them the way I spoke to the boys, low and steady, about names we kept rolling around in our mouths, about vines pulling tight against the trellis, about the soreness lodged deep in my hips and back. The butterflies lifted, circled once, and settled again. They did not leave.

In March, the month the redbuds split open and the wind ran wild down the valley, those boys arrived. Shortly after, we lost Big Granny, and the order of things shifted. It did not crack in half. It tilted. I felt it in my knees when I climbed the porch steps, in my hands when I washed bottles at the sink. The stories I had scribbled for years in spiral notebooks began tapping my shoulder while I folded laundry, while I stood at the stove stirring beans. They pressed close. They wanted out, the way real stories push out, muddy, loud, unfinished, showing up with a fiddle scraping in the background and animals talking over one another.

I live in a small Oklahoma valley where the land clears its throat and expects an answer. Spring comes in green and restless, pushing up through fence lines and flowerbeds. Summer lays its weight on your shoulders and watches what you do with it. Autumn eases the light back a notch and sets smoke in the air from burn piles out past the creek. Winter pulls folks toward one another; you see it in the way neighbors linger at the mailbox, in the way soup travels house to house in mismatched bowls.

My house sits near the edge of town, easy to find by the pink door. The paint has chipped near the bottom where boots catch it. Animals pass through often. Some rap their knuckles polite on the frame. Some swing the door wide with their hip and step in calling my name. Most carry feelings folded tight in their pockets. They set them down on my kitchen table between the salt shaker and the stack of mail.

Life here refuses straight lines. It cuts across fields, doubles back toward the lake, loops around old grudges and new babies. Families stay loud and tangled. A little strangeness earns you a chair at the table. Paying attention earns you another cup of coffee.

You might feel your step falter now and again on our gravel roads. Stay anyway. Laughter rises quick here. Music drifts from open windows. Lessons show up in the middle of a fishing trip or while sweeping the porch, and nobody hands you a test afterward. We lose track of time. We find it again at supper.

If you are reading this, step through. The pink door stands open. Wipe your feet on the mat. Notice what follows you inside.

PART ONE

spring

spring journal: bent but determined

I used to think spring asked for hope. Now it asks for a steady hand.

The first iris pushed up along the fence line, bent near double, green blade cutting through clay still hard from winter. It held there three days before the sun warmed the ground enough to loosen it. By week's end others rose beside it, thin and stubborn, and the valley took notice. Windows lifted on their tracks. Screen doors slapped wood against wood. Pollen settled on porch rails and truck hoods in a fine yellow film.

In spring I lie in bed longer than I mean to, listening to the house come to life before I swing my feet to the floor. The heat clicks on, then off. A pickup barrels down the road faster than good sense allows. Sleep leaves in its own time. When I stand, the day has already arranged a few matters without consulting me. Light presses through the curtains. The coffee pot waits empty on the counter.

Across the valley, families keep their practiced

rhythm. School mornings hold firm. Backpacks thud against the wall by the door. Calendars crowd with pencil marks, rubbed out and written over. A quiet counting hums under everything. Days narrow. The end of term sits close enough to taste. Folks keep moving, stirring pots, signing forms, tying shoes, because stillness invites too much thinking.

Oklahoma weather rewards attention. Morning opens wide and soft. By afternoon the air tightens its jaw. You see it in the way neighbors glance up from their yards toward the west. Blankets get folded and stacked on the arm of the couch, not carried to the closet. The weather report runs longer than supper requires. Radar maps glow blue and red in darkened living rooms.

On Spruce Street, a notice went up crooked on the board outside the bookstore. Thumbtack bent at the corner. No one planted their feet in front of it, yet each passerby slowed. One hand reached out and pressed the paper flat. Another pair of eyes moved across the lines twice, then drifted toward the street as if the words might step off the page.

Nothing has happened.

Still, the season leans forward. We lean with it. We watch what rises from the ground and what slips onto bulletin boards. We give thanks for irises pushing through clay, for doors left open a crack.

A scratch at the back door. Beans, again, asking out, nails ticking against the hardwood.

No-Skip Albums for Spring.

Tracy Chapman — Tracy Chapman
Bon Jovi — Slippery When Wet
Taylor Swift — Folklore

THE CHICKS — FLY
THE STORY— BRANDI CARLILE
TYLER CHILDERS — BOTTLES AND BIBLES

5

when the market wakes up

SPRING ENTERS LAWHOMA HILLS QUIET, stepping onto the porch before anyone reaches for the knob, leaning close enough to murmur something meant for those already inside. Spring draws a long breath; the farmers market lets one out, slow at first, then sudden and full.

I came down the steps with tulips and daffodils tucked beneath one arm, a basket of lettuce and radishes dragging the other low. A worker bee moved through the sweet peas, legs thick with yellow dust, flying a straight line toward work already claimed.

"Morning, pretty girl," I told her. "Mighty glad to see you earning your keep. Some of us fixing to catch up."

My old truck roared awake. Windows down. Carly Simon slid out of the radio smooth and steady, settled in the cab as though she had paid rent there for years. Wind tugged my ponytail with purpose. Hope rose up beside nerves and gratitude and a thin ribbon of worry, all of it crowding the same small space, which is how a Saturday worth remembering tends to begin.

The road kept me company. Trees leaned toward the ditch. Fence posts held their line. Indian paintbrush flared red along the shoulder, announcing the day whether we stood ready or not.

I tapped the horn once and lifted a big wave. The valley answered in fragments. Casey Jo shouted something about the wind stealing hats. Larry laughed at a joke still forming in his own head. A shop door banged open. Stevie traced slow circles on her bike tire. Music drifted from the Everett place, and Wilder Kate tuned her guitar, warming the morning before it asked.

The twins tore down their walk as I eased past, all knees and elbows, speed outrunning sense the way it does at twelve.

"You get the booth sign?" I called.

"We got it," Jasper said, holding his end high.

Hank yanked back. "It's my side."

"There is no my side."

They stared as though I had outlawed breathing.

They climbed in still arguing over the cash box, certain dollars sit straighter in chosen hands. Our money rides in a cigar box with a stubborn latch and a habit of staying shut. That earns my trust.

WHEN WE TURNED into the market lot, the day opened wide. Tents stood half raised. Ropes pulled tight. Hootie wrestled a canopy leg that refused to mind him. Beeswax caught the early light. Mason jars clinked into tidy rows. Kettle corn announced itself without apology. Ozzy tilted his sign left, then right, then back again, chasing a balance only he recognized.

Near the honey jars stood a new booth, white cloth pulled crisp, sharp heels pressing into grass not used to them. Two women smiled and passed out buttons and glossy cards stamped Aperture Developments, LLC. The regulars traded looks. No one had spoken their names ahead of time. I marked it in my mind to ask Ross later. Nobody sets up at our market without someone saying who they are.

We took our place three rows down from the popcorn, close enough to smell sugar, far enough to behave. I snapped my faded gingham cloth once, sharp. Flowers first, because they greet. Greens and roots next, because they hold steady.

A gust cut through as I slid the buckets into line. One tipped toward the edge.

Wyatt Chapman cartwheeled past and caught it mid fall without missing rhythm. Reed met my eye, nodded once, and kept moving.

"Thank you, baby."

"Was not even thinking," she said, grinning.

"That right there concerns me," I answered, and her laugh rang loose across the aisle.

Butter and Sasha clipped their tablecloth down with wooden pins carved by hand. Tally barked a laugh when the wind tried lifting her bread tray. Stewart chased flyers skittering across the gravel lot.

Jasper lunged after one, arms wide, full rodeo clown. Hank followed close behind, unwilling to concede even paper to his brother.

Jasper returned with the flyer crushed in his fist. "What's this?"

I read the heading without blinking. County notice. Planning meeting. Harmless words until they gather weight.

"Something grown folks adore," I said, folding it smaller. "Meetings about meetings."

BY NOON THE LOT HUMMED. Hats swapped heads. Faces leaned together for photographs. The STEM club selfie booth stayed crowded, children stretching their mouths into shapes they would deny by supper. I tried one myself. Jasper caught me.

"Yaya, you cannot."

Hank groaned.

"Hush. This face belongs to me."

"There are age rules," Jasper insisted.

"There ought to be. I plan to break them."

They pointed at me, laughing hard enough to bend at the waist. When grandbabies laugh at you, you stand on solid ground.

Sound check shifted the air. Chairs scraped open. Folks settled where they landed. Wilder Kate stepped onto the small wooden stage, sun striking her fur while she adjusted the mic. The first song drifted gentle. By the second, feet moved of their own accord.

People bought. Lingered. Sang under their breath. Clapped when rhythm found their palms. Beneath it all another current ran.

Not music.

Conversations stopped mid sentence. Numbers surfaced twice in the same breath. Rosemary lowered her voice when those high heels clicked past. Fragments reached my ear without effort. A company looking west. Land near Blue Creek Lake. A baby shower. The weather turning.

No one named the thing whole. We kept arranging produce. Folding extra bags. Holding spots in line. Making space.

The air pressed low, unsettled.

AT PACK UP, Ranger and Carly folded my tables with practiced ease.

"You hear anything?" Carly asked, light in tone.

"I heard talk. Talk differs from truth."

Ranger glanced toward the road. "Folks speak before they act."

"They do."

While we loaded the truck, memory rose without warning. Another spring. A young armadillo boy tugging my sleeve, offering a red apple from his family orchard, telling me it matched his little brother's favorite hat.

I took it and thanked him. Felt its weight long after sunset, heavy for a piece of fruit, heavier for what it meant.

The last crate slid into place. Engines turned over. Hands lifted in farewell.

I dropped the boys at home and drove on with the windows down, market fading in the mirror, a suitcase of worry riding silent in the back seat. I reached over and buckled it in. Some things require strapping down before they travel home with you.

SATURDAY, APRIL 12
MY PEN FEELS TIRED TONIGHT. MIGHT BE ME.
WE FACETIMED PAPA J ON THE WAY TO THE MARKET. HE LIKES SEEING THE BOYS WHILE THE MORNING STILL BELONGS TO THEM. HANK AND JASPER WERE ALREADY ARGUING OVER THE BOOTH SIGN, EACH CERTAIN THE OTHER HAD MISSED SOMETHING IMPORTANT.

Papa J leaned close to the screen. "Y'all behave."

"Yes, sir," they chirped quick, meaning it for about three seconds.

"And if either one of you loses Yaya's cash box," he added, "you're coming to live with me and eating fried bologna."

I believe him.

I called him afterward about the $78 we made. His pride traveled clean through the speakers, straight out of that West Texas drawl that knows where to land.

"Don't you go acting different."

I ate saltines with butter at the sink and called Annie to ask if she still had any of those high heels. My toes crinkled in my flip flops, already started practicing the pain.

I drew a small red apple in the corner of the page. I did not plan to. It steadied me.

Beans slept on the rug while I soaked. Steam climbed the walls. Music stayed long enough to loosen what had tightened.

Big Granny arrived the way she does. Give it to God and go to bed.

I heard her.

Tonight's listen
"Past Life" - Maggie Rogers

To Do:
call Lolli and Pop Weds to make sure they are ready for Thursday

TWO

run amuck rules

"GRAB HOLD," Arthur called over his shoulder. "No tumbling till we stop."

Wyatt hung upside down in the aisle before the sentence finished. Juan Carlos held up a fruit snack in the name of peace.

The bus carried more bodies than it deserved. Knees overlapped. Wings pressed the windows. A steady beat thudded against the glass. Laughter burst out in pockets. Trip shouted, "I'm first!" though nothing waited to be won. Avery swore she would not touch creek water and three voices rose at once, "Yes you are." Feelings ran loose. No child on that bus tried to rein them in.

When the hand painted Camp Run Amuck sign broke through the dust, noise shook the frame.

Gravel crunched under the tires. The bus rocked to a stop. Lolli turned her head toward me and gave that look, the one she wears before she names the weight she carries.

"Those signs in town," she said, tone plain.

Pop kept his grin steady, though his eyes moved quick. "We do not know what they mean yet."

"We will, then we answer how we always do."

"Not today," Lolli replied. "Today belongs to creek mud and children acting brand new."

Pop tapped the bus side, soft. "Kids first. Grown worry later."

The doors folded open and the children spilled out in a rush of tails, feathers, fur, and sneakers. RJ barked at the surge. Beans whined, front paws dancing at the edge of gravel.

I wiped my palms on my jeans and stepped forward. "Welcome to Camp Run Amuck."

They settled enough to hear.

"Today you get a preview of summer."

"Goats again?" Sasha whisper yelled, already braced.

"Yes," Jasper hollered, face lit up at the thought.

I shook my head. "Different this year."

Pop drummed his hands on the picnic table. I pulled the canvas from the sign.

HOW WE TAKE CARE OF OUR WORLD

A hush fell, the strong kind. Jessi sneezed so hard a sparrow shot from the rafters, and laughter cracked the quiet wide open. Around here, affection arrives tangled with noise.

I crouched and scooped a handful of soil, let it sift through my fingers.

"This is where we start."

Ruby lifted her paw. "Getting dirty?" she asked. "We play in dirt to take care of the world?"

"That belongs in it," I said.

Juan Carlos raised his lunch sack. "Fixing stuff?" "My abuela says throwing things away does not help."

Micah lifted both hands, eyes steady. Caitlyn nodded once. "Listening."

"Yes," I told them. "Listening most of all. Mini camps run this summer with the Oklahoma Department of Wildlife Conservation. We learn together."

Pop leaned toward Lolli. "I listen best when someone mentions pie."

She smacked his arm without glancing over.

The children laughed, the kind that loosens shoulders and makes space for trying.

.   .   .

WE WALKED toward the creek in a loose line. Dust curled around ankles. Wind moved through leaves with a low rub, sound of hands warming up.

At the bank, Bet Sinclair knelt and skimmed the surface.

"Some animals stay when things shift. They remain and trust the water to hold."

"Snakes and fish?" Boone asked.

"Yes. Many," Matty answered. "Even insects small enough to miss unless you slow down."

Several children leaned closer. A few stepped back. Whip pointed at a flicker in the shallows. "Baby snake?"

"Do not start," Ellie muttered. I let the spark die on its own.

"This summer," I told them, "you learn to notice. You care without taking over."

Hank narrowed his eyes. "So we do not grab what animals need."

"Right."

"And we teach others?" Sasha asked.

She had it.

"We practice, we pay attention. We ask before we reach. We mend what sits broken. We leave ground better than we met it."

The creek answered low and steady against the stones.

No cheering followed. Still, something moved through them. Hands lifted. Wings adjusted. Dust settled.

WHEN THE BUS pulled away that afternoon, shoes wore thick mud. Voices rasped. Each child carried something unseen.

I shut the camp door and stood in the quiet. Tents waited stacked. Check in lists lay half written on the table. Summer worked its way here fast.

THURSDAY, APRIL 17
GOODNESS GRACIOUS, AM I TIRED TONIGHT.
CAMP DUST IS STILL IN MY HAIR. CREEK MUD ON MY SHOES. RJ

STRETCHED ACROSS THE PILLOWS AT THE TOP OF THE BED, FULL LANDLORD ENERGY. BEANS HAD ALREADY TUNNELED UNDER THE COVERS AND GONE OUT COLD, TIRED AS IF HE PUNCHED A TIME CLOCK AND MEANT IT.

I ATE A SPOONFUL OF PEANUT BUTTER STRAIGHT FROM THE JAR WHILE THE SHOWER HEATED AND CALLED IT FUEL. TOMORROW WILL BE CINNAMON ROLLS AND REGRET IF I DON'T GET MYSELF TOGETHER.

ANNIE AND THE BOYS CALLED TO SAY GOODNIGHT. WE HUNG UP WITH ONE MORE "I LOVE YOU," SAME AS ALWAYS, JUST TO MAKE SURE THE DAY LANDED WHERE IT SHOULD.

I STEPPED IN THE SHOWER AND LET THE MUSIC PLAY WHILE THE STEAM CLIMBED THE WALLS AND THE HOUSE SETTLED INTO ITSELF.

TONIGHT'S LISTEN
"VAGABOND" - CAAMP
TO DO:
CALL ANNIE ABOUT SATURDAY LOGISTICS
CHECK THE PANTRY FOR CINNAMON ROLL SUPPLIES
ALARM SET FOR 4:30 A.M.
FRIDAY MARKET, PICK WHATEVER'S BLOOMING

cross country coyotes

BY THE TIME race season reaches us, Birch Creek smells of damp leaves and grass pressed flat under too many shoes. Spring sports drag the whole valley out of bed early and keep us past sense. Blankets fly into truck beds. Coolers ride up front. Everybody arrives carrying something, even when it is only a paper cup of lemonade and a tight hope lodged under the ribs.

I parked beneath a stand of scrub oaks while the runners warmed along the field, shadows stretching thin, then folding back in. Edie Claire bent to tie her shoe, untied it, tied it again. Frankie traced a short loop, breath sliding in and out through her nose, calm and deliberate. Joey stretched, sprang up, stretched again. JJ bounced in place, spending fuel she would wish for later.

The Flanagan sisters gathered close without matching one another. Four coyote girls sharing one name, each holding her own strain of grit. One steady in the jaw. One wound tight. One narrowed in focus. One grinning, ready to outrun her own stride.

Tucker Brewster warmed near the tree line, long bear boy limbs folding and unfolding with care. He rolled his shoulders once and then grew still. A quiet settled over him, the kind that comes when direction sits firm inside the chest and needs no witness.

. . .

PETE HILL STOOD at the start, cap tucked beneath his arm, wings twitching while he tested the wind. Dr. Bridget checked the first aid table, hands steady, turtle calm. Foster hovered close enough to lift a cooler or hold a towel without being summoned. Dahlia walked the edge of the course, deer eyes scanning roots, loose stones, low branches waiting to catch a careless foot.

"Runners to the line," Pete called.

Chatter thinned. Breath sharpened.

A bike bell chimed. A banner lifted and sagged in the same motion. Cheers rose ahead of their time.

A mother's voice cut through. "Run smart, not mad." A few runners laughed, filing the words where they would matter.

The whistle split the air.

They launched together, shoes striking dirt in a rush before the pack stretched long. A ribbon pulled thin. Dust lifted behind them and lingered.

Midway stood the hill everyone named and pretended to dismiss. It rose plain and unyielding.

Edie Claire climbed steady, refusing to chase anyone else's pace. Joey powered upward with a shout that startled two field sparrows into flight. JJ gave a quick yip and laughed in the middle of the climb, then leaned forward and drove her legs, joke carrying her higher. Tucker followed, face set, breath even, mounting the slope the way some folks meet hard work, without spectacle.

When they crested and curved back toward us, the crowd split wide. Names flew across the field. Whistles shrilled. Wings lifted. Mayflies scattered as the runners traced the creek's bend.

They crossed flushed and grinning, lungs heaving, pride plain on their faces. Families surged. Water bottles passed hand to hand. Tucker laughed too hard, swiped dirt from his knee, waved off concern.

NO ONE HURRIED HOME. Blankets spread beneath the oaks. Sandwiches unwrapped. Orange slices emerged from plastic bags, bright against the grass. Whoever remembers orange slices each year earns a ribbon of her own.

The afternoon stretched loose and warm.

I sat with Annie and the boys, creek flashing silver between leaves. A little way off, Rosemary Rodriguez stood apart, phone pressed to her ear, shoulder turned from the crowd. Guarded.

"…confirmed it."

"…northeast corner."

"…do not put it in writing yet."

She stilled, nodded once, slid the phone into her pocket, eyes on the ground where the grass thinned near the bank.

The creek kept moving. Children chased one another along the edge. Laughter snapped through the trees.

I stayed seated longer than needed.

My hand closed around my water bottle. I twisted the cap tight until it squeaked, then eased it back, trying to quiet the sound it made.

SATURDAY, APRIL 19
THE MIRROR CAUGHT ME RUBBING NIVEA INTO MY FACE, FINGERS FOLLOWING LINES THAT ALREADY KNOW WHERE A SMILE GOES.
DIRT CLUNG TO THE CUFFS OF MY JEANS. MY LEGS ACHED IN THAT EARNED WAY I DON'T ARGUE WITH.
DINNER WARMED WHILE TRACY CHAPMAN PLAYED LOW IN THE KITCHEN. THE DOGS SETTLED AT MY FEET—HOPEFUL, PATIENT. I LIFTED THE LID ON THE POT AND LET THE STEAM ROLL UP INTO MY FACE. TOOK IT AS A BLESSING. SAT DOWN.
I WROTE ONE LINE AND STOPPED.
STAY THE COURSE.
I LEFT THE NOTEBOOK OPEN ON THE TABLE AND STARTED SORTING MY LAUNDRY WITHOUT MEANING TO.

TONIGHT'S LISTEN:
"SHE'S GOT HER TICKET" – TRACY CHAPMAN

To Do:

Tue - Call ODWC to confirm camp dates
Wed - Text Larry re: Papa Max at shop on 26th
Let Ross know you're doing Thurs/Fri market — harvest
+ finish paintings to sell

FOUR

*haircuts and
headlines*

LAWHOMA HILLS CARRIES certain sounds that tell you summer is leaning close. Cicadas grinding at dusk. Screen doors snapping against their frames. Wet flip flops slapping porch steps.

Still, nothing marks the turn the way the steady hum drifting out of Larry's Cuts does.

Larry Brewster has trimmed this town longer than my tomatoes have climbed their stakes. His shop sits on Maple Bend, windows thrown open so warm air slides through, mixing aftershave with the mint Casey Jo keeps grows out back.

THE BELL JINGLED when I stepped inside, balancing a pan of cinnamon rolls and a tub of snap peas for Papa Max's birthday.

Papa Max glanced up from his paper before I cleared the threshold. "Well, there she is."

I leaned in and he hugged me quick, careful of the pan.

"You brought cinnamon rolls."

"For your birthday."

He nodded once, satisfied.

The shop already brimmed with bodies. Eli Everett reclined in the chair, surrender finally winning after he had dodged a haircut since

March. Larry drew a comb through Eli's auburn fur.

"Same as usual?" Larry asked.

"Do not make me look cheap or like I got clipped at a drive through," Eli said, crossing his fingers.

Larry snorted. "I have rescued worse."

Chase Everett waited off to the side, legs bouncing, faint choir music leaking from his backpack.

"You nervous?" I asked.

"Wilder Kate thinks I need something bold for summer concerts."

Eli groaned. "Please do not let my children become trendsetters."

"Too late," I said, patting his shoulder. "You married their fashionable Momma"

Foster Flanagan stepped from behind the rinse curtain, rubbing his freshly trimmed muzzle.

"Larry, Emma Mae is going to swear I look five years younger."

"That is because I cut the gray. You grow more every month."

The bell rang again.

Pop walked in wearing sandals and patched shorts, grin wide enough to hint at mischief.

"Larry," he called, clapping once, "make me aerodynamic."

Larry raised an eyebrow. "Full shave?"

Pop nodded. "Tradition. Same as Yaya's watermelon."

"You know shaving your head does not make you faster."

"Wrong. Two miles an hour. Three downhill."

Larry motioned to the chair. "Let us bring out the speed."

Clippers buzzed low. Hair fell in soft drifts. Papa Max folded his paper, glasses sliding down his nose.

"Hmph."

Larry kept working. "Good hmph?"

"No such thing anymore," Papa Max said. "Not in ink."

Pop leaned forward. "What is it?"

"Same tune. New verse. Outfit out of Tulsa wants to reimagine the west side of Blue Creek Lake. One hundred sixty three acres."

Larry muttered, "They reimagine places where they have never eaten lunch."

"They brought drawings," Papa Max said, tapping the page.

The room shifted. Not silent. Thinner.

Eli's phone buzzed. He checked the screen and stood. "I need to take this."

Outside, he leaned against the brick wall.

"I know, I am reading it too."

A pause.

"No, nothing is settled."

Another pause.

"Let's not borrow trouble Ginger. We will talk later. Love you."

He remained outside a breath longer than required, then stepped back in, face composed.

Chase looked up. "Is something happening to the lake?"

Pop met his eyes. "People are talking."

"Talking is how doing begins," Papa Max said.

He returned to his paper without turning a page.

"We will see what the council says," he added.

Chase frowned. "So we talk to find out why they are talking?"

Pop smiled. "That is the shape of it."

Larry flicked the clippers back on. "Alright, philosophers."

He caught my eye and winked, steadying the air.

When Pop's shave finished, Larry brushed the loose hair from his shoulders and turned toward Chase.

"You are up."

Pop slid free of the chair and stood tall.

As Larry angled the mirror, Pop narrated, "Observe the barber approaching the crest. Precision. Art."

"Pop," Eli said, laughing, "you are scaring customers."

"Nonsense."

Hair drifted to the floor. Chase lowered his voice. "I think I want bold too."

Larry paused. "Define bold."

Chase considered. "Lead singer. Also future scientist. Someone who could pilot a spaceship if necessary."

Larry nodded once. "I can work with that."

"I am not watching," Eli whispered, covering his eyes.

He peeked anyway.

When Larry finished, Chase's hair sat clean and sharp, a small faux-hawk rising with intention.

"Oh wow," Chase breathed. "I look official."

"You look great," Eli said. "Trendy and great."

Pop rubbed his bare head in the mirror. "Champion material?"

"You look smooth," I said, "but close to a man who might forget his paddle."

He laughed and squeezed my arm. "Text Lolli when you get home. She wants to chat."

"I will."

Pop headed for the door. "Larry, money is under the notepad."

Larry nodded. "I see it."

The shop returned to its hum. Papa Max carried his cinnamon rolls toward the back room.

"Do not ask. I am not sharing."

I plucked a snap pea from my container on the way out, just to keep from fainting of righteousness later.

The bell jingled behind me. The screen door snapped shut. The hum followed me halfway down the sidewalk.

SATURDAY, APRIL 26

IT WAS QUIET WHEN I PULLED INTO MY DRIVE.

I CALLED PAPA J AFTER I SHUT THE TRUCK OFF. SAT THERE A MINUTE WITH MY HANDS ON THE WHEEL. I TOLD HIM ABOUT THE TALK CIRCLING THE BARBERSHOP, ABOUT VOICES DROPPING LOW. TROUBLE HAS GOOD EARS.

"YOU HAVE TO LET IT GO FOR NOW, NOTHING YOU CAN DO." HIS VOICE SOFTENED UNDER HIS TEASING. "NOW GO SOAK IN THAT TUB. SCALD YOUR SKIN WHILE YOU'RE AT IT, BECAUSE WE BOTH KNOW YOU WILL."

I LAUGHED—THE FIRST REAL LAUGH ALL DAY.

"LOVE YA," HE SAID, SETTING SOMETHING STEADY DOWN WHERE I COULD REACH IT. "CRAZY WOMAN."

"LOVE YA TOO," I SAID, AND MEANT IT IN ALL THE WAYS THAT

STILL COUNT.

I WATERED THE BEDS UNTIL THE SOIL DARKENED AND SETTLED. THE PAINT WAITED WHERE I'D LEFT IT, BRUSH STIFF IN THE JAR. I STOOD THERE LONGER THAN PLANNED, THINKING ABOUT THE MORNING. ALL THOSE MEN PACKED INTO LARRY'S SHOP. PAPA MAX, WITH HIS NEWSPAPER AND HIS HMPHS, FELT CLOSE AS MY OWN HANDS.

THEN MY DADDY CROSSED MY MIND WITHOUT ASKING—THE WAY HE STILL DOES SOMETIMES. SUDDEN AS A SMELL. I PICTURED HIM IN A BARBER CHAIR, SHOULDERS SQUARED, PRETENDING NOT TO CARE HOW IT TURNED OUT.

I RINSED MY HANDS, WIPED THEM ON MY JEANS, AND CHECKED MY PHONE. NO MESSAGES.

I TEXTED LOLLI.

> home now, holler when you can chat

TONIGHT'S LISTEN:
"SUNDAY MORNIN' COMIN' DOWN" — WILLIE NELSON

To Do:
ASK LOLLI WHAT TIME ARE THEY COMING FOR CAMP, ASK POP TO BRING HIS DRILL

coffee, camp, and diet coke

POP AND LOLLI rolled up my driveway before the sun had pulled its britches on, waving wide, grand as parade marshals whose float lost and who decided to start their own procession anyway.

Pop carried his clipboard, taped corner flapping, title written thick and square across the top.

THINGS TO FIX BEFORE CHILDREN ATTEMPT TO BREAK THEM.

Lolli held a canvas tote heavy with ribbons, folded recipes, and three notebooks she swore served three separate purposes.

"Morning, Yaya," Pop called, letting the screen door snap hard behind him. "Where do we begin saving the world?"

"Coffee. Then cabins."

He snapped a salute, solemn as a cadet.

The grandkids trailed behind them, Hank Miller, Jasper West, and Millie, eyelids heavy but pride upright. The boys had turned twelve and carried it in their shoulders. Millie, not twelve until July, matched their stride, jaw set firm.

The morning held itself steady. Cut grass sweet in the air. Warm fritters on a plate. Sunscreen already rubbed into arms. Coffee cooling on the counter because somebody shouted your name.

· · ·

THEN THE REST arrived the way they always do, all at once.

Ranger made for the goat pen without waiting for instruction. Carly followed with an armful of camp linens stacked high. Stewart Sweetstripe laid out seed trays for the pollinator patch, setting each square into the dirt with careful hands. Emma Mae gathered the youngest near the hose, turning water into laughter.

Juan Carlos hauled two coolers of tamales into the shade, nodding once as though hunger had been handled before it could stir trouble. Shia swept the craft barn porch in wide strokes. Ricky studied the power boxes, gaze sharp, remembering what happens when a fork wanders where it does not belong. Liam rolled in two new picnic tables, lowered them into place, refused thanks, resisted my hug and lost anyway.

Pop herded the boys toward Cabin Blue Jay.

"We start here," he declared, tapping the clipboard. "This door slammed so hard last year I nearly went bald"

"You are bald Pop," Hank said.

"Technicality," Pop replied.

They set to work. By midmorning Blue Jay stood ready. Weeds gone. Hinges tightened. Porch swept clean. Millie dipped a brush into sky blue paint and edged the trim with steady strokes.

"I added pizzazz."

"You did," Lolli said, sliding the lid aside before a boot stepped square into it.

DOWN BY THE CREEK, the Waddell children cleared brush in tidy piles. The Simmons boys tied knots and untied them, arguing over which held best. The Flanagan girls walked the trail with markers, placing them at bends and dips. Butter and Sasha hung book slings in the reading tree, stepped back, adjusted the angle until it felt right. Bees moved through wildflowers without complaint.

Lolli and I claimed an empty picnic table and cracked open cold Diet Cokes. She opened her notebooks, pages already divided with neat lines.

"Menus first."

"Crafts next."

"Emergency snacks last."

"Those matter most."

We bent over the page and filled it.

BERRY CRUMBLE BARS.
VEGGIE PASTA WITH BOOTSIE HOWARD'S BASIL.
POPSICLE DAY.
TACO NIGHT WITH ABUELITA SHYRA'S SALSA.
NATIVE PLANT CRAFTS.
GRATEFUL JOURNALS.
FLORA AND FAUNA NOTES.
BIRDING SCAVENGER HUNT.
CAMPFIRE SING-ALONGS.

EVERY so often Pop's voice cut across the grounds.

"Cabin Finch handrail secured."

"Cabin Sparrow front step replaced."

"Cabin Roadrunner inspected and approved."

BY NOON the smell of cut grass tangled with food. Shyra's tamales steaming under foil. Paul's cucumber sandwiches lined neat on a tray. Lolli's chocolate bread sliced thick. Iced tea sweating through glass pitchers. Nick told the same story twice, hands moving wide. Nobody corrected him.

Then the air shifted.

No announcement. No signal. A few adults leaned closer over paper plates.

Council surfaced in the talk. Then the west side. Then one hundred sixty three acres spoken low and flat.

Rosemary stood with her plate untouched. Bet and Matty stilled beside her. Dahlia's eyes moved to the tree line, measuring without a ruler.

Pop set his clipboard down. The metal clip struck the table with a small ping that traveled.

"Alright," he said, voice easy on purpose. "We do what we always do. Eyes open. Facts straight."

Lolli's pen hovered above her page.

"Just in case," she said.

"Just in case," I answered, throat tight.

No one used the word fight. No one drew up plans. We named tasks, plain and practical.

Rosemary would walk the area under the banner of routine work.

Bet and Matty would check the creek and water lines the same way they always had.

Dahlia would mark trail edges and note what shifted.

Lolli would keep the lists, dated and tidy.

I would watch traffic along my stretch of County Road 40, count trucks, wave when needed.

None of it looked new. It looked like us.

AFTER LUNCH we stepped back and studied what we had finished. Cabins straight. Tables steady. Trails cleared.

Pop eased down beside us with a long sigh. "If this is not the most prepared camp we have run, I will shave my beard."

"You do not have a beard."

"Then we are ahead already."

Lolli pressed her notebooks into my hands, pages thick with ink and intention.

"This summer will be something," she said.

I looked over the row of cabins, the creek flashing under sun, the quiet hum of people who understand shared work.

Camp Run Amuck stood ready.

So did we.

SATURDAY, MAY 3

I TINKERED AROUND THE HOUSE AFTER EVERYONE LEFT, SETTING THINGS BACK WHERE THEY BELONGED. THE DOGS AND I HAD A LIGHT SUPPER TOGETHER. THEY ATE FIRST, OF COURSE,

THEN STATIONED THEMSELVES AT MY FEET WHILE I ATE—FULL OF THE PARTICULAR ENTITLEMENT ONLY WELL-FED DOGS CAN MANAGE.

I PUT THE MUSIC ON SHUFFLE AND LET THE KITCHEN TURN INTO A PLACE WHERE MY SHOULDERS COULD FINALLY DROP.

I REFILLED THE SWEET TEA PITCHER WITHOUT THINKING. TIGHTENED THE LOOSE SCREW ON THE BACK STEP. SET THE CLIPBOARD WHERE I'D REMEMBER IT IN THE MORNING

TONIGHT'S LISTEN:
"HAND IN MY POCKET" — ALANIS MORISSETTE

TO DO:
DOUBLE-CHECK WITH ABUELITA SHYRA ON ANY NEEDS FOR CINCO
FRIDAY MARKET: BEANS, CUKES (IF READY), PEAS, CHARD, DAFFS, TULIPS, IRIS

cinco de mayo celebration

SUNDAY MORNING I found Abuelita Shyra in the dining hall, sleeves pushed high, a bowl of masa wide enough to wash a child in resting firm against her hip. She worked in rhythm, palms pressing, folding, turning. The story lived in her hands before it reached her mouth.

Ruby stood beside her slicing peppers with sharp focus, jaw set. Juan Carlos stirred a pot with pride, wooden spoon steady. The Sweetstripe girls drifted in carrying flowers for the tables. Behind them came the duck children, jugs of agua fresca knocking against their knees, liquid bright with citrus. One jug bore a strip of masking tape marked in thick letters: LAWHOMA STANDS TOGETHER.

I laid my bouquet on the counter, early grasses and snapdragons, marigolds catching light. Abuelita Shyra nodded once and folded the color into her plan without breaking pace.

"Today," she said, smiling at the helpers, "we learn why we celebrate here, not only how."

BY MIDAFTERNOON the dining hall had turned into the gentlest classroom I have known. Toasted masa hung in the air with roasted chiles. Laughter rose and settled without anyone shushing it back down.

When the time came, Abuelita Shyra called us close. Humans.

Animals. Even Beans and RJ found their way beneath the tables, eyes fixed on the kitchen, convinced they held invitations.

"Cinco de Mayo is not Mexico's Independence Day," she said, voice clear. "It marks the Battle of Puebla. A smaller force defended their city against an army that expected victory."

She let that rest.

"Courage is not measured by size. Bravery carries dignity. It is standing together when something worth protecting faces harm."

Her gaze moved across the room. "That lesson belongs to more people than history often names."

Then she clapped once and laughed. "Now. Who wants to cook?"

Hands, paws, wings shot upward. Larry, hovering near the doorway, lifted his before he caught himself and lowered it halfway.

We worked in steady lanes. Dough pressed flat and filled. Chicken and vegetables seasoned with care. Empanadas folded tight, some neat, some lopsided. The turtles bent close to their work, tongues peeking out in concentration. Bees hovered near the sweet trays. Ginger arranged platters with painter's precision, shifting color and shape until balance pleased her. Dahlia tucked edible flowers along the rims. Foster lined up paletas with slices of fruit frozen clear inside. Dr. Bridget set stations, watched knives, adjusted spacing, never dimming the joy.

At one point Beans snatched a scrap of tortilla from the floor and vanished under a table, swallowing without a single chew.

When the sun dipped low we carried plates outside to the long wooden tables. Lantern light warmed the food and softened faces. Papel picado fluttered overhead. The air carried masa, chiles, citrus, bread.

We ate. We talked. We learned without calling it a lesson.

After plates cleared and the last of the tres leches and churros disappeared, Abuelita Shyra stood again.

"Cinco de Mayo is not about pretending sameness," she said. "It honors where we come from. It invites us to share it."

I looked across fur, feathers, scales, skin. The meaning settled in the space between us.

Heritage belongs on the table, visible and offered.

Sunday, May 4
My house still smells inviting with toasted masa and citrus, even after I washed the dish towels twice. I don't mind. Some things earn the right to linger.
Beans stole a tortilla scrap and strutted off to be sneaky and not show he'd pulled something clever. RJ looked offended she hadn't thought of it first.
I folded the sign from the dining hall and set it on the counter without deciding where it goes yet.
My brows stayed knit. I caught myself chewing my lip and made myself stop.

Tonight's Listen:
"It's a Great Day to Be Alive" — Travis Tritt

To Do:
Text Abuelita Shyra thank you
Check camp pantry list
Find out what Annie wants to do for recital — ride together? peek in on dress rehearsal?
Market Fri & Sat: clean out baskets, get singles for the cash box. Maybe we can break $100 both days.
Fingers crossed.

SEVEN

5, 6, 7, 8, again!

BY THE TIME recital week arrived, Wiggle Worm Dance Studio felt less like a business and more like a body with its own pull. Folks circled it all day long, drawn in whether they meant to be or not.

Music slipped under the doors, vanished, then returned down the hallway off count and stubborn. Hairspray hung thick. A lone tap shoe sat on the front desk, partner missing. May light cut through the windows and caught rhinestones, safety pins, and adults moving too fast while insisting calm.

Annie stopped in Monday to return an algebra book to Kelly. I rode along, drawn to the noise the way I am every year.

She would have slipped back out clean if Kelly Chen had not stepped sideways into the doorway, clipboard pressed to her ribs.

"You are not dropping that and disappearing," Kelly said.

Jordan Hill came down the hall behind her, steamer hissing, cord dragging like a tail.

"If you leave now," Jordan called, "the finale unravels."

Annie laughed. "That sounds dramatic."

Jordan tilted her chin toward Studio A. Winnie and Jessi ran a diagonal for the fourth time, stopped, reset, frustration clear in their shoulders.

"Watch," Jordan said.

Annie did.

One rushed the diagonal. Shoes slid. Another tried to fix it mid turn and clipped her partner.

Kelly exhaled slow. "We need fresh eyes."

Annie shifted her weight. I saw the flicker at her hip, quick and gone. Years ago surgery had carved its lesson into her. Trust the body. Listen when it speaks.

"I will help," she said. "No dancing." "That'll work. We need your twin-boy-mom skills."

Annie flexed her arms, joking. They laughed together, that shared-motherhood laugh that says: we're tired, but we're still here.

DRESS REHEARSAL at Birch Creek Auditorium arrived loud and unfinished.

Parents lingered in the lobby, folding and unfolding programs, gripping coffee cups as if they steadied something deeper. At the edge of my hearing, talk broke off when Ricky passed with his phone pressed close. The lake. Money. Low voices.

Inside, sound bounced off concrete and bleachers. Chairs scraped. A speaker shrieked until Jordan slapped it back into line.

Behind the curtain a box of headpieces tipped. Sequins scattered across the floor, bright as loose change.

On stage, the jazz dancers ran the finale.

They knew the steps. Spacing drifted. Arms reached into empty air. A turn finished early. Then late. Eyes darted sideways. When dancers start watching each other instead of the floor, the piece cracks.

Kelly clapped twice. "Hold."

Annie stepped forward without ceremony.

"You are rushing the diagonal," she said, voice steady. "Not because you are late. Because you are watching each other."

Jordan crossed her arms. "They anticipate the turn."

"Run it again. Spot the landing."

Annie counted them in. She did not miss a beat.

They ran it. Again. Again. Water bottles passed. Tempers flared and cooled.

Annie clapped three times. "Breathe. Let yourself breathe first."

The shift came clean. The next pass settled. Lines tightened. Timing shared instead of chased.

Across the lobby, Studio B unraveled in a different way.

The youngest hip hop class bounced in neon sneakers. Goldie lay flat on the floor.

"I am the beat," she declared.

Another child launched a cartwheel and nearly toppled a stack of water bottles.

Clover Hill caught Annie's eye, half laughing, half pleading.

Annie stepped between the speakers and clapped once.

"Freeze. Eyes here."

Most obeyed. Goldie finished her jump and froze late, grin wide.

Annie crouched. "Face front. Feet wide. Knees soft."

Smith shot his hand up. "Can I jump?"

"On seven."

They counted. Five. Six. Smith jumped on six, gasped, then laughed.

Annie smiled. "You found seven. Let's try eight."

They ran it again. Loud. Messy. Closer.

When the final freeze landed almost together, the teachers cheered as if they had filled a Broadway house.

I watched from the side, counting each eight count with her. Annie did not hover. She stood steady. When someone looked up, she met their eyes.

RECITAL NIGHT ARRIVED warm and clear. Lawhoma showed up dressed in a collision of church clothes and glitter. Programs rustled. Bouquets rested on laps. Children peeked through curtains and waved as if fame had found them.

The lights dimmed. The room drew one shared breath.

Kelly stepped to the microphone.

"Wiggle Worm Dance presents our Spring Recital."

Then she added, plain as wood laid across a creek.

"A couple dollars from every ticket goes into the just in case fund."

No drama. No naming.

"We do not know what we will need. We know we will need something. So we begin."

Two sentences. Solid.

The curtain rose.

Backstage ran on its own weather. Zippers tugged. Safety pins snapped. Whispered counts floated. A child searched for a missing shoe while wearing it.

Annie crouched near the wings, counting under her breath, nodding when rhythm landed.

Tap burst first, silver shoes flashing, sound clean and sharp. Kip stole the number. Lolli squeezed my hand. "I remember when he was born."

Jazz followed. Winnie and Jessi moved with control.

"They are holding," Annie declared.

Kelly squeezed her arm. "Because you stayed."

Then hip hop hit.

Clover and the children exploded onto the stage. Pops and locks landed close enough. Sage waved at Nanny, then froze a beat late, eyes wide.

The audience laughed and clapped in that rare rhythm that carries pride and delight together.

Annie laughed too, hand flying to her mouth.

Later Jordan stepped into the light for her solo.

She moved in muscle and memory. Weight grounded before the turn. Nothing wasted. Control carried resilience. Pauses carried sweetness.

Annie stood in the wings without shifting.

I watched my daughter from the audience and felt my breath catch, not from fear, but from the quiet astonishment of seeing her stand inside her own shape.

When the final note faded, silence held one heartbeat.

Then the room rose.

The finale filled the stage. Little ones scattered joy the way a paycheck moves through a household in minutes.

Afterward, the lobby swelled with flowers, photographs, glitter ground into carpet.

Kelly pulled Annie into a long hug.

"We needed you."

"You had it," Annie said. "I brought bossy and muscle."

They held on a second longer than required.

Outside, I squeezed my girl's hand and let her see the pride on my face.

Across the parking lot the boys shouted.

"Night, Yaya. Love you to the Milky Way."

SUNDAY, MAY 11

WHEN I GOT HOME AND SAT DOWN WITH THE DOGS, THE QUIET ARRIVED ALL AT ONCE. THAT'S USUALLY WHEN IT FINDS ME.

I WATCHED ANNIE TONIGHT FROM MY SEAT IN THE AUDITORIUM, COUNTING UNDER HER BREATH, STEPPING IN WHEN SHE WAS NEEDED AND STEPPING BACK JUST AS EASILY.

I RECOGNIZED THE STEADINESS IN HER BEFORE I RECOGNIZED THE RELIEF IN MYSELF.

SIS DID GOOD TONIGHT. REAL GOOD.

I LET THE SONG PLAY ALL THE WAY THROUGH BEFORE I CLOSED MY NOTEBOOK

TONIGHT'S LISTEN: "AND I LOVE HER" – PASSENGER

To Do:

WEED FLOWERBEDS BY PORCH, FEED SHRUBS BLOOD/BONE MEAL

ORDER SUNSCREEN SPF 50 FACE AND LIPS

DIRECT SOW—CUKES, HYACINTH VINE, COW PEAS

ORDER THE FRUIT AND NUT BIRD SEED FROM CHEWY

goat yoga survivor

SOME MORNINGS on my farm the air wakes up talkative, already whispering with the sun about what sort of day we are walking into. Goat yoga mornings arrive that way.

Before I reached the porch with my coffee, Ranger had backed his trailer in and begun unloading goats, stagehands dropping off small comedians for their shift. Carly followed with a stack of yoga mats and that wide, ready smile that means she has made peace with chaos ahead of time.

"Morning, Yaya," she called. "They are feeling bold."

She set a mason jar on the picnic table, fitting into the scene as natural as the fence posts. A strip of paper taped to the glass read, LAWHOMA STANDS TOGETHER, a small goat sketched beneath it, legs planted firm.

"For goat snacks," Carly said, "and whatever else shows up."

Jasper studied the drawing. "That goat looks hungry."

"I believe that," I called back, watching one of them nose deep into my flower bed. "That one has design ideas."

ACROSS THE PASTURE folks unrolled mats and tied back hair. Sandals scattered near fence lines. Paddy and Jon Lucas stretched like they had medals on the line. Bootsie arrived with herbs for relaxation, brave offering under these circumstances. Casey Jo and Shay were already on the ground laughing, stroking whichever goat drifted near. Dr. Bridget, Bet, and Matty settled with clinic calm, surprise long retired from their vocabulary.

Harry and Charlotte eased down careful, Charlotte guarding her belly, the most sacred cargo on the field. Millie—eleven going on twenty-five—pointed at Hank and Jasper, their impatient coach with a clipboard.

"Downward dog," she ordered, "and don't knock into each other."

POP STRODE in wearing a shirt he had lettered himself in thick marker. GOAT YOGA SURVIVOR.

Lolli followed prepared for flood, drought, or alien landing. Towels. Sunscreen. Water bottles. Spare patience.

Carly clapped once. "Balance. Breath. Coexisting with animals who ignore both."

Laughter traveled through the grass. The goats approved.

We attempted simple stretches.

Two goats claimed Stevie's mat and struck poses of their own. One sniffed Foster's ears without hesitation. Another rooted through Beck's backpack with the focus of a banker auditing accounts. A determined goat squared off with me, nose nearly touching mine.

"You will not win," I told her. "I raised children."

JJ lifted into tree pose while a baby goat butted her knee with persistent inquiry. She steadied and cheered for herself anyway.

Ranger's voice guided us. "Inhale. Exhale. Ignore the goat sampling your mat."

Wilder Kate hummed low across the field, smoothing the edges of noise.

Then Sheriff leapt onto Pop's back mid cat cow.

Pop froze in place.

"Lolli," he said, voice tight, "move slow."

Lolli laughed outright. "You signed up."

"I did not expect today," he answered, fighting the urge to buck.

Sheriff adjusted his footing with confidence. Pop held steady, spine flat, dignity intact.

Hank, Jasper, and Millie dissolved into laughter. Sheriff startled and sprang off, landing with a tidy roll onto Ranger's mat.

Ranger barely blinked. "Standard occurrence."

Eventually we lay back in the grass, clouds drifting overhead, goats grazing beside us as though they had planned the lesson from the start. Bootsie's butterflies crossed the sky. Wilder Kate hummed once more. Carly passed around small jars of lavender lotion.

Pop lay still, two goats curled against him, solid and unbothered. He made a fine rock.

I breathed in rosemary and basil and watched the sky shift in its own time.

SATURDAY, MAY 17

I soaked in the tub long enough to fog the mirror and give myself a new face. Painted my toenails after, just to prove I still could. Then I sat down long enough to catch the day before it slipped away.

The mason jar from this morning was still on the counter. Lavender smudged the rim. I set it beside the sink and left it there.

This evening, three white trucks passed my fence row headed west. Same logo on the doors. A black sports car flew by after, fast enough to stir dust and make the goats lift their heads.

I slowed what I was doing without meaning to.

Harry Styles felt right tonight. I tease Annie about my love for him and she rolls her eyes. I don't care.

TONIGHT'S LISTEN:
"GOLDEN" — HARRY STYLES

TO DO:

Tue: STEM fair — riding together? Group text Lolli + Annie
Skate night too — one car or separate?
Thu/Fri: Greenhouse inventory for Saturday
Fri: Text the usuals coming Saturday
Refill Meloxicam. Do not forget.

math, science, and gekkering

THERE'S a particular kind of pressure that settles over Lawhoma Hills at the tail end of the school year—a mix of nerves and sparkle. You can feel it in backpacks that won't zip, pencils worn down to nubs, knees bouncing under bleachers. Kids carry hope and worry like matching bookends, not always sure which is which.

That energy filled the gym today for the Lawhoma Hills School Math & Science Invitational, the final academic showdown of the year. Folks talk about it in the Red Foods aisles; all proclaiming this is the academic Super Bowl. All the while swapping lightning-round scores and picking out tomatoes and discount bread.

By the gym doors, Jordan Hill had posted a fresh Cricut sign:
LAWHOMA STANDS TOGETHER
T-SHIRTS
Below it, in blocky Sharpie:
KIDS $15 | ADULTS $20
Ask me at Wiggle Worm
As if anyone in town didn't already know.

I found a seat near the back with Pop and Lolli, who were handing out trail mix, might as well had a paid booth as vendors for the championship game.

Apparently, I'd misunderstood the tone of the day.

It was a Super Bowl.

Just with more calculators and fewer shoulder pads.

Pop nudged me, proud as a king. "Protein and peanuts," he said. "Keeps the nerves from eating the children alive."

"And keeps the parents from fainting," Lolli added.

Millie sat in front of me, bow already crooked.

"You ready for the big day?" I whispered.

She nodded with full-body seriousness. Millie wasn't competing this year, but she cheered her heart out. Her eyes stayed fixed on Ruby Rodriguez, that quiet, starry focus girls get when they've already chosen who they want to grow into.

Jasper scanned the room. "Don't it feel quiet? Is this gonna be so boring? No one is even breathing."

Hank leaned forward. "They're in concentration mode. Nerd brain fully activated."

I gave him a look. "We'll revisit that word later—with your momma, Henry Miller."

The full name landed.

"Yes, ma'am. I didn't mean it mean, Yaya."

Lolli reached across and rested her hand on his. "Even when we don't mean harm, words can still land heavy."

Hank nodded. That kind of correction always does its work softly— and then stays.

Millie whispered, "He got Lolli'd," like it was a verb.

Jasper tried to hide his laugh and made it worse.

AT THE FRONT of the gym, Ruby Rodriguez stood ready, pencil gripped the same as a sword. Her tail twitched. Her jaw set. She looked prepared to duel the universe.

Across the aisle, Juan Carlos waved a glitter sign:

RUBY, YOU'VE GOT THIS!

She tried not to smile.

She failed. Thank goodness.

Ophelia and Eugene sat quietly a row over. No signs. No noise. Just that steady love you give kids who speak in numbers and patterns instead of speeches.

On the science side, Chase Everett ran his team with the confidence of a four star general. Lab coat crisp. Hair sharp. Eyes darting, then settling. Bravery often looks a little unsteady when you're close enough to see it.

Mr. Banerjee tapped the microphone, antlers catching the lights, smooth as polished wood.

"Today we honor curiosity, courage, and learning. Let's hear it for the students representing Lawhoma's STEM programs."

Applause rolled through the gym—whistles, woo-hoos from folks not built for inside voices.

Ruby exhaled.

Chase straightened his notes.

From a few rows back, Wilder Kate leaned into the aisle and whisper-shouted, "Lettttsss Goooo, Chase!"

Lightning round.

Pencils flew. Brows furrowed. Erasers squeaked. The room held its breath the way parents do when they're praying panic doesn't win.

Ruby hit a snag.

Her pencil hovered.

She stared up at the rafters. Her eyes searched for the answer up there.

"She's stuck," I whispered.

"She's spiraling," Lolli said, hands twitching. Her teacher's hands trying to wring the answer loose.

Ruby looked to the crowd.

Manuel winked.

Abuelita Shyra met her eyes—calm and clear.

Juan Carlos bobbed his sign and pulled a ridiculous face that said, I love you and I'm right here.

Ruby breathed.

Answered.

Not perfect. But brave.

That mattered.

. . .

SCIENCE DEMONSTRATIONS FOLLOWED. Chase's team rolled out their catapult and they were unveiling royalty. They talked about trajectory, weight, velocity–all sounding as gospel from the pulpit of STEM.

Then Chase froze.

Notes slipped. Words vanished.

From the back, Wilder Kate let out a quick burst of fox chatter—sharp, strange, unmistakable.

Chase blinked.

Nodded.

Picked up right where he left off.

The catapult fired clean across the gym. The front row flinched, then laughed.

Judges disappeared to tally.

The room exhaled.

Barbara Chen tapped her foot until her shoe squeaked.

"Nervous?" Paul asked.

"A little. I've got a Algebra test later and my brain cannot get straight on variants or coefficients for my life."

Paul smiled. "Smart, kind brains wobble. You just learn to dance through it."

"That man could teach a master class in gentleness," Lolli said.

Pop nodded in understanding he might need to sign up for that class.

THE JUDGES RETURNED. Silence dropped with a curtain of held breath.

"First place, Math Division: Ruby Rodriguez."

The gym erupted. Juan Carlos jumped so high his sign folded in half.

"First place, Science Demonstration: Chase Everett."

Everyone stood. Abuelita Shyra wiped her eyes. Eli high-fived Manuel. Ginger and Rosemary laughed through tears because sometimes joy doesn't fit inside one body.

Ruby stared at her medal.

"Oh em gee that was such a freak out of my entire body," she whispered.

I crouched and cupped her cheek. "I didn't care if it was right. I cared that you stayed steady. We saw you. You made us proud."

Her tail wagged hard enough to tip her sideways, then she hugged me quick, she needed the feeling stored somewhere permanent.

HANK TUGGED MY SLEEVE. "That fox noise? It was amazing," he whispered. "Me and Jasper got twin stuff, but nothing close to that, can I ask Wilder?…never mind she will think I am a goob."

We caught Wilder Kate by the doors. Somehow Hank mustered the nerve.

"What was that sound?" Hank asked.

"It's called gekkering," she giggled. "Fox families use it when we wrestle, call for our moms, or need to say: Hey bro, you know, just stuff we need to holler."

Jasper lit up. "So it's a secret language?"

Wilder nodded. "Exactly."

Hank looked at Jasper, together they solved something sacred.

"We got that," he said softly. "We just never named it."

Jasper answered with a noise that was half snort, half burp.

Wilder laughed. "Twin counts."

OUTSIDE, the May air was warm, summer waiting just offstage.

Hank squeezed my hand.

"We came to see the smart kids," he said. "But we got some work to do on our bro sounds."

He paused. "I didn't mean the nerd thing, Yaya."

"I know," I told him. "Still good to learn how a word lands."

Up ahead, Jasper called out in twin-code.

Hank answered back—loud, proud, absolutely ridiculous.

I laughed out loud and thought:

How in the world am I going to spell that in my journal?

TUESDAY, MAY 20

I've added gekkering to my personal dictionary.
Now the boys are out in the yard inventing the twin
version of gekkering, it has always belonged to them. I'm
debating whether to spell it phonetically in my journal
or draw two lightning bolts and call it close enough.

Tonight's Listen:
"Keep Lookin' Up" — Kacey Musgraves

To Do:
Launder thick socks for skating
Order seed starting mix (Floret's Recipe)
Bathe dogs
Pick up Meloxicam before Friday
Friday Market if possible — extra $75-120 straight
into the just-in-case jar until we know what we're up
against

neon, popcorn, and wobble

ANY NIGHT DIPPED in 1980s Technicolor will send us out humming. Skate nights at Whippoorwill Wheels are always one of them.

The rink's older than most of us can remember. The wood floor has been polished smooth by decades of wheels. The disco ball still works—no one knows how—and scatters light the moment the sun dips. The neon sign flicks on after waiting all day.

It was already dark when I pulled into the lot. Families streamed toward the doors. Wheels clacked and music thumped through the walls.

Inside, everything moved at once. Colored lights looped across the ceiling. The disco ball sprayed silver dots over the floor. The snack bar was stacked with striped popcorn bags. Skates of every size lined the shelves, toe stops scuffed and hopeful.

Wesley and Whip Simmons ran the front desk. Whip wore aviator sunglasses indoors, committed to the look. Wesley handed out skates with the seriousness of someone practicing responsibility.

"Welcome to Whippoorwill Wheels," Wesley said. "Safety first. Fun is tied for first."

"Do you have my size?" I asked.

Whip leaned across the counter. "Flower stickers. Same as last summer."

Of course they were.

. . .

WHILE I WAITED FOR POPCORN, a dad behind me leaned in, voice lowered to compete with the noise.

"If they build over there, County Road 40's going to be a mess."

The popcorn machine hissed and swallowed whatever followed. I let it stay swallowed. Tonight belonged to wheels and kids and music that didn't ask questions.

Annie and Stetson dropped the kids off in a rush, jackets half-zipped, promising to collect them later from Lolli and Pop after date night. Hank and Jasper barely paused for goodbye before racing to the skate racks. Millie stayed close to Lolli, already lacing her skates because in fun and fashion that girl had a system.

The boys zipped past me, clinging to each other and determined not to fall.

"Yaya!" Hank hollered. "I'm gonna go the fastest!"

"No, you're not," Jasper yelled, grabbing his arm just before Hank drifted toward a trash can.

Millie sailed past both of them, steady as if she'd been born on wheels. Her pink bow stayed put, glitter flashing under the lights.

AROUND THE RINK, familiar faces found their rhythm. Butter and Sasha Sweetstripe held hands, circling carefully. Butter tried out footwork from music class. Ruby Rodriguez read a book while skating and made everyone nervous. Stevie Brewster practiced backward laps. Wyatt Chapman spun too fast, crashed into Beck Hill, and got hauled upright without anyone breaking stride. Jessi Howard sang as she passed, loud and off-key.

In the middle of it all, Pop stood very still, skates strapped to feet that did not trust him.

"You don't have to skate," Lolli said.

"I want to skate," Pop replied, swaying as he tested a step.

"Do you remember last year?"

"Selective memory."

She guided him toward the wall. His legs moved, a new recruit still negotiating the job.

Near the DJ table, Chase Everett and Shia Goldberg set up speakers and a laptop. When the next song hit, the beat kicked in and the floor filled again.

Halfway through the night, the lights dimmed. Cosmic blues and purples washed across the rink, neon patterns sliding under spinning wheels.

The kids gasped like the ceiling had opened.

Wesley and Whip followed the chaos with whistles bouncing, pretending to maintain order through conga lines and limbo while Chase and Shia kept the music rolling.

Laughter echoed. Wheels hummed. The disco ball spun tiny galaxies overhead.

Eventually, the pace slowed. Lolli and I stifled yawns after our own mini jam session. Kids crowded the snack bar for last sips of lemonade. Pop sat down to unlace his skates with the satisfaction of a man who'd survived something worth bragging about.

Outside, the neon sign buzzed soft and steady.

"Yaya," Jasper asked as we walked to the cars, "why does skating make my feet feel weird, now they still are flying even in my shoes?" "Because you keep moving," I told him. "Even when your feet argue for taking the skates off."

Pop paused long enough for Jasper to climb onto his shoulders, then reached back for Hank's hand. Millie curled into Lolli's arms, power drained right on schedule.

The parking lot lights flickered once, then steadied, and the night behind us kept humming—bright as a pocketful of stars.

FRIDAY, MAY 23
AFTER I BUCKLED THE KIDS INTO POP AND LOLLI'S BACKSEAT, I HEADED HOME TO RJ AND BEANS AND REACHED FOR MY JOURNAL.
I STOPPED.

Tonight, I let the fun outweigh the worry.

RJ's head settled heavy against my knee. I scratched behind her ear.

"Some things, don't need to be written down."

Tonight's Listen:
"Faith" — George Michael

To Do:
Up 04:30/ get seed trays out
Pull the rest of the hoses out of shed
Call OSU Extension—ask about soil results in new
West beds

dirt in your bra

THAT FIRST WARM Saturday brought bird calls from the tops of the trees and a sun bright enough to feel instructional, the kind that says get up and do something worth the daylight.

So we did.

GARDEN DAY CAME EARLY. Wheelbarrows lined the paths crooked and proud. Seed packets fanned out across the potting bench. Starter trays waited in their flats, tomatoes, basil, marigolds, cucumbers, okra, peppers. Fresh trays stacked beside them, empty and hopeful.

Hank Miller and Jasper West circled me already dirt streaked.

"Where do we start?"

"Which ones go first?"

"Can we use the big shovels?"

"Compost first," I told them. "Big shovels earn themselves."

Hank trailed Ross to the worm bins. He scooped up a fistful of black soil and let it sift through his fingers, eyes narrowed serious.

Ross talked scraps and heat and turning time into food. Hank nodded along, wearing that look he gives grown men, halfway between puzzled and pretending he grasped every syllable.

Tata rolled up in Lolli's car wearing a sun hat crowded with fabric flowers, gloves bright as traffic cones, neon apron shouting DON'T MESS WITH MY TOMATOES.

She stepped out and struck a pose.

"Gardening waits on nobody."

"Mom," Lolli sighed, not even halfway to noon and already tired.

"I'll rush at ninety, today I stroll."

The boys ran to her.

"Tata, help us plant sunflowers."

"I was born for this," marching toward the seed trays without checking if they followed.

NEIGHBORS DRIFTED IN STEADY WAVES.

Bet and Dr. Bridget came shoulder to shoulder, voices low.

"Passed one of them white construction trucks on West County Road 40," Bet said. "Big A on the door. Shaped like a camera lens."

Harry followed behind, jaw tight. "Some slick black sports car near shoved me into the ditch. We know the cars that belong out here."

I did not answer. My gaze slid to the road anyway. Thought of those high heeled gals at the market smiling too wide.

Carly and Ranger backed up a truck bed full of goat manure. Ranger hoisted a bag and nodded once. "Gold standard."

The Sweetstripe sisters arrived with fry bread dough wrapped in cloth. Abuelita Shyra carried pepper starts swaddled in newspaper. The Rodriguez children hauled flats of milkweed and coneflower. Bootsie showed with lavender starts and jars of compost tea. Nanny and Hootie brought pollinator plants bundled in twine. Dahlia came last with tubers tucked in crates from her namesake fields.

Ross worked the warm season beds with a broad fork, back straight, rhythm steady. Ricky and Gus crouched over hoses and drip lines. Reed and Daphne scrubbed birdbaths until they sparkled. Gladys knelt in the native acre, pressing soil firm with the side of her hand, checking tags twice before moving on.

The farm smelled alive, damp earth and sun warmed leaves rising together.

At the potting bench, Tata took charge.

"Fill the trays. Not packed. Soil breathes same as you."

She leaned toward the boys and lowered her voice. "Seeds need confidence."

Water followed, gentle and even.

Jasper leaned toward me. "Tata thinks she runs this whole place."

"She does!"

We moved down the rows without pausing. Heirloom tomatoes first. Malabar spinach for climbing trellises. Peppers in every color of the rainbow. Herbs tucked along edges, chive, rosemary, parsley, dill, sage, thyme, basil wherever a hand found space.

Zinnias next, Queeny and Oklahoma, mixed with last year's saved seeds shaken loose from paper envelopes. Cosmos and nasturtiums in the corners. Okra, cucumbers, pole beans, bush beans, sunflowers, lavender, gayfeather. Each planted and covered before debate could flare over spacing.

Gladys stayed faithful to the native acre. Oklahoma penstemon and Blackfoot daisy went in first. Dutchman's pipevine along the fence. Blue grama, sideoats grama, hairy grama to finish. She pressed each root home firm, palm flat, nodding to herself.

MORE HANDS KEPT JOINING.

Charlotte and Harry set a serviceberry in place, dirt firm around its base. Nick and Lindsay planted annuals in pots. Bootsie mixed tinctures on the porch, glass jars catching light. Darla leveled rain barrels. Jordan and Ozzy argued over milkweed placement.

"It needs sun."

"It needs space."

"It needs both," Jordan shot back.

Rosemary and Juan Carlos labeled rows with careful script, Latin names curling neat on wooden stakes. Beans dug more holes than required and fell asleep with his nose in one.

Hank and Jasper crouched over squash seeds, foreheads nearly touching.

"How do they know what they are supposed to be?" Hank asked.

"They already know, we only give them ground."

Jasper pressed a seed into place. "All that inside that tiny thing. Reckon that's one of them mysteries we ain't meant to solve."

"Reckon so."

BY EVENING TATA climbed onto the porch step, gloves dusty, hat tilted.

"Gardeners," she called. "We planted beauty and food. May it grow tall. May the goats mind their manners."

A goat bleated loud in protest.

We ate Tally's beans and fry bread, shared easy. The sky slipped pink into gold. Tools rested where they had fallen. Greenhouse shelves filled tray by tray. Children sat where they landed.

Hank and Jasper leaned against me, dirt still packed beneath their nails.

"It feels good getting this dirty knowing all the good eating we will have," Jasper said.

Hank nudged my arm. "Yaya loves garden talk."

"I love any day in the garden with you."

Evening settled in close around us.

SATURDAY, MAY 24
MY HANDS HURT IN THE GOOD WAY.
SOIL UNDER MY NAILS. DIRT SHAKEN OUT OF MY BRA.
EVERYBODY LEFT CARRYING SOMETHING—CUTTINGS, STARTS, LEFTOVERS, SORE BACKS. THE BEDS ARE FULL. THE PATHS ARE CLEAR.
I STOOD ON THE PORCH LONGER THAN I PLANNED, LOOKING OUT AT THE NATIVE ACRE AND THE WARM-SEASON BEDS EACH ARE DIFFERENT KINDS OF PRAYER.
SOME DAYS I FORGET HOW MANY HANDS IT TAKES TO HOLD A PLACE TO THE GROUND. SOME DAYS IT ALL COMES BACK AT ONCE. I THINK ABOUT CLEAN DESKS AND LAND THEY'VE NEVER KNELT BESIDE.

I shut the journal.
Tomorrow, we water.

Tonight's Listen:
"Strange Magic" — Electric Light Orchestra

To Do:
Sunday/ laundry, vacuum, fertilize houseplants before
they move outside
Monday/ call Annie: dinner before show choir Tuesday
or meet there?

decades under one roof

SHOW CHOIR NIGHT at Birch Creek Auditorium carries a hum in its bones. Last hurrah of the school year, and it takes your whole body to hold it steady.

Kids ran in loose bunches, wild as starlings, while teachers hovered with reminders. Hairspray hung in the air stiff, an invisible force field. The lights flickered through their checks and balances, impatient to earn applause.

I settled between Hank Miller and Jasper West. Hank leaned close to his brother, listening hard, expecting the stage might hand out instructions.

"This is really gonna be something," Jasper declared with his eyes locked on the curtain. "Wait till Prince."

Hank nodded so fast I feared for his spine. "We are gonna jam."

The theme this year ran through decades, a musical time machine powered by young voices, shaking knees, and the kind of courage that shows up under bright lights in front of everybody you know.

THE CURTAIN LIFTED on doo wop.

Middle schoolers stepped out in soft pastels, shoes flashing when they shifted weight. They swayed together, earnest and careful, and sang

"Sh Boom," "Blue Moon," and a tender "Earth Angel." Harmonies floated up and popped bright.

Beck, Sage, Clover, and JJ snapped fingers in time. Jessi, Lacey, and Butter dipped low on the bass line. Ruby and Juan Carlos blended smooth and steady, standing side by side like they had practiced since birth.

Pop leaned toward Lolli, voice carrying three rows. "Now that's music."

Lolli cut him a look sharp enough to slice cake and kept clapping.

Tata sat with her eyes closed, smile soft, songs turning keys somewhere deep.

Then the mood shifted.

High school choir members filed in wearing jeans and rhinestone trimmed pearl snap shirts. Lights warmed to orange.

Shep and Brick Banerjee stepped forward with guitars slung low. "Gentle on My Mind" came out steady. "Wichita Lineman" stretched long and lonesome across the room.

Wilder Kate took the solo. Her voice rose clean and strong. Even the stagehands paused.

Hank leaned into me. "Yaya… she sounds how summer feels."

"She does, baby."

They closed with "Rhinestone Cowboy." Vests shimmered, Gus and Connie Franklin's late night stitching shining clear. Applause rolled in heavy, no one wanting to sit back down.

Then the lights dropped.

Deep purple washed the stage. Spotlights hit the stage.

Drums kicked. Guitar answered. The air shifted.

Will Franklin stepped out in a purple military cut coat, Jordan's work, buttons flashing. Wilder Kate and Chase Everett flanked him, harmonies pulling the room forward.

"Purple Rain" rose slow and thick, older than their voices. Behind them the choir moved in ripples, lanterns glowing, auditorium turning sea and sky at once.

Then "I Would Die 4 U" snapped bright.

Snaps. Spins. Hollers from the elementary rows. Pop threw both hands up, shoulders rolling, caught clean in the Spirit. Lolli laughed and let him have his moment.

The finale hit hard. "Let's Go Crazy," all stomp and joy. Shep pounding drums. Will on keys. Brick's guitar slicing clean through the dark.

Shep grinned wide enough to light the stage if power failed.

The crowd did not clap alone.

They moved.

Tata rose first. Pop followed. Lolli and I danced in place with the boys, shoulders knocking, knees already planning revenge.

When the final note dropped into purple quiet, the ovation came up like a wave and refused to fall.

The kids stood sweating, with glowing faces lit from somewhere inside.

Mr. Ashe stepped to the mic.

"Thank you," he said, voice catching.

He tried again. "You have no idea how proud I am of your children."

IN THE LOBBY, joy spilled everywhere. Glitter stuck to sleeves. Bouquets crushed against chests.

Behind me two parents leaned close.

"Saw another one of them white trucks on County Road 40," one whispered. "Big A on the door."

"Yeah," the other said. "Something's moving."

"DID YOU HEAR THAT SOLO?" Jasper said, breathless.

"And the drum crash," Hank added. "And the lights, Yaya, the lights."

Tata fanned herself. "I haven't danced like that since 1989."

"We could tell," Lolli teased.

Mr. Ashe passed by wearing his tired that came from carrying something heavy and good.

I caught him in a hug.

"You made magic tonight, Bridger."

He shook his head, still catching his breath. "They did it, Yaya. I just steered the ship."

On nights like this, Lawhoma Hills beats as one heart, all of us moving to the same rhythm, even when none of us can count past eight without losing track.

MONDAY, MAY 26
SHOW CHOIR NIGHT ALWAYS MAKES ME FORGET MY AGE UNTIL THE NEXT MORNING REMINDS ME, QUICK AND THOROUGH.
SOME SOUNDS DON'T BELONG TO AN AGE. THEY JUST BELONG.
TATA DANCED LIKE SHE'D BEEN WAITING ALL YEAR FOR PERMISSION. POP ACTED EXACTLY LIKE POP. THE BOYS CAME HALF OUT OF THEIR SEATS, FEET ANSWERING THE MUSIC BEFORE GOOD SENSE CAUGHT UP.
I CAME HOME STILL BUZZING. STOOD IN THE KITCHEN WITH THE LIGHTS OFF AND LET THE HOUSE SETTLE ME BACK INTO MYSELF.
SOME SEASONS ASK FOR MORE ENERGY THAN ORGANIZATION. I'M HOPING THAT COUNTS FOR SOMETHING.

TONIGHT'S LISTEN:
"JINGLE AND GO" — RYAN BINGHAM
TO DO:
WED /CALL OPHELIA: ANYTHING SHE NEEDS FOR THURSDAY?
CALL ANNIE ABOUT THE LAST WEEK OF SCHOOL—— IS STETSON PICKING UP THE BOYS?
CHECK CAMP SUPPLY LIST AGAIN (WHY DO I KEEP DOING THIS).
FRI /EMAIL ODWC WITH EXPECTED ATTENDANCE NUMBERS.

these walls listen

THE MONA SITS at the corner of Spruce and Chestnut, modest brick wrapped in vines and years of footsteps. The doors wear a deep blue that makes you tug your collar straight before you step through.

Ophelia Goldberg stood at the entrance, glasses sliding down her beak, feathers lifted with expectation.

"Welcome, young artists," she waved her arms upward. "These walls listen."

Eugene stood beside her, one wing folded careful behind him, posture quiet in respect to the space.

"Inside voices," he told the children. "Even your thoughts."

The moment we crossed the threshold, street noise dropped away. Jasper, Hank, and Millie paused just beyond the doorway, still as fence posts, the hush resting on their shoulders.

"It smells like old books and new paint," Jasper whispered.

Hank studied the sign near the door. "It smells like we better not touch."

The first gallery opened wide with landscapes. Sunflowers tilting toward heat. Blue Creek washed in watercolor. A charcoal sketch of the creek during cross country season, runners ghosted along the bank.

Then I saw it. A pastel of my farm. Goats mid leap. Fence line bent familiar. Carly's hand in every stroke.

I stood longer than intended.

Butter Sweetstripe lifted her hand halfway. "I do not always know what I am looking at."

Ophelia nodded. "Looking comes first."

Butter leaned against her leg, content with that.

IN THE SCULPTURE ROOM, Mr. Chapman stepped forward, magpie feathers catching the track lights. He gestured toward a carved oak deer, muscles cut clean from wood.

"Some pieces mirror life," he said. "Some refuse to."

He stopped at a bronze twisted tight upon itself.

JJ Flanagan cocked her head. "What is it?"

Mr. Chapman smiled without answering.

JJ narrowed her eyes. "Spaghetti breaking out of a bowl."

"Then it has done its job," he replied.

Micah Quinn rolled near a cluster of hanging glass flowers. Air shifted when we passed. The pieces chimed, thin and bright. He kept his hands anchored at his sides, eyes following each tremor, listening through sight alone.

IN THE TEXTILE GALLERY, Wilder Kate Everett stood before a quilt divided into four stitched panels.

"This one feels loud," she said.

Ophelia's mouth curved. "Good."

Ruby Rodriguez lingered over a pattern spiraling inward.

"Is this a fractal?"

"Yes."

Ruby's grin broke wide. "Finally."

While the children moved ahead, Ophelia fell into step beside me.

"We do not fret," she whispered low, gaze still on the room. "But the west end of County Road 40 sits close. I think about what that brings."

Before I could answer, Eugene's voice entered gentle and steady.

"What did we tell Shia? We do not borrow trouble. And we do not hand it to children."

Ophelia dipped her head once. "It may come to nothing."

We closed the distance to the others.

THE FINAL ROOM held the studio. Long tables draped in butcher paper. Jars thick with brushes. Slabs of clay waiting for hands. Watercolors bright enough to quiet even JJ.

"Create something that shows Lawhoma Hills today," Ophelia said.

The room leaned into work.

Millie layered blues until the creek took shape. Jasper molded a goat bent into yoga, tongue out in concentration. Hank washed the sky in gold and violet, the hour before dark. JJ drew herself breaking a finish line ribbon. Barbara Chen sketched her family mid kick, motion caught in pencil. Butter pressed charcoal into a careful portrait of her great grandfather, shading his eyes with reverence. Sasha drew Butter mid bite, cookie crumbs suspended in triumph.

Micah shaped a small clay goat curled beside a sleeping human. He smoothed the edges slow, palm moving in circles, guarding the quiet he had made.

When they finished, Ophelia and Eugene arranged the pieces along a long table under steady lights. No applause. No hurry.

Outside, afternoon had turned soft.

"Can we put easels at your house?" Hank asked.

"And more clay?" Jasper said quick behind him.

"Can we come back?" Millie asked.

"Yes," I told them. "Those doors stay put."

WEDNESDAY, MAY 28

AFTER I DROPPED THE BOYS OFF, I DIDN'T GO INSIDE RIGHT AWAY.

I SET UP A CANVAS INSTEAD.

USED THE GOOD BRUSHES—THE ONES I KEEP TUCKED HIGH SO THEY DON'T END UP IN THE BATH WITH DINOSAURS OR DOGS.

THE PAINT CAME EASIER THAN WORDS.

One shape, then another.
Color where there wasn't any.
It didn't make a picture so much as a feeling—but it steadied me.
I'm proud of those boys.
They're starting to notice things that don't make noise.
They stay still long enough to look—really look.
That's not small.
I cleaned the brushes slow, careful with the bristles, they were something sacred.
Sometimes that's all a day asks: Clean the brushes when you're done.

Tonight's Listen: "Wildflowers" — Tom Petty

To Do:
Order groceries (we are out of everything)
Sat/ call Charlotte if no baby yet—what do they need?
Don't forget belly band + compression socks

batteries, blankets, and sirens

LATE SPRING in Lawhoma Hills changes the air before it changes the sky. Wind shifts tone. Clouds stack up in odd formations, tall and uneven, enough to make even the calm ones pause mid step and look twice.

We do not fear storm season.

We prepare.

READINESS RUNS through this town the way tomato stakes line a garden row. You learn weather the way you learn a hymn. Repetition. Call and response. Memory held in the body.

Annie and Stetson dropped Hank and Jasper off one Saturday morning on their way to meet Silas and Addie for lunch. The boys spilled out of the car already wound tight, backpacks bouncing against their shoulders.

"Yaya," Hank said, breath short, "Momma heard storms on Tuesday."

Jasper's eyes stretched wide enough to hold the horizon. "Will we be ready? Is it rain or bad?"

I set my palms on their shoulders and kept them still long enough to land my words.

"Storm season is not about fear. It is about being smart."

Their spines straightened. They looked ready to square off with a thunderhead.

Storm Readiness Day had already swept through town. You could sense it in the clipped pace of folks crossing parking lots.

Gus Franklin checked roof straps and cleared gutters. Dr. Bridget ran the clinic generator, steady hands, no rush. Rosemary walked the power line edges with Ricky and the Lawhoma Power crew. Limbs earned bright paint marks before wind had a chance to claim them. Near the lake, Ricky tipped his chin toward a fresh sign hammered into the dirt.

APERTURE DEVELOPMENT, LLC

Land Survey in Progress

Rosemary said nothing. She lifted her phone, took a picture, and kept moving.

Eugene passed out weather radios at Red Foods, stacking them neat beside the register. Sweetstripe Floral delivered comfort kits to Willow Creek. Wade secured the lake equipment. The Banerjee twins closed the creekside trails. Bridger and Arthur reviewed shelter plans with parents who asked careful questions. The Quinns checked stock at the community food bank. Nanny and Hootie tied down their hives.

Storm season draws Lawhoma Hills close.

AT HOME, Hank and Jasper followed me with purpose. Pop had handed them a clipboard marked in thick black letters.

OFFICIAL WEATHER BUSINESS

We checked window latches, barn locks, flashlight batteries, feed bins. I walked the tree line and studied the branches. Tested the weather radio. Oiled the shelter hinges until they swung smooth. The boys scribbled notes as though the valley depended on their handwriting.

Shared preparation turns into ritual. It reminds you that effort holds value, even when the sky does what it wants.

That afternoon, Pop and Lolli hosted a check in at Spruce Street Books. Pop sketched a storm track on a napkin with such authority he nearly convinced himself.

"Pop," Lolli said, leaning close, "that shape is Kansas."

He rotated the napkin without shame. "Then Kansas stands in for Lawhoma."

The boys laughed, whatever unnamed worry they carried loosening a notch.

Then Tata burst through the door in a windbreaker and hiking boots, goggles perched on her head.

"I am ready for anything."

"Mom," Lolli said, patient and tired at once, "we are reviewing shelter plans."

"I said anything."

Children watch how adults hold themselves. Capability steadies more than panic ever will.

Back home we ran the plan again, not as lecture, but rhythm.

Pay attention to David and Lacey on Channel 9.

Tell your people where you are.

Gather what you need.

Shelter early.

Stay calm.

Then the rule every Oklahoma child learns:

DUCK.

Down to the lowest level.

Under something sturdy.

Cover your head.

Keep shelter until the all clear.

They repeated it because repetition plants courage deep.

Evening fell soft and gold. Goats settled in the pasture. Wind held its line. We drank lemonade on the porch, hands idle for once.

AT DUSK we drove out near Birch Creek for the siren test. The warning tower stands tucked among bur oaks, plain until it finds its voice.

When it sounded, the air split wide.

Not danger.

Practice.

A reminder that watchfulness lives here.

Jasper tightened his grip on my hand. "It is loud."

"It is meant to be."

Hank kept his gaze on the horizon. "No storm today?"

"No storm. A test."

The sound faded. Leaves rustled back into place.

Practice lays roots under courage.

In Lawhoma Hills, we listen for one another.

SATURDAY, MAY 31

AFTER I FED THE DOGS, I SAT WITH WHAT WAS LEFT OF MY ANGER. MAYBE THAT'S WHAT IT WAS.

WE DIDN'T HAVE SIRENS OR RADAR WHEN I WAS GROWING UP. NO ALERTS. JUST THAT LOW GUT-FEELING WHEN THE AIR WENT STRANGE. BIG GRANNY HAD A BONE-DEEP FEAR OF STORMS, AND SHE NEVER DID LEARN HOW TO HOLD IT. SO NONE OF US DID EITHER.

FEAR WAS OUR FAMILY LANGUAGE—LOUD, INHERITED, FLUENT.

I'M GRATEFUL WE GET TO TEACH THESE KIDS A BETTER VERSION. THAT THEY CAN RESPECT THE WEATHER WITHOUT PANIC. THAT PREPAREDNESS DOESN'T HAVE TO MEAN HYSTERIA. CHAOS WAS FAMILIAR TO US.

I'M NOT MAD AT HER ANYMORE. NOT REALLY.

BUT I AM GLAD WE GET TO DO IT DIFFERENT.

TONIGHT'S LISTEN:
"CARRY ON WAYWARD SON" – KANSAS

To Do:
STORM PREP RESET. WASH SHELTER BLANKETS; SWAP BATTERIES; CHARGE POWER BANKS; RESTOCK DOG GO-BAG
PRINT DUCK RULE SHEET FOR DINING HALL
RED FOODS RUN/ STORM PANTRY BASICS + BOTTLED WATER
FRIDAY MARKET IF POSSIBLE—SET ASIDE 20% FOR THE JAR

the newest windsor

SUMMER HAD ONLY BEGUN to stretch her green fingers over Lawhoma Hills when the news came tearing across the valley.

"Charlotte's going into labor."

In a town this size, word travels the way a storm front does. Fast. Shared. Impossible to ignore. A grocery cart stood crooked in the cereal aisle. Pruning shears dropped into turned soil. Phones pressed tight to ears, voices lowered and lifted in the same breath.

At the farm, Tata called first, breathless and commanding at once.

"Yaya. The baby's coming. The baby's coming."

I caught my keys from the counter, told RJ and Beans to mind the place, and rang Lolli.

"Let's go."

Some sentences require no decoration.

LAWHOMA HILLS REGIONAL carries a different air when a child prepares to arrive. The halls soften. Light turns warmer against the tile. The scent of antiseptic meets something tender beneath it, clean in a way that steadies the pulse.

The waiting room had already filled by the time we stepped inside.

Not loud. Simply full. Sunday shirts beside work boots. Hands gripping paper sacks. Eyes fixed on the maternity doors.

Food covered the side table. Tally's containers stacked neat, labeled in her careful script. Abuelita Shyra sat still, beads sliding through her fingers with practiced rhythm. Ranger paced, paused, paced again. Carly pressed snacks into his hand until he accepted one out of surrender.

Arthur arrived mid stride, antlers slightly askew, superintendent thoughts still lining up schedules somewhere behind his smile. Ophelia and Eugene carried a banner rolled tight beneath one wing.

Tata planted herself in a chair.

"I am not leaving until I meet my baby."

The building did not argue.

Hours moved the way labor hours do, stretching thin, snapping tight, stretching again. Pop fetched ice. Tata topped off water cups. Carly let out one sharp laugh and covered her mouth quick, eyes wide, worried she had crossed a line no one had drawn.

After school, the children poured in, energy bright and unfiltered.

"What's his name?"

"Will he have hair?"

"Do babies open their eyes?"

"Can we name him Sheriff Junior?"

Ranger attempted that last suggestion with a straight face and lost it halfway through.

I leaned back and watched the doors.

An old part of me stirred, the one shaped by years in labor and delivery. Not the part that directs traffic. The part that reads silence. The cadence of footsteps. The pause before a nurse speaks. The pitch of a fetal monitor filtering through drywall.

You never forget that sound. A steady gallop. Here. Here. Here.

Inside, Dr. Bridget worked steady and sure. Charlotte gripped Harry's hand and rode each contraction with grit plain on her face. Foster moved through the room with quiet efficiency, hands ready before anyone called for them. Somewhere strings played low, music soft enough to support without stealing breath.

. . .

BACK IN THE WAITING ROOM, the naming debate flared and dimmed in cycles. Tata argued for sparkle. Papa Max favored tradition. Ranger proposed a goat themed compromise that earned no votes and encouraged him further.

Then the maternity doors swung open.

Dr. Bridget stepped out, cap tilted, eyes bright.

The room leaned forward.

"It's a boy. Perfect and healthy. Meet Beau Charles Windsor."

The floor seemed to lift.

Noise followed, joyful and overflowing. Tally let out a squeal. Abuelita Shyra wiped tears without hiding them. Ranger crushed Carly in a hug. Pop pumped his fist as though a trophy had landed in his hands. Tata circled the vending machines in triumph, claiming the hallway for celebration.

Lolli and I held each other the way we had when Annie delivered the twins, a grip that carries memory of older battles and fresh mercy.

Hank and Jasper launched into my arms.

"We get to meet him soon?"

"When the nurses say so, and when his parents say so."

We waited right. The first quiet belongs to mother and father. It belongs to the baby learning air, light, sound.

AT LAST FOSTER cracked the door.

"Small groups."

Charlotte sat propped in bed, exhaustion and radiance sharing her face. Harry stood close, eyes red and unguarded.

Beau lay in her arms.

Small. Warm. Wrapped in the pale blue blanket Lolli stitched herself. A strip of damp chestnut hair clung to his head. His nose carried Charlotte's shape.

"Oh my," Lolli whispered.

Tata hovered behind us, already mapping a future.

"This baby will do great things."

Charlotte laughed, tired and proud. Harry wiped his cheeks and did not excuse it.

Hank and Jasper stepped forward and stopped short of the threshold.

"Go on," I told them.

Charlotte lifted Beau slightly.

"He's so little and fuzzy," Jasper said.

"I love his little teeth," Hank added, wonder plain in his voice.

"He's a gift," Harry said.

The boys nodded, silence settling over them like a shared blanket.

When my turn came, Charlotte placed Beau in my arms with the trust earned between women who understand cost.

He fit against me as though carved for the space. Warm weight. Newborn softness. His ear rested velvet under my thumb.

"Welcome to Lawhoma Hills," I whispered. "We have been waiting."

His fingers curled around mine, grip small and fierce.

My heart steadied.

By the time we stepped back outside, the waiting room had thinned. Folks drifted into late sunlight, tired and satisfied. Tata walked with bounce untouched by the long hours. Hank and Jasper talked the entire drive home, sketching Beau's future in grand strokes.

"I'll teach him rodeo."

"I'll read him stories."

"What if he drums?"

"What if he plays baseball?"

I watched the hills roll past, green laid thick over them.

"Let him grow, he will show you."

New life carries that promise.

SUNDAY, JUNE 1

A GOOD WAY TO START JUNE.

I LOVED EVERY YEAR I SPENT IN THE BIRTH CENTER DURING MY EARLY NURSE DAYS. TODAY REMINDED ME WHY—THE FIRST BREATH, THAT SMALL SOUND THAT CHANGES EVERYTHING WHETHER YOU'RE READY OR NOT. I SENT PAPA J A TEXT.

my birth-center nurse heart is full-up 🩶

I GOT A THUMBS UP—HIS UNIVERSAL SIGNAL THAT HE'S EITHER BUSY OR DOESN'T WANT TO HEAR ME GUSH. BOTH CAN BE TRUE.

BEAU IS CHESTNUT FUZZ AND SOFT SKIN. I STILL CAN'T QUITE BELIEVE HOW PERFECT HE IS.

NEXT WEEK IS GO-TIME FOR SUMMER. I NEED SLEEP AND A GOOD TUB SOAK, BUT TONIGHT I FEEL WRUNG OUT IN THE BEST WAY—FULL, QUIET-HAPPY. I WANTED FAMILIAR LYRICS TO CARRY ME, SO IT'S TAYLOR ON SHUFFLE AGAIN.

TONIGHT'S LISTEN:
"NEVER GROW UP" — TAYLOR SWIFT
TO DO:
EYE DOCTOR (CITY)/ MONDAY, 10:00
ODWC/ TUESDAY, 9:00
BIRDING SCAVENGER HUNT PREP: BINOCULARS + JOURNALS
FRIDAY MARKET /GOAL: $200!!
BLUE CREEK OPENS SATURDAY/ CHECK LIFE JACKETS; CALL
LOLLI

PART TWO

summer

SUMMER ARRIVES AND THE LIGHT REFUSES TO LEAVE. DAWN BREAKS EARLY AND ALREADY WARM, THE SUN PUNCHING A TIMECARD BEFORE MOST OF US POUR COFFEE. THE GARDEN SWELLS AGAINST ITS TWINE AND STAKES AND STARTS ISSUING ORDERS. TOMATOES HANG HEAVY AND SMUG, SPLITTING THEIR SKINS WHEN YOU TURN YOUR BACK. ZINNIAS SCATTER COLOR ACROSS THE BEDS, BOLD HEADS TIPPED TOWARD THE ROAD. EVEN THE WEEDS RISE STRAIGHT AND CERTAIN, ROOTS SUNK DEEP IN RED DIRT.

OUT HERE, SUMMER SHOWS NO RESTRAINT. SHE PRESSES HER WEIGHT INTO THE FIELDS UNTIL THE GRASS LIES DOWN IN SURRENDER. SHE TRAINS YOUR EYE ON THE HOSE LEFT RUNNING TOO LONG, ON THE SHADE SHRINKING INCH BY INCH ALONG THE PORCH FLOOR, ON SOIL TURNING PALE AND POWDERY BETWEEN YOUR FINGERS. SHE SENDS YOU DOWN TO THE LAKE AND DARES YOU TO STUDY THAT BRIGHT SKIN OF WATER WITHOUT WONDERING WHAT MOVES BELOW IT. THE SURFACE GLITTERS. THE DEPTH KEEPS ITS OWN COUNSEL.

MOST YEARS, THAT FILLS THE DAYS.

PORCH MORNINGS WITH A SWEATING GLASS ON THE RAIL.

Camp Run Amuck racket drifting over the pasture, whistles and hollers carried on thick air. Popsicles bleeding down small wrists. Scraped knees dusted off with spit and the hem of a T shirt. Boys running half wild until supper, sunburned noses peeling, hair slick from the lake, laughter ricocheting through the door I forgot to shut.

I tell myself to fix my gaze there. Keep hold of what feeds us. This summer came hard won. We earned it in long winters and tight springs.

Still, another sound threads through the music.

It begins small. A white truck idling too long near Blue Creek, tires too clean for a road that stains everything rust red. Bright ribbons knotted to low branches where no child has played. Words dropped quiet at the feed store, picked up louder at Ginger-snaps, carried careful to kitchen tables. Survey. Appraisal. Development. Soon.

Nothing stamped with a seal. Nothing nailed to a post. Nothing I can lay my palm against without inviting trouble through the door.

Summer already brings heat, thunderheads building tall over the ridge, mosquitoes whining near your ear before you reach the screen.

I have lived long enough to recognize the feel of eyes measuring distance.

In Lawhoma, when noticing begins, we do not charge the fence. We drag extra chairs from the shed. We set them in a loose circle. We pour tea. We listen for the space between words, the breath someone holds a second too long.

No-Skip Albums for Summer:

Harry Styles — Harry Styles
Brothers Osborne — Port Saint Joe

Ed Sheeran— Divide

Eric Church — 61 Days of Church, Volumes 1-5

Kings of Leon — Come Around Sundown

Ashley McBryde — Ashley McBryde Presents:
Lindeville

blue creek lake opens its arms

ON THE FIRST real hot days of summer, everything happens fast in Lawhoma Hills. Fans start humming again on front porches. The smell of catfish frying slips out of kitchen windows. And most mornings, a kid dives into Blue Creek Lake before breakfast—because the day itself is a dare.

By the time I made it to the shore, the place was already buzzing. Bright sun scattered across the water like loose change. Wind rolled off the lake carrying that murky algae scent that shows up right on time every year, unfolding its arms and settling in right where it belongs.

OPENING DAY ARRIVED the way it always does—generous and a little unruly. Coolers packed too full. Towels draped over shoulders and railings. Children raced ahead and left their shoes behind before the sand even warmed. Music drifted from somewhere near the docks. Ross burned the first batch of hot dogs, and nobody said a word about it.

It was Darla who noticed first.

She stood with her hands on her hips, squinting toward the south side of the lake, where a cluster of vehicles sat just beyond the tree line.

"You see that?" she murmured.

I followed her gaze. The distance shimmered in the heat, door markings unreadable, but I could read posture. Those trucks weren't parked. They were waiting. The fancy black sports car too.

Darla's phone buzzed once. She didn't linger over it. Just typed, slipped it back into her pocket.

A few minutes later, Matty came over from the Nature Center, his walk easy, his eyes not. Around us, a few adults checked their phones—nothing urgent, just enough to register something, send something, tuck it away again.

"Come on!" Trip called, already knee-deep and splashing toward shore.

I clapped once, bright as I could make it. "Sunscreen check, then we eat." I realized, too late, that I hadn't counted heads in a while.

My eyes swept the water once—quick, practiced—and landed on Jasper's wet hair just as he popped up beside Hank, laughing.

Nothing wrong.

Still, my chest stayed tight longer than it should have.

And whatever sat across the water stayed where it was.

WADE WADDELL STOOD PROUDLY beside his line of shiny canoes and kayaks. His feathers stuck out at odd angles in that classic first-day-of-summer way, but his smile stretched wide enough to make it feel as though he'd personally unlocked the lake.

"Yaya, you are just in time for the safety speech," Wade called.

Trip, Smith, and Goldie skipped in excited circles, darting in and out of the water, little mallards that can't decide which part of summer to start with. Each wrestled a life jacket that was too big and not really needed anymore.

I crouched to help Goldie, turning the jacket the right way before she went in upside down.

"We will fix that," I told her.

Farther down the dock, Kolby Sweeney demonstrated wakeboard adjustments, talking to the older kids knowing they were capable of learning something real. He checked the straps, then checked them again —steady, patient.

His younger brother Boone tested each board by hopping between them until their daddy, Nick called out in that perfected father tone that goes straight to a child's bones.

"Feet on solid ground, buddy."

CLOSER TO SHORE, Clover and Sage Hill gathered the smaller kids, leading stretches before swimming. Their honeybee wings fluttered in the sun as they counted.

"One, two, three. Reach for the sky. Now wiggle your toes."

On an overturned bucket, Beck Hill wrote in his Blue Creek Rule Book, which I'm fairly sure he keeps entirely in his head. The boy treated the lake as his kingdom and himself, its King.

Nearby, Ranger tested a rescue rope, tugging hard enough to prove the knots could hold a grown-up. Carly arranged wildflowers along the picnic tables, turning the snack area into something that felt—a porch party, not a public lakeshore. Wilder Kate Everett warmed up her singing voice for the Blue Creek Summer Song she insists on performing every year, humming until the notes drifted out over the water.

Watching it all, my heart did what it always does when the community finds its rhythm. Even with that small, quiet weight sitting across the lake, this place still knew how to be itself.

"All right, all right, all right," Wade announced, flapping his wings and puffing his feathers. "Number one, life jackets. Number two, listen for whistles. Number three, have fun, but think first. The lake is your friend—and she deserves respect."

Smith took off running before anyone said his name, feet slapping hot boards.

"Hey—" Wade started, already moving.

Smith skidded at the edge, laughed, and stopped himself short before flying head first off the dock.

Wade crouched in front of him, voice low enough not to carry. "We don't test the water without asking first."

Smith nodded, feathers settling, and reached for his life jacket without being told.

I caught myself thinking about how differently we raised kids once, before TV and social media made safety its own language.

"You sound like a real old lady," I whispered to myself.

Even the kids who'd been swimming here since they learned to walk listened, it mattered.

The first canoe slid into the water with Tucker Brewster paddling smooth while JJ Flanagan rode up front, still glowing from her cross-country finish. JJ's strokes were powerful, a little chaotic, and full of joy.

"You are splashing me on purpose," Tucker laughed.

"That is impossible," JJ shouted. "I am paddling the best I can Tucker!"

DOWN THE DOCK, Millie and Hank Miller practiced knots Pop had shown them during camp workday. Jasper West tried too, but whatever he tied looked so complicated it belonged in a wizard's handbook.

"That is impressive," I told him. "Not useful, but impressive."

At the far end, Kolby skimmed across the water in a practice run, light as a skipped stone, then coasted back in.

"I don't have to be going fast to have fun," he said, pushing water off his forehead. "But fast is awesome! The best thing Stetson taught me, you gotta pay attention."

A lesson that landed without trying.

At the picnic tables, Lolli and Bootsie Howard organized snacks—strawberries, cucumber sandwiches, little jars of honey, and Bootsie's herbal iced tea that smells like a warm porch evening. Pop oversaw the berries, which mostly meant Pop ate more than he supervised.

Everything felt alive. Splash after splash. Laughter bouncing off the water. Locusts buzzing like they'd signed on as cheerleaders.

This was the kind of day that tucks itself into memory without asking permission.

. . .

LATER, I sat on the dock with my feet in the cool water and looked around at our small world—kids learning, families helping families, animals and humans sharing the same sun. All of us tending ourselves, the water, and each other.

That was Blue Creek at its finest. Summer doing what it does best, giving us everything at once, and daring us not to ask what it might cost us later.

SATURDAY, JUNE 7

TUESDAY'S MINI CAMP WITH THE OKLAHOMA DEPARTMENT OF WILDLIFE CONSERVATION LANDED BETTER THAN I'D HOPED. THURSDAY BROUGHT THE BEST BIRD SIGHTING DAY WE'VE HAD YET. I FLIPPED THROUGH THEIR NOTES AGAIN BEFORE DINNER: TUFTED TITMOUSE, CAROLINA CHICKADEE, RUBY-CROWNED KINGLET. CAREFUL HANDWRITING. LITTLE BURSTS OF PRIDE IN THE MARGINS.

MY FACE STILL FEELS TIGHT FROM THE SUN. BY MORNING IT'LL SETTLE INTO A TAN, SOFTEN THE LINES A BIT, MAKE MY WRINKLES LOOK MORE HONEST THAN APOLOGETIC.

TONIGHT'S LISTEN: "SHINE" — COLLECTIVE SOUL

To Do:

NEXT WEEK IS FULL UP

CALL POP ABOUT TENT BUILDING FOR TUESDAY / CONFIRM 0900

CHECK FRIENDSHIP BRACELET SUPPLIES

CALL REED AND DAPHNE ABOUT JUNETEENTH FOOD ITEMS

for those about to rock, we organize you

SUMMER IN LAWHOMA Hills has a way of gathering people without asking permission. The sunshine does it. The long evenings do it. The sound of sprinklers ticking does it. By the second week of June, excitement was growing faster than zucchini in July, and everywhere I went, the same conversations followed me.

At Red Foods, leaning over the laundry soap:

"Will Wilder Kate sing again?"

At Gingersnaps, half-buried in the shoe aisle:

"Think the Banerjee boys will play bluegrass this year?"

At the post office, Pop stood too close to the stamp counter and announced to no one in particular, "We need a grunge night."

That last idea wasn't met with immediate rejection—which told me summer had already softened everyone's judgment.

SO WHEN GINGER EVERETT called a town planning meeting to talk about expanding the Summer Concert Series, the community poured into Town Hall like it was free air conditioning and permission to be loud on purpose.

Hank Miller and Jasper West came with me, each carrying a Summer Ideas notebook like they were junior council members. They sat in the front row, backs straight, eyes serious—ready to vote on matters they weren't old enough to fully understand but absolutely old enough to care about.

The room buzzed with that specific mix of joy and chaos only music can stir. Wilder Kate warmed up softly in the corner, her voice testing the ceiling. Shep and Brick Banerjee tapped drumsticks against their legs. Bridger Ashe carried a stack of sheet music tucked under one arm. A few school jazz band kids spread arrangements across a table like they were laying out a treasure map.

Carly and Ranger whispered excitedly about goat-yoga flash mobs. I pretended not to hear them.

At the front of the room stood Gus Franklin, wearing his tool belt like a badge of honor.

"I hear we need a proper stage this year," Gus said, tapping the podium. "Well. You've got your man."

The room erupted like he'd just promised free lemonade forever.

Ginger flipped open her clipboard. "Genres first."

Hands shot up.

"Old-school country."

"Bluegrass."

"Student jazz band."

"Early 2000s hits."

Wilder Kate stood, cheeks pinking the way they do when she's about to be brave.

"I'd love to do a night of covers," she said, "and maybe one or two of my own."

"She is getting good," Shep said, loud enough for half the room to hear, like he'd personally raised her voice into being.

Ideas poured out from there. Chase Everett offered lighting help. Ruby volunteered poster designs using math patterns. Bridger proposed a student showcase. Eugene raised his wing to sponsor snacks—which earned applause, he'd already fed us.

It was joyful and unruly and exactly what community planning looks like when nobody's pretending not to care.

. . .

WHEN THE MUSIC talk finally slowed, Gus stepped forward and pulled down a large sheet of paper taped to an easel—a detailed drawing of a brand-new outdoor stage.

The room went still.

Then gasped.

"It'll go here," Gus said, pointing to the grassy area near the Farmer's Market lawn. "Covered roof. Built-in lighting. Storage for sound equipment. Reinforced flooring. Steps on both sides."

Ranger leaned toward Carly and whispered, dead serious, "Can goats climb up there?"

Gus squinted at the drawing. "Probably."

The kids cheered. The adults applauded. Hank leaned toward me, eyes wide.

"Yaya," he whispered, "it really does look like a fancy concert stage."

"It is a fancy concert stage," Jasper said reverently, as if purpose itself had just arrived.

Before the room could settle, Arthur Banerjee lifted a hand—the same way he does on the school bus when the back row needs reminding.

"BEFORE WE ADJOURN," he said, smiling like he hated to interrupt joy, "we need five minutes for Blue Creek."

The shift wasn't heavy. Just attentive.

"We've had vehicles on the south side the last two weekends," Arthur said. "Marked. Professional. Not fishing. Matty confirmed they're surveying."

Matty nodded once from the side of the room.

"Surveying what?" Gus asked.

Rosemary Rodriguez stood. Calm as someone who's spent a lifetime reading land.

"The west-side tract," she said. "One-hundred-sixty-three acres. We don't know the full scope yet. But we know enough to start acting like grown-ups."

Pop muttered, "I am acting like a grown-up."

Lolli pinched his elbow.

Arthur tapped his pen. "Bet and Matty are gathering documentation.

Rosemary's team is mapping plant presence. We need a legal consult—before fall."

Ginger didn't hesitate. She flipped to a fresh page and set a sign-up sheet on the table.

"If you can give time, skills, or money, write your name. If you can't—write your name anyway. We're better together. Boots on the ground. Ears to phones. Call attorneys. Find someone who knows city code. Or just show up."

Pens scratched. The room breathed. Confusion flickered, then steadied. Faces softened. People nod the way they do when a place starts deciding to defend itself.

Something in my chest shifted.

JUST AS QUIET began to return, the back door flew open and in walked Tata—late, dramatic, entirely unbothered.

"Did I miss roll call?" she asked, adjusting her scarf.

"No, Mom," Lolli said. "We don't take roll call."

Tata marched down the aisle anyway. "I would like to propose a theme night," she announced. "Songs from every decade I've been alive."

Pop leaned toward me. "This will be a very long concert."

Wilder Kate smiled. "I actually love that idea, Tata. Maybe you can sing one with us?"

"Well," Tata said, pleased, "I could try. I was a wonderful singer in my youth."

WE VOTED THE OLD-FASHIONED WAY—HANDS raised, voices counted, arguments that weren't really arguments. Just passion wearing a smile.

Gus would build the stage.

Concert nights were approved, plus a student showcase.

Afterward, the Blue Creek sign-up sheet stayed on the counter. People circled back. Names were added. Numbers written. Grandma Bertha asked where donations should go, and Ginger pointed to a jar like she'd known all along she'd need one.

Outside, the evening air felt charged. Crickets tuned up. Summer leaned in close enough to listen.

At home, the boys sprawled across the couch, scribbling song lists.

Jasper wanted banjo music, guitar solos, and "the one with the howling coyote Flanagans."

Hank wanted drums, Wilder Kate originals, and "any song where Pop may yell-sing."

At the bottom of Hank's page, in smaller letters, he wrote:

ask yaya what surveying means

I wrapped blankets around them as the porch lights flickered on.

"Yaya," Hank asked, already half asleep, "do you think the concerts will be cool?"

"I think," I said, brushing his hair back, "they already are."

Down by the water, bullfrogs harmonized, keeping time with a hopeful, steady rhythm.

MONDAY, JUNE 9

AFTER WE GOT HOME FROM THE MEETING, WE STAYED OUTSIDE AND LET GOLDEN HOUR HAVE ITS WAY.

THE OKLAHOMA SUNSET PUT ON A SHOW. PINK SO VIVID IT MATCHED MY FADING SUNBURN—THE KIND OF COLOR THAT COULD BE BOTTLED AND SOLD AS A LIPSTICK CALLED TRY ME, HONEY. BEANS AND RJ SETTLED CLOSE, WARM BODIES PRESSED INTO MY LEGS, AND I PETTED EACH OF THEM SLOW, LIKE I MIGHT SMOOTH THE WHOLE DAY FLAT WITH MY HANDS.

I LOVE MUSIC. I FILL MY EARS WITH IT EVERY CHANCE I GET. CONCERT PLANNING DIDN'T CHANGE THAT. ALL I COULD SEE AHEAD WERE NIGHTS FULL OF SOUND AND LAUGHTER. THAT PART FELT EASY.

IT WAS THE OTHER PART—THE BLUE CREEK PART—THAT TRIED TO EDGE IN WHILE THE SKY WAS STILL BRIGHT. I LET IT TRY. THEN I LET IT GO. I SAT THERE WITH THE DOGS AND DIDN'T BORROW TROUBLE. NOT TONIGHT.

TOMORROW IS TENT-BUILDING DAY, AND MY BED WAS ALREADY

CALLING MY NAME, BUT I LET A '90S GRUNGE MOOD SETTLE THE
EVENING INTO SOMETHING STEADIER.

Tonight's listen: "Hard Sun" — Eddie Vedder

To Do:
Alarm 0430/ water, move drip line, deadhead
Pull tents out to the picnic area
Harvest for Friday Market: peppers, eggplant (if
ready), zinnias, cosmos, lisianthus, snaps, yarrow/ go out
late Thursday or early Friday
Run to TSC for more harvest buckets

EIGHTEEN

juneteenth gathering

BY MID-JUNE, the heat in Lawhoma Hills had settled into its routine. It rose early, leaned heavy by noon, and stayed long after supper. The Chapman yard took it without complaint. Red dirt baked smooth between patches of grass. The pecan tree dropped shade in wide, reliable pieces. Ronnie had dragged a picnic table closer to the house and tilted it just enough that one leg needed shimming with a flat rock.

We weren't on the calendar date this year. Summer schedules scattered people, so the Chapmans hosted when folks could come.

I pulled up with my windows down and my potato salad sweating in its bowl. Reed had told me to come early if I wanted a job. I always want a job at other people's gatherings.

The yard was already in motion.

Reed Chapman stood at the grill, sweat darkening his chest feathers. Wyatt barreled around the side of the house trailing a length of ribbon.

"Don't run with that," Reed called, not looking up.

"I wasn't running," Wyatt said, skidding to a stop. "I was testing speed."

Ronnie followed more carefully, carrying a cardboard box with hand-lettered signs taped to the sides. One read FREEDOM DAY. Another had been crossed out and rewritten twice, marker lines thick.

Daphne sat barefoot on the porch steps snapping beans into a metal bowl. Each one broke clean.

"You girls are going to knock the flags over," she said.

"They're sturdy momma, I won't." Wyatt said.

"They're cardboard," Daphne replied.

"Ok, I won't bend the cardboard," Wyatt huffed.

I set my dish on the porch rail and grabbed folding chairs leaned against the house.

"Under the pecan," Daphne said. "Leave a path. Kids will run no matter what."

"I've met these wild kiddos," I laughed.

Ronnie crouched beside the box, sorting supplies. Paper fans. Red ribbon. Programs Daphne had printed at the post office, ink still faint.

Wyatt picked one up and squinted. "Why does it say Oklahoma?"

"Because it mattered and no-one came on time," Ronnie said. "Texas heard the news June nineteenth, 1865. Other places heard even later."

Wyatt frowned. "That stinks and was totally unfair."

Daphne looked up. "It was."

Wyatt tied the ribbon to a fence post, knot pulled tight.

BY THE TIME GUESTS ARRIVED, the yard shifted. Chairs filled the shade. Coolers clanked open. Children darted between legs already sticky with popsicle juice.

Butter appeared near the compost bin dragging a scrap of red fabric, then disappeared again.

"Butter stole the ribbon!" Wyatt said.

"She likes crafts sissy, leave her alone," Ronnie said.

Butter returned wearing the ribbon looped around her neck like a scarf. She paused, met Wyatt's eyes, flicked her tail.

Daphne laughed. "Let her be."

Music rolled in from County Road 40 and settled into the yard. Old gospel. Blues. A little 90s R&B that made the teenagers pretend not to like it while moving anyway.

Reed clapped once. "Food's almost ready."

People drifted closer without being told. Bootsie smoothed the tablecloth. Daphne set the beans down and scanned the crowd—family first, then friends, then newer faces still learning the shape of things.

When she caught my eye, she nodded once. You're here. Keep going.

AFTER EVERYONE MADE THEIR PLATES, Reed cleared his throat.

"Thank you for coming."

When he lifted his hand again, the music cut.

Ronnie stood, holding the microphone with both hands.

"Juneteenth marks the day freedom was announced in Texas," she said. "Two years late. In Oklahoma, later still. People were already moving, building lives, making plans before the words reached them."

Wyatt shifted.

"We gather because freedom delayed is still freedom claimed," Ronnie said. "Because names matter. Because remembering matters."

Katydid song filled the space between her sentences.

Daphne stepped forward. She didn't use the microphone.

"My grandmother said you could tell the truth by watching what people carried," she said. "Food. Songs. Stories."

She gestured to the tables, the yard.

"We're still carrying all of it," she said. "Eat. Talk. Ask questions. Let the kids run."

Applause followed, easy and unperformed.

Wyatt ran toward the creek with the younger kids, shoes abandoned near the porch.

Later, Daphne found her sitting on the picnic table folding her program into a paper boat.

"Do you know why I like Juneteenth?" Wyatt asked.

Daphne waited.

"Because it's loud with music and people," Wyatt said. "And nobody pretends it wasn't important."

Daphne nodded.

As lanterns were lit and fireflies stitched the yard's edges, Butter returned dragging a strip of cloth tied to a stick. She planted it by the compost bin and sat beside it proud.

Wyatt saluted.

When the chairs were folded and the yard emptied, Daphne picked up the ribbon Butter had dropped, folded it once, and slipped it into her pocket.

Some things were meant to be kept.

SATURDAY, JUNE 14
THE CHAPMANS' YARD STAYED WITH ME AFTER I LEFT—
LANTERN LIGHT, CICADAS, THE SOUND OF BEANS SNAPPING INTO
A BOWL.
WYATT'S PAPER BOAT RODE HOME ON THE DASHBOARD.
BUTTER'S RIBBON DIDN'T.
I'M LEARNING WHEN TO SPEAK AND WHEN TO CARRY SOME-
THING QUIETLY INSTEAD.

TONIGHT'S LISTEN:
"CELEBRATION" — KOOL & THE GANG

TO-DO:
TEXT DAPHNE THANK YOU
RESTOCK CAMP SUPPLIES
WASH TABLECLOTHS BEFORE THE NEXT GATHERING

careers, committees, and care

BY LATE JUNE, the heat in Lawhoma Hills is here to stay awhile. Slow. Stubborn. We moved gatherings indoors when we could, which meant Spruce Street Books. The air conditioning worked. The shelves smelled of paper, tea, and use.

Thursday nights carried another scent.

They smelled of futures not yet lived.

By the time I arrived, my shirt clung to my back and I ignored it. Rosemary and Manuel slid shelves aside to make room. Jordan lined up folding chairs in straight rows, treating order as a form of care. Bootsie came in with a tin of cookies shaped into briefcases, trees, and airplanes and taped a sign to the door.

THURSDAY CAREER NIGHTS

Come see how your neighbors do what they do.

Hank Miller and Jasper West flanked me, each holding a small notebook.

"I hope this isn't boring Ya, I am not ready to know my career, I am barely thinking about clean socks." Hank announced.

"This is when you can plan your future, find what you like…. That's what Lolli told me yesterday." Jasper added, solemn and sincere.

"You're allowed to change your mind ten thousand times," I said.

They nodded and gripped their notebooks anyway.

The room filled fast. Children cross-legged on the floor. Adults claiming stools and cushions. Tata took a front-row seat and uncapped a pen she did not need.

"Could this become my favorite Thursday night?" Lolli whispered.

"It might be mine too," I said. I meant it.

The speakers had agreed to answer three questions:

What do you do?

How did you learn it?

Why does it matter?

CARTER SIMMONS WENT FIRST. Pilot. Snake dad. Wings pinned to his shirt.

"I fly planes," he said.

The room held still.

"I started with toys. Then simulators. Then instructors who didn't let me forget the rules."

"There are a lot of rules, I bet." Jasper whispered.

Carter nodded. "Because when people trust you with the sky, you don't get careless."

Dahlia Banerjee followed, steady and unhurried.

"I'm a forest ranger," she said. "I care for land that doesn't belong to one person."

"I check trails. Help people who get turned around. Watch animals who cannot ask for help."

"You protect trees?" Lacey asked.

Dahlia smiled. "Trees. And the lives tangled in them."

Casey Jo Brewster stood in scrubs, headband on, she had come straight from work.

"I'm a nurse," she said. I was an LPN for many years and became an RN later on. Most days I help people do things they used to do alone."

She let the quiet work.

"Eating. Walking. Remembering."

"I learned science, math, and lots of practice caring for others," she said. "I learned patience from the people I care for."

"A good day is when someone feels steadier than they did that morning."

Tata's mouth pressed thin. Not disapproval. Recognition.

"I could do that, maybe," she thought out loud.

Casey Jo met her eyes. "We could use you."

Tata nodded once.

Manuel Rodriguez adjusted the badge on his jacket.

"I work security," he said. "Which mostly means planning for what I hope never happens."

"Lost kids. Medical emergencies. Weather turning fast, finding lost keys, locking doors, and keeping my eyes open."

"My job is to stay calm so others can enjoy themselves."

Juan Carlos sat taller.

Harry and Charlotte Windsor stood together. Beau slept between them.

"I design outdoor spaces," Harry said. "I studied horticulture at Oklahoma State, and learned from my parents when they started our nursery." Charlotte explained her role as a civil engineer, "my job is drawing the plans and looking at safety, maintenance, and if projects can remain sustainable."

"Plants. Paths. Places to gather."

"Drainage. Materials. Safety."

"If we do it right," Harry said, "people don't notice."

"They just feel safe," Charlotte said.

Tallulah Sweetstripe stepped forward, hands dusted with flour.

"I own Running Waters Café. I feed people."

"I learned by failing mostly," she said. "Repeatedly."

"When do you know a recipe is good or when it's ready?" Juan Carlos asked.

"When it tastes like care," Tallulah said.

Butter the skunk sniffed. "Now I'm hungry."

Laughter moved through the room. Easy. Earned.

WHEN THE SPEAKERS FINISHED, I stood. The boys were watching.

"You don't need certainty to begin," I said. "You need care and the willingness to learn."

Hank and Jasper held their notebooks like maps.

The chairs shifted. The room quieted.

Bet Sinclair stepped forward. Matty stood beside her, hands in his pockets.

"Tonight wasn't about jobs," Bet said. "It was about care."

"We work in conservation," she continued. "Which means we look at places people love

and ask how to keep them whole."

Matty nodded. "Blue Creek Lake is one of those places."

"We're preparing research," Bet said. " Documentation. Mapping what already exists."

"It takes time," Matty said. "And people who know this land."

Hands lifted.

"I am happy to help, if I can" Dahlia said.

"I can review plans," Charlotte offered.

"The lake raised our kids," Darla Waddell said. "Count us in."

Rosemary lifted her binder. "I have a pretty decent amount of records going already."

Paul Chen cleared his throat. "I teach biology."

Paddy raised his hand halfway. "Does this count toward Eagle Scout credit?"

"It counts toward being useful," Matty said.

Paddy raised his hand all the way.

Bet took a breath. "There's one more thing."

"The vehicles near the lake and County Road 40 and the booth we've all seen at the Farmer's Market."

A murmur passed.

"They're surveyors," Bet said. "From a development firm in Tulsa, Aperture Developments.

They look to be an urban renewal firm, building on empty space across the state."

Silence settled.

"It is apparent they have funding and approvals," she said. "Which means speed."

"Money does that," Matty said.

"But speed is not care," Bet said.

I looked around the room. No panic. No speeches. Just people awake.

"This," I said, "is how good things begin, the talking and awareness starts whatever Lawhoma folks need to do."

Pens came out. Names were written.

Outside, the evening waited.

Thursday, June 19

Camp is running full-tilt.

Pajama Day became a parade of flannel and stubborn bedhead. Flashlight stories pulled kids shoulder-to-shoulder. S'mores landed everywhere except where intended. The goats watched without comment.

Wilder Kate led sing-alongs and pulled even the too-cool kids in. Voices cracked. People tried anyway.

Tomorrow is the first summer concert. July is already leaning in.

Summer moves the way creek water does after a hard rain. Fast. Loud. Committed.

Tonight's listen: "Morning Comes Wearing Diamonds" —
Ray LaMontagne

To Do:
Market tomorrow
Harvest early
Call the boys
Highest so far: $232.00
I would like to see $250.00.
Saturday city trip with Annie. Sunscreen. Lawn chairs.
Lanterns.

tata finds new purpose

I WENT to open the front blinds and found Tata already awake, rocking slow on the porch swing. A teacup rested in her hand, gone cold, which told me everything I needed to know. Tata does not abandon tea.

She wasn't crying. That was never her way. But her thoughts had been pacing all night, and she wore the look of someone who had followed them to the end.

"You alright?" I asked, sitting beside her.

She nodded once. "Last night stayed with me," she said. "All those people talking about how they serve others."

Her thumb circled the bracelet she'd worn since Doc passed, keeping time with something only she could hear.

"Doc," she said, voice tightening just enough to notice. "A man who filled rooms. A man who left them slowly."

She looked out over the yard, eyes searching the ground like the answer might be tucked under the pecan leaves.

"I realized I'm not finished," she said. "I still have something to give."

I waited.

"I want to volunteer at the Lawhoma Hills Care Center," she said. "The memory unit. Families too. Lolli suggested I ask you, since you did the work–can I volunteer, I don't need pay."

She rattled off questions then finally, took a breath. "I know what it is to lose someone a memory at a time."

That was it. The truth, said plain.

LATER THAT AFTERNOON, Lolli called laughing so hard she had to start over.

"Tata walked into Larry's and ordered Casey Jo," she said. "Like she was hiring a roofer."

When Tata came back to my place, she reenacted the scene with courtroom authority.

"Put me to work," she said, slapping the porch armrest.

"And?" I asked.

"She hugged me," Tata said, chin lifted. "Hard."

ON HER FIRST VOLUNTEER DAY, Lolli and I went with her. Not because Tata needed help. Some beginnings deserve witnesses.

She carried a tote filled with small comforts. Scarves folded neat. Oversized playing cards. A photo album from the good years. And a tin of lemon bars, powdered sugar drifting every time she moved.

Inside, Tata moved without hesitation. She learned names quickly. Sat beside people, not across. A woman stroked the edge of Tata's scarf, whispering, "Pretty," again and again.

Tata stayed still. Let it be enough.

A man studied the photo album for a long time. "I knew someone like him once," he said.

"He was wonderful," Tata replied. "Sometimes wonderful things stay even when memory doesn't."

I watched Lolli press her mouth tight, swallowing back what rose.

Casey Jo stood in the doorway, hand over her chest.

"She belongs here," she said later, quiet as truth.

A week after that, Tata stood in front of a room full of families.

She wore a coral blazer she'd purchased that morning, because Tata refuses to grieve quietly. Her hands rested easy on the podium.

"My name is Tata," she said. "I walked this road with my husband."

The room settled.

"You lose them before the goodbye," she said. "But you learn to love who remains."

She spoke of repetition. Of mercy. Of days when clarity returned without warning.

"We don't honor people by remembering who they were," she said. "We honor them by loving who they are today."

A woman reached for her hand. Tata took it without pause.

Those talks stayed on the calendar.

Now Tata stops at Gingersnaps before each one. A sweater. A jacket. Something bright enough to remind tired rooms that color still exists.

Ginger set aside a section labeled TATA'S CLOSET.

Tata approved.

That evening, Tata sat beside me and Lolli on the porch and sighed, long and settled.

"I thought the world was done with me," she said. "Turns out I was wrong."

She didn't look busy. Or braced.

She looked whole.

THURSDAY, JULY 3

TATA SPOKE TONIGHT WITHOUT SOFTENING ANYTHING. PEOPLE NOTICE THE JACKETS FIRST. WHAT THEY MISS IS THE PATIENCE UNDERNEATH.

AND DOC.

NOT MEMORY. NOT LESSONS. PRESENCE.

A VOICE IN A ROOM. A HAND OFFERED.

I DON'T FEEL FINISHED. BUT I FEEL AWAKE.

THAT WILL DO.

TONIGHT'S LISTEN: "AT LAST" — ETTA JAMES

TO DO:

ASK GUS ABOUT BUSY BOARDS FOR CASEY JO/ COST ETC.

TEXT CASEY JO

PICK OKRA

ronnie's wings

MY PHONE LIT up early the morning after the pageant, the way it does when somebody's already lived through their feelings and come out the other side.

> Reed: Breakfast at Running Waters? Our treat.
> Ronnie wants to ask you something. Also,
> Backstage hot topics.

I smiled into my coffee. Reed doesn't add emojis unless something has shifted.

RUNNING Waters Café sat cool and dim against the July heat, air conditioning humming, the smell of coffee and warm bread doing its quiet work. Daphne waited at a corner table with Ronnie, a bowl of fruit between them. Reed stood when I walked in, tired-eyed and proud, like he'd been guarding something delicate all night.

"Yaya," he said, pulling me in. "Thank you for coming."

"I saw our girl shine," I told him.

Ronnie's feathers still held a trace of stage polish, sleek and careful, but she didn't look like someone clinging to it. Her white wing rested folded and bright against her side. She looked steady in a way that had nothing to do with applause.

Daphne slid a mug toward me. "We ordered you the good stuff."

I took a sip. It tasted like being let in.

Wyatt arrived late and loud, breathless with updates she was told to save for later. Reed gave her a look. She sat. Mostly.

"Star stole the show," Wyatt finally blurted.

Ronnie smiled. "Star had the biggest tutu."

"A very serious tutu," Wyatt added.

I laughed. "And you," I said to Ronnie, "belonged up there."

Ronnie tipped her beak down, then up. "I tried."

"You were strong," Daphne said, smoothing Ronnie's shoulder once. No drama. Just a fact.

The pageant had been polished. Sparkle and choreography and stories meant to stay neat. Ronnie's hadn't. It had weight. When the lights hit her, she didn't shrink or perform small. She held herself like someone who knew she deserved the space.

She didn't take the crown.

She took Most Photogenic.

Not consolation. Recognition.

Back at the table, Reed watched me closely. "You saw her."

"I did," I said. "All of her."

Ronnie's smile softened, then shifted. She looked at her hands, then back up.

"Yaya," she said, voice careful and brave at the same time. "Can I ask you something?"

"Always."

"I got made fun of for my look, I talked to mom and dad and well....I think I should start a club?"

Wyatt vibrated. Daphne's hand covered Ronnie's.

Ronnie kept going. "Not a school club. A place for kids who feel different and are tired of bullying or embarrassed by stuff they don't need to be about, you know what I mean? Like a club we can be ourselves. Does that make me more weird? I don't know but..."

I set my mug down slow, so she knew she had my full attention.

"What would you do there?"

Ronnie's shoulders eased. "Talk or make things, maybe older kids could show younger kids how to stay themselves, like we are our own kind of super hero."

The room went quiet in the good way.

"That," I said, "sounds like a necessary club."

Reed exhaled. "We told her you'd understand."

"I do," I said. "We'll talk about the details. We'll build it right."

Ronnie nodded once. Decided.

Outside, the heat was already pressing in. Inside, we sat with our plates and the feeling that something had just been named.

That's how courage shows up sometimes. Over breakfast. With good coffee. With someone saying, tell me more.

SUNDAY, JULY 6

I CAME HOME AFTER BREAKFAST AND CALLED WILDER KATE ABOUT TOMORROW'S CAMPFIRE SING-ALONG.

THE YARD WAS IN FULL SUMMER MOTION. BEANS FOLLOWED ME IN HIS SUPERVISOR HAT; IT WAS HIS JOB. RJ BLOCKED THE DOORWAY AND DARED ME TO SIT STILL.

I KEPT THINKING ABOUT REED AND DAPHNE. THE WAY THEY DON'T JUST TELL THEIR GIRLS THEY'RE ENOUGH. THEY BUILD A WORLD THAT AGREES.

I FELT A FLICKER OF ENVY.

I DIDN'T HAVE THAT KIND OF COVERING GROWING UP. I HAD LOVE. JUST NOT THE KIND THAT STAYED WITHOUT CONDITIONS.

I LET THE FEELING PASS THROUGH ME.

I ATE GREENS FOR SUPPER AND DANCED IN THE KITCHEN WITH BEANS STEPPING ON MY TOES. THERE ARE MANY WAYS TO BE SEEN.

TONIGHT'S LISTEN: "FAMOUS IN A SMALL TOWN" — MIRANDA LAMBERT

To Do:
Call Harry about drip line leaks
Can okra and pickles/ no excuses
Order new garden shoes

To Do:
Call Harry about drip line leaks
Can okra and pickles/ no excuses
Order new garden shoes

roping, wrangling, and jasper's lesson

MOST ADVENTURES DON'T SHOW up with banners or warnings. Some just appear—quiet as a goat on a fencepost—waiting to see if a kid's got enough curiosity to reach out.

That was the rodeo for Jasper West.

It started like any summer day at my place, with the boys bouncing between Camp Run Amuck, the farm, and whatever project Pop had left halfway done. But then Ranger's truck rumbled up the drive—goat trailer in tow—and the air changed.

He wore that smile that means he's been thinking too long and finally decided to do something about it.

"Yaya!" Jasper shouted before the truck even stopped. "He brought the goats!"

Hank squinted at the trailer, suspicious. "Why are there ropes?"

Ranger hopped down, brushing dust off his jeans like it had insulted him. "Just an idea. Thought Jasper might want to try junior goat tying."

Jasper froze—one foot forward like he was about to run, but not sure if it was toward or away. "Me?"

"You," Ranger said, nodding slow. "You've got quick feet and a steady eye."

. . .

RANGER SET up a practice area out back—simple stuff. A soft patch of ground, a chute, some cones, shade pulled together from whatever trees we had left with branches worth using.

But before he handed Jasper a single rope, he crouched down beside him. And something about his posture made even the goats pause and watch.

"Listen close," Ranger said. "Rodeo is tradition. But tradition only matters if it keeps getting better."

Jasper eyed the goats. "Will it hurt them?"

Ranger shook his head. "Not when it's done right. We don't do this to a goat. We do it with a goat. That means calm hands. Respect. And if that goat says no? You stop."

Jasper nodded, slow. "I don't want to hurt them."

"That's why you're out here," Ranger said, and gave his shoulder a squeeze.

Practice didn't start with ropes. It started with time.

Jasper brushed the goats until their coats shined. Fed them apple pieces and learned which ones took bites polite and which ones snapped like they were mad at the air. They sniffed his pockets, his hands, his shoelaces—like they were deciding if he could be trusted.

He learned their names.

Cricket and Moonpie were the flirts.

Munchie was a follower.

Sheriff—though the smallest, he ran the precinct.

"Sheriff doesn't ask for respect," Ranger said. "He demands it."

Jasper squared his shoulders, realizing he'd just been handed an official challenge. "Yes sir, I will try Ranger, yes sir." I saw the tenderness, excitement, and respect land in his eyes at the same time.

When the rope finally came out, Jasper's focus narrowed. Ranger showed him the sequence with slow, practiced hands.

"Approach calm. Keep steady. Tie quick. Release quicker. And no celebrating till the goat's okay."

His first try landed him tangled in his own rope while Hank applauded from the fence. "Ten out of ten. Pure chaos."

Jasper stuck his tongue out and tried again. And again.

Soon enough, the rope stopped fighting him. Ranger adjusted his posture, his stance, the way his face pinched when he got nervous.

"Goats feel tension," he reminded him. "They'll mirror you."

"Safety first. Calm second. Skill third," Jasper mumbled, over and over, like a private creed.

They practiced in little clusters. Tied. Rested. Checked the goats. Watered. Sat under the shade without speaking. Ranger kept the pace gentle. Enough to challenge, not crush.

At one point, Jasper and I shared an upside-down bucket seat in the dust.

"Yaya," he said, "why do people do rodeos?"

"Lots of reasons," I told him. "Some for tradition, it is a tough sport but long time rodeo folks can earn a living too, and it sure is fun to watch."

He frowned. "Is it mean to the cows, bulls, horses or goats?"

"It can be," I said honestly. "That's why the how matters. You stop when something feels wrong. You ask questions. You decide what your part looks like."

Jasper looked at the rope in his lap. "I want to do it right."

"You already are," I said, brushing a smudge of dirt off his cheek.

BY LATE AFTERNOON, his movements had softened. He wasn't rushing. His hands moved fast, but never sharp. His release was clean. His face was steady. Even Sheriff seemed to notice.

"You question the hard stuff," Ranger said, arms crossed, watching. "Not everybody does."

Jasper shrugged. "I just want the goats to be okay."

"That," Ranger said, "is exactly what makes a cowboy worth knowing."

At the end, Ranger clapped his hands once. "One more. Ready?"

Jasper took a breath. "Sheriff, you rascal… let's do this!"

Sheriff strutted out like he'd been waiting for the encore. He zig-zagged, then—because goats love drama—held perfectly still.

Jasper moved like he'd practiced: calm, sure, fast, kind.

The tie was solid. The release was clean.

He didn't cheer. Just stood there watching Sheriff stroll off, unimpressed as ever.

"Did I do it?" Jasper whispered.

"You did," Ranger said, smiling with his whole face.

Sheriff ignored them both and went looking for something else to dominate.

WHEN ANNIE and Stetson pulled up, Jasper ran to the truck like he was carrying state secrets.

"Dad!" he shouted. "I worked with goats and I didn't hurt anyone, I landed a full tie like a champ!"

Stetson scooped him up like he was still small enough to hold. "That's my boy."

Annie leaned down and kissed his head. "You smell like goats and dirt."

Ranger tipped his hat. "You've got a good one here. He's got the right kind of grit."

As the truck pulled away, Jasper leaned out the back window and waved like something in him had shifted for good.

There are a dozen ways a child learns courage.

Sometimes it's a dusty afternoon, a stubborn goat named Sheriff, and a kid choosing kindness even when the rope's in his hands.

WEDNESDAY, JULY 16

IF YOU WANT TO KNOW WHAT KIND OF SEASON IT IS, YOU DON'T CHECK THE CALENDAR.

YOU WATCH THE BOYS.

THEY DON'T FIT ON MY PORCH SWING ANYMORE. KNEES EVERYWHERE. ELBOWS SHARP. ON AUGUST 11TH, THEY'LL WALK INTO THAT BUILDING WITH BACKPACKS AND THAT BRAVE SWAGGER KIDS WEAR WHEN THEY'RE HALF EXCITED, HALF TERRIFIED, AND UNWILLING TO ADMIT EITHER.

ANNIE, THEIR MOMMA, WHO CRIED HER EYES OUT WATCHING

Old Yeller like she was personally responsible for the ending. She packs lunches. Signs papers. Carries worries so practiced they don't slow her down.

I watched Jasper today, rope in his hands, choosing care over speed.

I'm lucky to witness the in-between moments.

The ones that don't announce themselves.

Tonight's Listen: "Tough Little Boys" — Gary Allan

To Do:

Find Junior Goat Tying Events near us

Find compression socks + stethoscope (Lord help me, where did I put it)

Dr. Bridget needs you Thursday

Pick green beans and cucumbers. More pickles, whether I feel like it or not

measured, weighed, still wild

EVERY YEAR, right when the garden turns heavy and the heat refuses to loosen its grip, Lawhoma Hills knows it's almost time to go back to school.

You can see it best in the hallway outside Dr. Bridget Sinclair's family practice. By late July, families line up with forms and backpacks and children who still smell faintly of lake water and sunscreen. I showed up in official Nurse Yaya capacity—the one day a year I pull scrubs from the back of the closet, slide my Danskos on, and let the Littmann hang around my neck like muscle memory. I don't come out of retirement for just anyone. I come out for Bridget and a hallway full of kids about to step into something new.

The clinic moved with practiced calm. Foster Flanagan had the rooms set before the first door opened, cuffs coiled neat, charts stacked square. Eli Everett presenting on Zoom, headset low, voice steady as he coordinated the remote nurse care navigators and confirmed their equipment deliveries. Dr. Bridget swept in like she always does, clipboard in hand, presence filling the space.

"Welcome to Back-to-School Health Day," she announced. "Our goals are simple: healthy, hydrated, and no one growing mushrooms between their toes."

Hank's eyes widened. "Gross, does that really happen?"

"No," she said sweetly. "But the fear helps."

She kept moving.

Kids cycled through fast. Tucker Brewster, sunburned and proud. JJ Flanagan, vibrating with opinions about what counts as hydration. Ruby Rodriguez arrived with a binder thick enough to stop a door.

"This is impressive," Bridget told her, flipping pages. "Also unnecessary. You are healthy."

Ruby exhaled, she'd been holding it since June.

Wilder Kate leaned against a doorframe humming scales while Foster checked her vitals. Some people don't turn their light off just because the setting changes.

NEAR MIDDAY, Bridget gathered the kids together.

"School works your brains hard," she said. "Your bodies need backup."

She counted it out. Sleep. Water. Real food.

"And kindness," she added. "Because healthy communities start with how we treat each other."

They nodded, solemn as if she'd handed them something sacred.

Frankie raised her hand. "What if we're nervous?"

Bridget didn't hesitate. "That means you care. We worry about kids who don't feel anything at all."

That settled something in the room.

When Hank and Jasper's turn came, they handled it fine—brave in that quiet way that doesn't ask for credit. Jasper squinted at the eye chart like it was personal.

"These letters are moving."

"They always do," Bridget replied. "Especially before school starts."

She signed their forms, told them they were growing fast, and slipped a pamphlet into my hand.

"Healthy Start Guide," she said. "For Pop."

"He'll pretend not to read it, then quote it later."

She smiled. "Good."

Outside, the heat wrapped around us again. The boys talked backpacks and teachers, voices already shifting toward fall.

In Lawhoma Hills, back-to-school isn't just forms and schedules. It's a town pausing long enough to check its children, steady them, and send them forward still wild, but ready.

114

THURSDAY, JULY 24
I CAME HOME TONIGHT SMELLING LIKE HAND SANITIZER, STICKER GLUE, AND THAT PARTICULAR KIND OF COURAGE KIDS CARRY WITHOUT REALIZING IT.
I SOAKED UNTIL THE ACHE SOFTENED. THE MUSIC CAME ON, AND MY FOOT FOUND THE BEAT UNDER THE FAUCET, EVEN THOUGH THE REST OF ME WANTED STILL.

TONIGHT'S LISTEN: "GIVE A LITTLE BIT" — SUPERTRAMP

To Do:
CALL ANNIE ABOUT SCHOOL SUPPLIES
INCREASE DRIP LINE TO 2 HOURS PER ZONE
ASK POP IF HE CAN HELP RICKY WITH SHADE CLOTH

the club of being different

A FEW WEEKS after breakfast with the Chapmans, Daphne called one morning.

"Is Camp Run Amuck open this Saturday?" she asked. "Ronnie wants to meet. And she's nervous."

"She doesn't need to be," I said. "But I'll help."

Ronnie came on the line, voice careful. "Would you text people? I don't want it to sound like I'm asking for something."

"You're not," I told her. "You're making space."

I sent the message.

> SATURDAY, 6 PM. Camp Run Amuck dining hall.
>
> Ronnie's starting The Club of Being Different. Everyone Welcome!
>
> Come eat. Come listen. Come as you are.

People answered fast.

> Carly: sure thing, will bring cookies!🍪
>
> Kelly: b there with bells on

ON THE FIRST MEETING EVENING, the dining hall held that low hum—chairs drawn into a circle, dishes set down without ceremony, string lights dimmed just enough to keep it from feeling like a stage.

Ronnie sat instead of standing. She smoothed her wings once.

"During the pageant," she said, voice steady but thinner than usual, "I realized how much I explain myself. Where I come from. How people don't understand my color and that makes people be awful sometimes. I'm tired of explaining myself so people can decide if I make sense."

She looked around the circle.

"I wanted to know if I was the only one."

Butter Sweetstripe immediately held up her hand and spoke first.

"My name is Aponi," she said. "Most of you call me Butter. My stripe's yellow instead of white like my whole family and every other skunk in the universe."

She shrugged.

"I used to wish it would change. Now I don't, because I am unique—period, it took a long time but I just don't explain it and that is way easier."

Carly cleared her throat. "People think labels equal truth," she said. "In high school, it was really hard dating Ranger made them louder. Folks think they know the whole story just by looking."

JJ leaned forward, eyes catching the lights—one gold, one blue.

"I spent so long hating my eyes," she said. "People thought it meant something was wrong with me, I got called really terrible names."

She paused.

"In coyotes, it's rare, in people too but it is not messed up or broken."

She rested her hand on Beans' back.

"There are some famous people with two eye colors and when I met Beans, I just fell in love with his big blue eye."

Beans lifted his head.

Will Franklin and Mack Ashe spoke together, the way they always did.

"We're tired of explaining the math," Will said.

"Half this, half that," Mack added.

"We're just family," Will finished.

Ellie stood. "Brother and sister is enough."

The quiet that followed held.

Kelly Chen raised her hand. "Ronnie," she said, "this matters. Kids carry labels I see every day at school and the dance studio. This opens a door."

Ronnie listened. Her shoulders lowered.

"THIS SHOULDN'T BE ONE NIGHT," she said. "I want younger kids to know they don't have to earn their place."

She looked at me.

"We can do that here," I said. "Consider officially on the camp calendar, you say when and the door will be open."

Outside, every bug in the valley chimed in. Inside, the circle stayed.

No one rushed to leave.

SATURDAY, JULY 26
AFTER THE LAST CAR PULLED OUT AND THE LIGHTS WENT DARK,
I STAYED BEHIND, STRAIGHTENING CHAIRS THAT DIDN'T NEED IT.
MY HANDS WANTED WORK.
LATE-JULY HEAT LEANED AGAINST THE WINDOWS.
I SPENT YEARS EDITING MYSELF BEFORE WALKING INTO ROOMS.
SOFTEN THE LAUGH. DULL THE EDGE. TAKE UP LESS.
TONIGHT REMINDED ME THAT SHRINKING ISN'T THE COST OF
BELONGING.
HONEST, I WAS RELIEVED THAT THE FOCUS WAS JUST THE KIDS.
NOT SHRINKING FROM WHATEVER FIGHT WE HAVE AGAINST

APERTURE OR THOSE RIDICULOUS HIGH HEELS, SELFISH MAYBE—
NICE TO SIT IN AND IT NOT BE THE TOPIC.

TONIGHT'S LISTEN: "YOU'RE ON YOUR OWN, KID" — TAYLOR
SWIFT

TO DO:
TEXT ANNIE ABOUT SCHEDULES
PULL DEAD VINES
CALL RANGER FOR COMPOST
CHANGE AC FILTER
SCHEDULE THE WORKS AT THE FORD HOUSE

knowing the land

BY THE TIME the second Career Night rolled around, Spruce Street Books didn't just feel full.

It felt claimed.

The bell over the door rang without rest. Chairs filled the aisles. Kids sat cross-legged on the floor, notebooks open, pencils scattered like seeds. This wasn't a career night anymore. Everyone knew it.

I sat between Hank and Jasper, their shoulders squared, listening hard. They were past beanbags and not yet old enough to pretend they didn't care.

When Ginger quieted the room, she didn't soften it.

"We're listening tonight," she said. "And we're leaving knowing what matters."

Rosemary Rodriguez stood first, binder hugged close. She didn't perform. She never does.

"I'm a botanist," she said. "I work with TORCH, the Texas and Oklahoma Regional Consortium of Herbaria."

She nodded to Manuel. "Lights, please."

The projector clicked on. Prairie greens and dusty purples filled the wall. Leaf shapes that looked ordinary until you understood what you were seeing.

"These are two protected species present on the west-side tract," Rosemary said. "Skinner foxglove. Earleaf foxglove."

She smiled once, quick. "I won't drown you in scientific names. Just know this: plants keep records."

"These tell us what's been here," she said. "And what still belongs."

Barbara Chen asked quietly if plants talked.

"They whisper," Rosemary said. "You just have to listen."

Eugene Goldberg stepped forward next. He didn't need the microphone.

"I was trained to protect people," he said. "And to stay steady when things shake."

He spoke about coming home changed. About choosing not to shrink. About feeding a town, stocking shelves, showing up anyway.

When the weight grew thick, he let out a rolling laugh.

"I am the wise old owl in that cereal commercial," he said. "And I will wear that corny crown with pride."

The kids laughed. The room breathed again.

"Protecting a place doesn't always look heroic," Eugene said. "But it is."

Ricky Howard followed in his Power and Light vest, all momentum.

"I keep the lights on," he said. "And sometimes I put them back on."

He nodded toward Bet. "Tonight, you need her more than me."

BET SINCLAIR STEPPED up with a stack of papers. The room leaned forward.

"I'm not sugar-coating this," she said. "So stay with me."

She spoke clearly. Ecosystems. Watersheds. The difference between scenery and home.

Then the slides.

We can pursue different avenues to protect land and water, non-profit and even grants.

Protected plant species confirmed.

Protected keystone animals present.

Enough research to form a nonprofit and seek federal designation, a list of grants available.

Legal work required. Funding required.

The applause came slow. Strong. Deliberate.

"This is direction," Bet said. "Not certainty. But something."

Outside, the heat pressed down, August heavy and unmoving.

Hank walked close, notebook tight against his chest.

"I'm confused," he said. "But I ain't scared."

Jasper frowned. "So do we pay the bad guys?"

"No," I said. "We pay someone to tell them no. In big words."

They nodded. That was enough.

Behind us, Spruce Street Books still glowed. People bent over paper. Names being written.

Lawhoma Hills wasn't finished.

We were just taking the work home.

THURSDAY, AUGUST 5

AFTER THE BOYS SETTLED AND THE DOGS FOUND THEIR PLACES AT MY FEET, I OPENED MY JOURNAL AND STARED AT THE PAGE. RJ'S BREATH ROSE AND FELL SLOW. BEANS SIGHED LIKE THE DAY HAD MET HIS STANDARDS.

THE BOYS ASKED HARD QUESTIONS TONIGHT. THE KIND THAT MEAN THEIR HEARTS ARE AWAKE. I WAS PROUD OF THEM—EVEN WHEN MY ANSWERS FELT THIN.

WE HAVE RESEARCH. WE HAVE A PLAN.

AND WE NEED MONEY.

AFTER MOST FOLKS LEFT, A FEW OF US STAYED ANYWAY. NO TITLES. NO MOTIONS. JUST NAMES, NUMBERS, AND THE UNDER-STANDING THAT WE NEED SOMEONE WHO KNOWS HOW TO SAY NO IN A LANGUAGE THAT HOLDS.

I HAD A GOOD OLD FASHIONED SHOWER CRY. DIDN'T RUSH IT. DIDN'T HIDE IT.

WHEN THE WATER TURNED COOL, I STOOD THERE UNTIL MY BREATHING MATCHED IT.

TONIGHT'S LISTEN: "REVELRY" — KINGS OF LEON

To Do:
Alarm 0430
Weed and clean by headlamp
Drink water, not Diet Coke
Pick what's still good and make baskets for neighbors

summer sounds

AT THE END OF SUMMER, the grass along the Farmer's Market lawn held a shallow groove where chairs had been planted and quilts unfolded. Lantern cords stayed strung between concerts. Lawhoma Hills found its rhythm and kept it.

The season opened with bluegrass and folk, music baked into harmony and muscle memory. The Banerjee twins strummed with steady pride while children spun loose circles at the foot of the stage. Goats were politely escorted off speaker wires. Pop wore his loudest shirt. The crowd sang every chorus without hesitation.

Country and porch-light songs followed. Wilder Kate's voice carried across the lawn, sure and grounded, the kind that makes people stop talking mid-sentence. She sang one of her own that night, "Creekside Wishes," and the hush arrived before the first line landed. Later, "Cotton Eyed Joe" pulled everyone to their feet, skidding across the grass in half-remembered steps.

The final nights turned toward jazz and blues. Gus fussed over stage lighting, adjusting shades of blue like weather depended on it. The school jazz band settled into a groove so rich it made the crickets sound underdressed. Eugene lifted a harmonica and left the lawn quiet in a way that wasn't silence so much as attention.

Each concert left something behind.

Not just melodies, but moments.

Bridger Ashe dedicating a blues ballad to anyone who'd lived through a hard season.

Millie stepped onstage beside Wilder Kate, steady enough to leave our whole family blinking fast.

Ruby Rodriguez tracking sound cues with the seriousness of flight control.

Harry and Charlotte weaving through the crowd with lemonade, Beau asleep against Charlotte's shoulder.

Tata boogie-woogieing across the stage during "Hound Dog," knees popping, joy intact.

Kids folded into their shoulders when the music went soft.

Pop declaring every set the best one yet.

Gus watching the clouds, just in case.

Everyone kept one eye to the west, even while they sang.

We didn't host concerts. We practiced gathering.

We sang with our whole chests.

ON THE FINAL NIGHT, lanterns swayed like applause. Shep and Brick closed with a new song written with Wilder Kate, "Moonrise Over Lawhoma." It didn't ask for an explanation. You stood where you stood, held whoever was close, and let the notes lift toward the tree line.

When the lawn finally emptied, Lolli counted the donation hat. Some bills folded. Some crumpled. One marked for the lake.

$2,409 for the Blue Creek Committee.

No one clapped for the number.

Music lifts a spirit.

Sometimes it also funds a fight.

FRIDAY, AUGUST 6

MUSIC RESTORES ME, AND THESE NIGHTS HERE IN THE GLOW OF IT, TALENT FLOWING FROM PEOPLE I ADORE, IT FILLED ME UP. I KEPT TRACK FOR H&J. MAYBE FOR MYSELF TOO.

Summer Concert Playlist - Lawhoma Hills Edition

Bluegrass & Folk Revival
"Jersey Giant" - Elle King (performed by Wilder Kate)
"Foggy Mountain Breakdown" - Earl Scruggs (performed by Bridger Ashe on banjo)
"Wildwood Flower" - The Carter Family (performed by Wilder Kate and Millie)
"Trail Songs at Dusk" - The Banerjee Brothers (original)
"Meet Me at the Meadow" - Lawhoma Community Folk Singers (original)
Country & Porch-Light Originals
"Good Hearted Woman" - Waylon Jennings & Willie Nelson (performed by Shep and Brick)
"Will the Circle Be Unbroken" - Nitty Gritty Dirt Band (performed by the High School Choir)
"Cotton Eyed Joe" - Asleep at the Wheel (featuring Eugene on harmonica)
"Creekside Wishes" - Wilder Kate (original)
"Moonrise Over Lawhoma" - Shep, Brick, and Wilder Kate (original)
Jazz & Blues Night
"Hound Dog" - Big Mama Thornton (performed by Wilder Kate, joined by Tata)
"Okie Dokie Stomp" - Clarence Gatemouth Brown (performed by the High School Jazz Band)
"Creekside Shuffle" - Lawhoma High Jazz Band (original)
"Eugene's Harmonica Blues" - Eugene Goldberg (improvised, legendary)
"Bridger's Ballad" - Bridger Ashe (original dedication)

PART THREE

fall

Fall keeps its own calendar. Some years November rolls in and the heat still clings to your back. Then one morning the grip eases, and the oaks and maples begin unpinning their hair, letting that heavy green slip down around their trunks. They trade ball gowns for plain dresses in orange and yellow, cloth a body breathes in without strain.

I feel the tug each time I haul the houseplants inside. All summer they lounge on the porch rail and steps, leaves wide, faces tipped toward the sun, sun drunk and swaggering. The moment I reach for their pots, soil crumbling against my palms, they stiffen. I line them up beneath grow lights. I set humidifiers humming. I move from leaf to leaf with a damp cloth, inspecting stems, trimming brown edges, murmuring under my breath the way I once did walking hospital halls, hands steady, eyes sharp. The fiddle leaf fig sulks. The monstera droops in protest. I keep tending.

This is the season we lift vine skirts and look beneath. Pumpkins squat in the dirt, round and stubborn. Gourds twist into odd shapes, necks craned. Squash hide under broad leaves, knobby elbows pressed into the ground, firm in their opinions. You pass that sprawl all summer and see only green confusion. Then one afternoon you bend down and find heft in your hands, weight grown in shade.

Across the valley, clotheslines wake from their slack. Sweaters snap in the breeze, sleeves flapping, airing out for evenings that cool before the last story finishes. The air carries a scrubbed scent, the smell of counters wiped down and windows pushed open wide. Folks here call it magic and move on, though gratitude sits plain on their faces.

Most years the first cool front sends us laughing for jackets buried in cedar chests. This year the chill settles deeper. It rests behind my ribs. The town holds still a beat longer than usual, hand resting on a door-knob, ear pressed toward the hall.

The unknown has taken up space again, shifting plates in my cabinets, sliding jars from one shelf to another. I open the doors and stand there, tea towel in hand, staring at what no longer sits where I left it.

I have had enough.

No-Skip Albums for Fall:

10,000 Maniacs – Our Time in Eden
Pearl Jam – Ten
Sturgill Simpson – The Ballad of Dood & Juanita
Tyler Childers – Live on Red Barn Radio I and II
AC/DC – Back in Black
Taylor Swift – The Tortured Poets Department: The Anthology

TWENTY-SEVEN

the great forking event

WE ALWAYS CAP off summer and back to school with one last overnight campout, the kind that's supposed to feel like a ribbon on a present. This year it was the boys, with Lolli, Pop, and me chaperoning at Run Amuck.

Pop handed out walkie-talkies the way he hands out life jackets—no arguing, no exceptions. One for the big tent, one for him and Lolli, one for me.

"If the woods get a vote, I want us louder than the woods."

The tents never line up right out there. No matter how many times Pop teaches setup, somebody pulls a guy line too tight or sets a stake crooked. One tent leaned toward the creek. Another sagged in the middle like it had given up on holding anybody's dreams. By dark, it looked less like a campground and more like a place claimed in a hurry.

We banked the fire low. Sparks travel farther than you think. The moon slid in and out of thin clouds, porch-light bright then gone again.

THE BOYS WERE in the big tent, telling stories—fear turned into a toy if you keep one hand on the zipper. Lolli and Pop were a few yards off, quiet now, pretending to sleep.

I was in mine with the dogs.

RJ claimed the left side like a bodyguard. Beans curled at my feet, long and warm, sighing the deep sigh of a creature convinced he'd met all expectations for the day. I lay there listening. I've never been good at letting a night go by without checking its pockets.

Whip's voice drifted through the canvas, low and dramatic.

"And then—dropping it further, they heard the scratching from inside the walls."

"You always do this part," Wes muttered.

"That's because it's the best part," Whip whispered. "The scratching means something's already in there."

Boone laughed, soft and forced. "You never scare us, Whip."

Tucker tossed a pair of socks, landing with a thud right next to Whip's head. "Quit!"

Then the tent went quiet. Not a pause for effect. A hush with weight.

Jasper's voice came thin. "Hold up."

Plastic clicked. A sleeping pad shifted. The soft clink of something lifted and set down—binoculars. Jasper always has his binoculars. The backyard of camp might offer him a headline if he waits long enough.

"What," Whip whispered.

"The yard," Jasper whispered. "The yard's…getting messed up."

RJ lifted her head. Beans made his Chewbacca sound—something that started in his chest and ended in mine.

Hank's voice followed. Flat. "Bro, what do you mean? What's out there?"

"What the heck," Wes breathed.

Shia gasped like he'd seen a ghost and a report card at the same time.

"Sycamore Valley," Jasper said.

Even through canvas, I felt the shift. Sycamore Valley isn't just a place. It's an attitude with teeth.

"Jerks are in Ya's garden," Hank whispered.

A decision moved through the tent without a vote.

Jasper keyed the walkie-talkie.

"Ksssshhh—buzz"

The walkie scratched in my pocket.

"G-parents," Jasper whispered. "We got visitors. Channel forty. Y'all copy?" "Ksssshhh—buzz"

I heard it and knew Pop would already be sitting up. I pulled on my boots instead.

Hank's voice came across, firmer. "Lights red. Low."

Canvas rustled. Feet padded.

I unzipped my tent and stepped out. The air was thick, keeping us honest. Above us, the moon slid free of the clouds and stayed.

The boys moved in a line, headlamps snapped to red. Little spies that had trained in discipline.

Hank led. Two fingers to his eyes, then toward the others. Watch.

Then the same gesture toward my tent. Go.

They crawled through leaves and grass, slow and low.

My walkie buzzed. "Ksssshhh——-buzz," Pop's voice came through, quiet and edgy.

"Yaya."

"Up?"

"Roger."

When Hank crossed my line of sight, RJ stood fully. Beans rose, growling.

I stepped into his view. He gave the eye signal again—smaller now, almost respectful—then pointed toward Lolli and Pop's tent.

WE MET THEM HALFWAY. They were already up. Boots half-laced. Pajamas on top, cut offs on bottom. Pop's shoulders squared.

"Boys?" Lolli whispered.

"In the garden," Jasper whispered back.

We walked. All of us together.

At the rise, the moon brightened and showed it plain.

Shaving cream clung to porch posts and slid down the rails. Toilet paper twisted in the pecan tree. Forks stuck up from the lawn, prongs catching the light.

Forks. In my yard.

Something old and ugly stirred in me.

The Sycamore Valley kids froze. A can clattered. Someone kicked at the forks like ignoring them might erase them.

"It's just a prank," a boy said, laughing too sharp.

I took in the smashed vines, the foam, the trampled beds.

"That's damage," I said.

"You'll live, we didn't break anything."

Pop stepped closer. "You don't get to decide that."

The boy lifted his chin. "We'll stomp you anyway. Wrestling. Field hockey. Cross country."

I looked at him closely then. Really looked.

He wore a gray tee-shirt, the logo clean and unmistakable in the moonlight—Lawhoma Regional hospital, printed sharp as a promise.

"Your last name's Harris," I said.

He hesitated. "So."

"I worked nights with your grandmother; Lawhoma Hospital. She brought lemon cake on everybody's birthday."

Recognition hit before embarrassment tried to cover it.

"She talked about you," I added. "Said you ran faster than anyone she'd ever seen."

The yard shrank.

Pop nodded once. "You're cleaning this up."

"All of it?" a girl cried.

"All of it," Lolli said.

They worked. Forks pulled. Foam hosed down. Toilet paper bagged. The pumpkin patch hurt worst—vines snapped, gourds split open and ruined.

HANK KNELT BESIDE THE DAMAGE, quiet.

"We can fix this in the morning, Ya," he said. "I promise."

By the time they left, wet and subdued, our fire was coals.

I sat on a bucket. RJ pressed to my leg. Beans stretched out.

"Do you call her?" Lolli asked.

"Not tonight."

"Grace," she said, "or avoidance?"

"Both."

We stayed near the dead fire until the sky lightened.

Saturday, August 7

After everyone went home and the tents were folded back into the storage building, I walked the garden again with the dogs trailing me. I picked up a few straggler forks and swore under my breath.

This wasn't the first time kids had marked our place like this. Years ago, when Papa J and I were still married, some friends of Elijah's pulled a similar stunt. Papa J was so angry he drove to the wrong parents' house before dawn, ready to unload a fury that turned out to belong to somebody else entirely. Wrong driveway. Right rage.

I keep telling myself this belongs in the chapter of youth rebellion, and maybe it does. Still, I was proud of how our boys carried themselves when those Sycamore Valley kids smarted off to Pop. Proud of their restraint. Their steadiness. Even so, there was a part of me that wanted to grab that Harris boy and give him a swat, hospital lemon cake be damned.

I called Papa J to tell him what happened. He was walking his dogs, already thinking about mowing.

"I'd have yanked them up by their ears," he said. "But there's nothing to do now. Get a nap. Don't let this eat at you. You can grow more pumpkins next year, crazy woman."

I cranked up music with some grit in it and took a long shower, letting the night rinse off.

Tonight's Listen (Morning Listen): "Barton Hollow" –
The Civil Wars
To Do:

Tues/ start harvest on remaining pumpkins and gourds
Wed/ pre-emergent on grass, clean windows

dust, speed, and stevie brewster

SCHOOL STARTING BACK ALWAYS MAKES Lawhoma Hills exhale, even the folks who pretend the calendar doesn't run them. We call it routine and act like it's ordinary.

Fall hadn't arrived yet—not fully—but summer had begun to back up. That morning, a breeze came down Birch Creek smelling of damp leaves and creek stones, and under my boots an old leaf finally gave up its grip with a crunch that sounded stubborn enough to matter.

Birch Creek's annual mountain bike race is the town's first real gathering after school begins. Sport, reunion, and excuse to stand too close to people you haven't seen since the last casserole emergency. There's always electricity in the clearing, but cinnamon too, because Bootsie Howard never arrives empty-handed. She carried in a tin of muffins like they were sacred objects, which in Lawhoma they are.

Dahlia Banerjee was already bent over a clipboard with Paddy Quinn, who took his Eagle Scout Citizenship in the Community badge like he'd been sworn into office. They'd walked the course before most folks finished their coffee.

"Morning, Yaya," Dahlia called.

I nodded at Paddy's clipboard. "Looks official enough to arrest me."

"We reviewed safety measures," Paddy said solemnly.

That's when I knew the day was in good hands.

Stevie Brewster waited at the start line astride her bike, still as a held breath. Her helmet was plastered with tiny mountain and lightning-bolt stickers. She wasn't nervous. Stevie rarely is. She had that look Papa Max gets before a big story breaks—eyes steady, mind already ahead of the truth.

"Don't blink," I told her.

"I won't," she said, and meant it.

NEAR THE ROPE LINE, Micah Quinn sat with Caitlyn and Aunt Carly in the best seats, clapping like joy was his full-time job. Every warm-up lap earned him applause, and somehow that made the riders pedal better.

Pop and Lolli stood near the start. Pop gripped his cowbell like a sacred instrument. Lolli carried emergency snacks, which is her version of preparedness.

"The key to sports," Pop hollered, "is cheering loud enough so the forest hears you."

The trees looked ready.

Riders lined up—raccoons from Deer Creek, rabbits from Hollybriar, coyotes from Fox Hollow. And Bernie, the Sycamore Valley duck, back after last year's crash, determination riding him harder than physics.

"Riders ready," Pete Hill called. "Set. Go."

They shot off in a rush of tires and leaves.

Birch Creek's trail twists through hollows and climbs that make grown adults reconsider their hobbies. Stevie took the first descent clean, line precise, trust built from skinned knees and practice.

Bernie narrated his survival out loud.

"I'm doing it!"

"I'm oversteering!"

"No wait—I'm okay!"

Micah clapped like he might lift off the ground.

At the bridge—the one everyone fears—the crowd went still. Stevie hit a gust, wobbled, corrected, and rode through on earned trust. A rabbit slid behind her, and another rider reached out, steadying them just long enough for the tire to catch.

When the riders burst back into the clearing, Pop rang his bell like a man conducting fate, and the hills answered back.

Stevie crossed, dusted and glowing.

"You saw me?" she asked Tucker, voice catching.

"Of course," he said. "I was the loudest one."

Bootsie passed muffins. Lolli handed out water. Pop interviewed muddy riders with an imaginary microphone. Even the trees sounded like applause.

I stood there longer than necessary, smelling creek water and cinnamon, thinking how easy it is to love a place that loves its children—and how hard it is to keep it.

THAT AFTERNOON, the attorney search met at Lolli's kitchen table.

"City-government law," Lolli said. "Not divorce."

"Anderson, Fuller and Smith—conflict," Ginger said.

"Schanck, Florence and Labore—no," Ophelia added.

Annie checked her phone. "Waiting on Murphy, Allen. Two more numbers coming."

Progress. No answers. Yet.

Outside, bikes leaned against trees. Inside, we kept going.

SATURDAY, AUGUST 14

THIS MORNING PRETENDED AND GAVE A HINT OF FALL, AIR SO CLEAN IT MAKES YOU BELIEVE YOU COULD REORGANIZE YOUR WHOLE LIFE BEFORE LUNCH. FOLKS WORE CUTOFFS ANYWAY. BY NOON IT WAS HOT AGAIN, BECAUSE AUGUST DOES NOT NEGOTIATE. WHILE POP HOLLERED AT THE FOREST AND BOOTSIE PASSED MUFFINS LIKE COMMUNION, I NOTICED A RIBBON TIED TO A SAPLING NEAR THE SPECTATOR PATH. NOT A RACE RIBBON. NOT DECORATION. JUST THERE. QUIET. WAITING.

TONIGHT'S LISTEN: "DOG DAYS ARE OVER" - FLORENCE + THE MACHINE

To Do:
UNPACK FALL CLOTHES
WASH THROW BLANKETS
TUES/ PULL LETTUCE AND SPINACH SEEDS
HARVEST BEANS

connected, not consumed

SPRUCE Street Books changes after dark.

In the daytime it's cheerful shuffling and the soft squeak of sneakers on the kid rug, people coming and going with paperbacks tucked to their chests like groceries. At night, the walls seem to lean in. Not to crowd you. To hold you.

Rosemary rolled up the children's rug and set the chairs in a circle. No podium. No stage. Just knees nearly touching, the way people sit when they're done pretending.

This evening wasn't about banning anything.

It was about learning how to live with tools that don't come with instructions.

TEACHERS HAD ASKED for the meeting. Arthur Banerjee was there, along with Paul and Kelly Chen and a handful of others with calm eyes and tired shoulders—the kind who can break up a hallway argument and still remember every kid's birthday. When teachers start gathering parents like this, it means something's already happening and we're late to it.

Parents filtered in. Teens followed, trying to look bored in that particular way that actually means I am listening. Younger kids clustered near the edges. Micah settled between his people, AAC device mounted and steady, exactly where it belonged.

Annie and I took seats with notebooks out of habit, old nurse reflex, listening for what wouldn't get said unless someone made room for it.

Eli Everett cleared his throat—not for drama, just to quiet the shuffle.

"I work in IT," he said. "So I want to be clear. Technology itself isn't the problem. The problem is giving kids powerful tools and never teaching them how the tools work."

That landed.

He didn't scare us. He didn't need to. He talked about screenshots—how fast they travel, how slow apologies are. About how once something leaves your phone, it doesn't come back just because you regret it. He said it the way someone does when they've watched the same mistake happen over and over and hated it every time.

Across the circle, a teenager underlined something hard in a notebook. Another nodded once, slow, already matching his words to lived experience.

Shep raised a hand. "Can we talk about gaming?"

Brick added, "Voice chat. It gets sketchy, we watched a thing on how it really isn't kids sometimes."

Half the parents leaned forward at once.

Megan spoke without waiting, because Megan doesn't treat concern like a private hobby.

"Most games aren't just games anymore. They're social spaces. Private messages. Voice rooms. And they're built to keep you there, often not knowing who is on the other end."

Boone said quietly, "Sometimes the game's fine. It's the chat that gets weird."

"Or mean," Kolby added.

"And logging off," Shep said, "can feel like you are a wimp if you are losing."

We wrote that down. When language finally fits the thing you've been worrying at, it feels like relief.

Micah tapped his device.

The voice came out clean and steady.

"Technology allows me to communicate what I need," it said.

"It allows me to participate."

The room softened. Even the teenagers went still.

Dr. Bridget smiled at him. "That's exactly right."

Micah tapped again.

"Technology works best when people listen."

And for a moment, everybody did.

That was when Megan shifted us deeper, where the water turned colder.

"We also need to talk about AI and schoolwork," she said. "Kids are already using it."

No one argued.

Eli nodded. "Use it to brainstorm. To organize. To understand. But if you turn in work you didn't create or don't understand, you're cheating yourself first." He paused. "And AI can sound confident while being wrong. Confidence isn't credibility."

Pens moved fast.

Carly took a breath that looked like courage.

"When I was in high school, I was bullied online, Facebook, even Instagram," she said. "Anonymous messages. Posts from fake profiles. Things people wouldn't say to my face."

Ranger didn't interrupt. He just took her hand.

"I stayed quiet too long," Carly said. "I thought silence made me stronger. It didn't."

"Silence protects the wrong people," Ranger said.

A couple of kids nodded.

"Boundaries aren't punishment," Megan said gently. "They're guardrails."

THAT WAS THE SHIFT. No bans. No panic. Just practical care. Phones out of bedrooms at night. Permission to leave a chat without explanation. Rules about posting faces and places. What to do when something feels wrong.

Nobody got shamed. Nobody got to pretend they were above it either.

When the room got heavy again, I asked the question everyone was circling.

"So how old were your kids when they got their first smart phone?"

Groans rolled through the circle, then laughter—the good kind, the kind that means you're not alone.

"I'm asking," I added, "because Hank Miller and Jasper West are already drafting a presentation for an upgrade."

That broke the tension clean in half.

When the chairs stacked and the lights dimmed, nobody rushed out. Teens lingered. Parents talked softer now. Not because things were solved, but because they'd been named.

AFTERWARD, the unofficial lawyer-search crew stayed.

Lolli opened her spiral notebook. Annie pulled up her call log. Ginger uncapped a pen. Ophelia slid cookies no one touched closer to the middle. Grandma Bertha Sweeney took the chair by the window and watched us like she always does—steady, unflinching.

"We need to expand statewide," Annie said.

"City-government law," Lolli added. "Land use. Municipal."

I wrote LAWYER SEARCH at the top of the page.

Annie read. "Carter and Carter. No go. Conflict."

"Cox, Waters, Jones, and McGovern," Ginger said. "Booked."

Ophelia slid her list across. "Two messages out. Waiting."

Grandma Bertha nodded once. "Keep going."

When we finally stepped outside, Spruce Street Books glowed behind us, windows lit the color of warm honey.

Tomorrow the world would still be complicated.

THURSDAY, AUGUST 26
NEVER DID I IMAGINE I'D BECOME A WOMAN WHO WORRIES
ABOUT A KEYSTROKE THE WAY I ONCE WORRIED ABOUT A FEVER.
PHONES ARE DIFFERENT.
PHONES ARE POCKET-SIZED DOORS.
I THOUGHT ABOUT MY NEPHEW HENRY. NONVERBAL. GOD REST

him. If we'd had something like Micah's device back then—would we have heard him better? Would we have known him more fully while we still had time?

That thought hurts.

I'm grateful the teachers opened this conversation before something ugly forced it open. We want to protect innocence, yes. But we also want our kids prepared.

Tonight's Listen: "Little Bird" — Annie Lennox

To Do:
Check parental settings on MacBook
Order new Muck Boots

paddy quinn, private eye

PADDY SAID he liked the west side of the land because it felt unfinished.

That's how he started when he told me, sitting at my kitchen table with dust on his calves and his phone laid between us like evidence. I'm writing it down the way he said it, because when a boy tells the truth with his whole face, you don't improve on it.

He rode past the Simmons place, the last mailbox—where the road narrows and the gravel starts popping under your tires. Dust lifted, then settled back onto his legs. The farther he went, the quieter it got. No porch radios. No wind chimes. Just grass moving in long bands and the low hills easing toward the lake.

He stopped at the section fence and leaned his bike against a post. The wire hummed when he touched it. Prairie dogs popped up along the ridge, watching him, still as punctuation.

"Hey," he whispered.

They didn't scatter.

That mattered.

He crouched and pulled his notebook from his backpack. The cover was soft from use. He flipped to the page marked Eagle Scout Project Research, though the list beneath it had grown sideways.

Prairie dogs.

Burrow clusters.

Water access.

He wrote fast, then slower. He liked getting it right.

Then the wind shifted.

He said he smelled canvas before he saw it, and that stopped him cold. He stood with the notebook still open and scanned the far rise.

Something pale broke the line of grass. Then another.

Tents.

Not the camping kind. Square. Rigid. Staked tight. One flap tied back. Orange tape snapping in the wind.

His mouth went dry.

He checked his phone. No service. Then one bar flickered and held. Enough.

He took a picture from where he stood, but it felt thin. Distant. His body knew more than the screen could hold.

He moved along the fence line, low, keeping the posts between himself and the tents. The prairie dogs went quiet.

"That was worse than the tents, I felt their fear, you know what I mean, I just felt it" he said across my table.

When he reached the first one, he paused. Canvas snapped overhead. He heard voices farther west. A laugh. Metal clinking.

His shoulders tightened. The fine hairs along his arms lifted.

"Eagle Scouts don't run," he said. "I felt myself bristle."

"I'm just looking," he told himself.

Then he went inside.

The tent smelled like dirt and coffee and plastic. A folding table sat crooked in the middle. Papers were spread across it, weighted with rocks. A map was taped to the wall.

Paddy stepped closer.

It was our land.

The creek bend. The cottonwoods. The slope where the prairie dogs sun themselves.

Red lines cut through it.

Circles marked thick.

Notes in the margins: Traps. Relocation. Mitigation.

"Oh no," he whispered.

He took pictures fast, hands shaking enough that he had to brace his wrist. A page slid. He froze, then eased it back like careful could undo the moment.

Outside, footsteps crunched closer.

He crouched and waited, canvas brushing his back, counting under his breath until the shadow moved on.

Then he ran.

HE DIDN'T STOP until the fence line, lungs burning, sweat dripping into the dirt. The prairie dogs were back, watching him like they'd never left.

"I saw it, I saw it all guys" he told them.

Then he texted me with fingers that wouldn't quite cooperate.

> You home? I need to talk. I did something I
> probably shouldn't have.

I answered because I was already awake.

> Come now. I'll be watching for you.

He rode hard all the way east. When he skidded to a stop at the gate, his hands were shaking again.

I met him on the porch with a bowl in my hands and set it down too fast.

"Inside," I said.

We sat at the kitchen table. The house smelled like tomatoes and warm bread, which felt wrong. Paddy slid his phone across.

I scrolled without speaking. When his hand started tapping, I reached out and stilled it.

"Breathe," I said. "Right here."

When I finished, I looked at him.

"You were brave," I said.

He nodded.

"And you were risky."

That landed.

"I had to," he said. "No one else even knows what they are doing."

"I know," I said. "That doesn't mean there isn't a next part."

I stood, walked to the sink, and turned on the water without needing it. Just needed something to do with my hands.

"This is serious," I said finally. "And it matters."

He waited.

"But it's also unfinished," I said. "And I don't want to move faster than the truth."

His brow furrowed. "Yaya, please don't call my parents, my mom will be p…well sorry but real mad."

I looked at him. Really looked. Dirt still on his calves. Eyes sharp and scared and proud all at once.

"Not tonight," I said.

His shoulders loosened, just a fraction. Relief, mixed with something like doubt.

"I'm not pretending this isn't real," I continued. "I just need time to be sure we understand what we're seeing before we pull more people into it."

He nodded slowly.

"You don't go back," I said. "You don't tell anyone else. Let me carry this for now."

"Ok, thanks Yaya, I didn't know what else to do" he said.

I rested my hand on his shoulder.

"Eagle Scouts don't work alone," I told him. "Even when it feels like they are."

The lantern came on as the light faded. Somewhere out back, prairie dogs called.

Paddy listened and let himself sit still.

For now.

SATURDAY, AUGUST 28
AFTER PADDY RODE HOME, I WALKED THE HOUSE THE WAY I DO
WHEN THE WEATHER'S COMING. RJ FOLLOWED AT MY HEEL.

Beans followed RJ. Nobody wanted to be the last one alone in a room.

I ran the vacuum on the rug three times. My hands kept trying to make order out of something that would not be ordered.

I didn't call anyone.

I told myself I needed more information. I told myself it was better to wait than to stir panic without proof. I told myself I was protecting him.

But if I'm honest, part of me just wasn't ready to know what it meant yet.

Tonight's Listen: "Broken Horses" — Brandi Carlile

To Do:
call Ross and Gladys about next year's market schedule
ask Annie what Hank needs for next week
text Arthur to confirm chaperone for Wicked field trip
launder kitchen curtains

henry miller, chairman

THE NEWS CAME in on a Tuesday afternoon, all string and momentum, no brakes.

Annie's SUV rolled into the drive and barely slowed before the passenger door flew open and Hank Miller launched himself out, backpack thumping behind him like it was trying to keep up. A LAWHOMA STANDS TOGETHER tee hung half out of the backseat, tangled with permission slips and snack wrappers.

"YAYA!" he hollered, shoes untied, grin reckless. "Guess what? Guess what? Guess—"

Jasper climbed out behind him, a little breathless, already laughing. "He did it."

I already got the call from Annie, I let Hank get the joy in saying it.

"What did you do, sweetie?" I asked.

He skidded to a stop in front of me, chest heaving, eyes bright enough to knock something loose in the air.

"I got elected Student Council Chairman."

Then he jumped straight into my arms, full-body celebration, no warning. I laughed and caught him, grateful my knees chose cooperation today.

Once the lemonade was poured and the shouting settled into a happy buzz, Hank began pacing my kitchen like a man with a schedule to keep.

"I have meetings," he said, counting on his fingers. "I have to help with school ideas. I have to make sure the money is counted, attendance is taken, I don't even know it all yet." He paused a big ol' breath…. "I have to give a speech at Friday assembly."

Then he stopped short, sock squeaking on the floor.

"What if I mess up in front of the whole middle school and maybe even the high school kids….. I bet Wilder Kate even?"

That voice. Quieter. Serious. The weight finding him.

I pulled out a chair and sat. "Come here."

Leadership looks shiny from a distance. Up close, it feels heavy and personal.

"Sweetheart," I said, "leadership isn't about getting it right every time. It's about being kind, paying attention, and doing the next right thing even when your stomach is doing cartwheels."

He swallowed. "Is that enough?"

"It's the whole recipe," I told him. "Everything else is seasoning."

THAT EVENING, Lolli and Pop came over and we walked the trail toward Blue Creek, the air just cool enough to make you breathe deeper without meaning to. Jasper marched ahead, chin up, shoulders squared, clearly appointed Hank's personal security detail.

Hank peppered Lolli with questions.

"How long should my speech be?"

"What if I forget something?"

"What if my voice cracks?"

"What if I sneeze?"

Lolli stopped right there on the trail and crouched like she was coaching a championship team.

"Close your eyes," she said. "In through your nose. Out through your mouth. Again."

Pop wandered past and stage-whispered, "Is he acting like he smells pizza?"

Lolli shot him a look sharp enough to stop traffic. Pop retreated.

Hank opened his eyes. "That helped."

"Your heart beats fast," Lolli said, "because it knows what you're doing matters."

Back at my house, the boys spread paper and markers across the table. Hank wrote, crossed things out, rewrote. After a while he looked up.

"What does a good leader say?"

"A good leader tells the truth," I said.

"And," Lolli added, "tells people how he wants them to feel."

Hank nodded and bent back over the page. When he finished, he climbed onto my step stool and cleared his throat.

"Hi," he began, voice unsteady. "My name is Henry Miller. I go by Hank. And I want our school to feel like a place where everyone belongs."

He paused. Kept going.

"Leadership isn't about being the boss. It's about noticing when someone feels left out and doing something about it. It's doing stuff even when it's hard."

Jasper clapped first, soft but fierce. "Bubs," he said, "that was really good."

Pop scooped Hank up like he weighed nothing. "Grandson! I'd vote for you on anything."

Lolli squeezed my shoulder in our shared grandmother language: Look what we're getting to witness.

FRIDAY CAME BRIGHT AND COOL, nerves riding the air. Annie hugged Hank tight. Stetson gave him one solid nod—the kind that says everything without wasting words.

The auditorium was filled. The principal introduced him.

Hank walked to the microphone.

I could see his hands shake. Then he started speaking, and his voice steadied the way things do when they're rooted in truth.

"I want our school to be a place where it's okay to try," he said. "Where new kids feel welcome. Where everyone feels safe being who they are and we have fun."

He finished. The room broke open with applause. Jasper cheered loud enough to earn a warning and wore it like a badge.

Afterward, Hank slapped me a high-five. "I wasn't scared once I started talking."

"That's because you meant it," I said.

He nodded, thoughtful. "Do you think I'll be a good Chairman?"

I hugged him hard, right there in public. "I think," I said, "you already are."

Watching him stand among his classmates, taller somehow than he'd been that morning, I felt that quiet ache that comes when children grow in ways you can't measure.

And I let myself breathe it in.

FRIDAY, SEPTEMBER 3

HANK AS A BABY. HE WAS THE KIND WHO LOOKED AT YOU LIKE YOU WERE THE WHOLE PLAN. SOFT EYES. GENTLE HANDS. A SHADOW OF ANNIE EVERYWHERE HE WENT. A MOMMA'S BOY IN THE BEST SENSE—THE KIND THAT MAKES YOU BELIEVE THE WORLD MIGHT STILL TURN OUT DECENT IF WE KEEP RAISING BOYS THAT WAY.

JASPER ARRIVED RUNNING NINETY MILES AN HOUR AND NEVER APOLOGIZED. IF HANK WAS A LULLABY, JASPER WAS A DRUM LINE. FULL-TILT. ALL MOMENTUM, HE WORRIED THE DAY MIGHT END BEFORE HE GOT TO THE BEST PART.

AND NOW LOOK AT THEM.

I FACETIMED PAPA J AFTER THE ASSEMBLY, SITTING IN MY CAR BEFORE THE FEELING COULD LEAK AWAY. HE ANSWERED WITH HIS SWEATY CAP ON, MOWER HUMMING BEHIND HIM, DOGS CIRCLING LIKE SUPERVISORS.

"WHAT'D I MISS?" HE ASKED, ALREADY GRINNING.

I TURNED THE CAMERA ON MYSELF. HE SQUINTED. "WHAT THE HELL. YOU BEEN CRYING"

"I'M ALLOWED," I SAID. "THAT BOY JUST STOOD UP IN FRONT OF HIS WHOLE SCHOOL AND SPOKE WITH PURPOSE."

PAPA J'S EYES SOFTENED.

"Tell Annie she's doing good. Tell Stetson too. Tell that boy I'm proud."

"I will," I said. "Ok Crazy Woman, I gotta get this yard done." The screen blanked, sometimes we don't have to say bye.

Tonight's Listen: "Rock Salt and Nails" — Tyler Childers

To Do:
Tues/ pull pumpkins
Weds/ order hay, get tractor fuel
Thurs/ hook up flatbed

wicked back row secrets

IF YOU'VE NEVER HEARD a bus full of schoolchildren headed to a musical "in town," as we country folks say, it sounds like popcorn popping.

Loud popcorn. Opinionated popcorn. Popcorn that sings off-key and refuses to stop.

I volunteered to chaperone because I needed a break from harvest festival work and because I'd seen Wicked years ago and wanted to watch the kids fall in love with it the way I did.

The bus rolled into the school parking lot with one long honk, brakes sighing like they already knew this was going to be a day. Arthur Banerjee leaned out the driver's window wearing sunglasses and that grin that says he enjoys chaos as long as it has a schedule.

"All aboard for Pumpkin Lane Entertainment," he called. "Seatbelts on. Expectations high. Voices"—he paused, letting the noise swell—"eventually lowered."

The kids cheered so loud the finches on the wires scattered skyward.

Bridger Ashe counted heads at the curb while the line folded and unfolded around him. Jackets half-zipped. Backpacks bouncing. Lacey already announcing she had to use the bathroom, the traditional opening number of any field trip.

I climbed aboard and took my post halfway down the aisle—half monitor, half Yaya, all vigilance. I know that's three halves. That's what a bus requires.

Jasper bounded up first, skipping the last step. "I can't believe we're seeing Wicked."

"Momma and Yaya love it, so who knows," Hank said, sliding in behind him. "I hope it's decent."

"I watched the movie but not all the way through," Jasper said. "And green people ain't real."

Millie followed, calm as a librarian. "It's about friendship and misunderstanding."

Jasper blinked. "That was fast."

"I read," Millie said.

THE BUS FILLED the way a kitchen fills when cookies come out. Joey and Frankie Flanagan argued over earbuds. Chase Everett bobbed along to something only he could hear. Ruby Rodriguez counted seats twice. Lacey and Barbara compared dance numbers like judges.

Arthur eased forward. The ramp unfolded. Micah Quinn rolled on smooth and steady, Arthur greeting him by name, Bridger securing the straps. Micah gave a thumbs-up, headphones already in place, fingers tapping rhythm against his knees.

Arthur cleared his throat into the intercom. "Sit safely. Sing quietly. Absolutely no reenacting scenes until we're off the bus and I'm emotionally prepared."

Twenty-four children tried.

They failed.

I made my aisle walk—seatbelts, jackets, a dropped bottle, a reminder that "quiet" is not the same as "quietly screaming." I passed out peppermints and got thanked like I'd handed out treasure.

In the back rows, the older kids had staked their claim. Paddy Quinn sat sideways, legs in the aisle, until Jon Lucas nudged them back.

"If Mr. Ashe trips," Jon Lucas muttered, "Mom grounds us all."

"Mine grounds us for breathing wrong," Wilder Kate said.

Shep leaned forward. "Did you hear? They won't let us see the Halloween anniversary cut."

"Because of 'sex and violence,'" Brick said, air quotes wide.

"As if kissing is shocking," Edie Claire said, "and violence is literally the news."

Boone held up his phone. "Parental controls again, I am blocked on installing a flashlight app."

"Flashlights are gateways," Wilder said solemnly. "First light. Then chaos."

That one nearly broke me.

But Paddy didn't laugh.

He stared out the window, fields streaking past. His knee bounced. He stilled it. Then it started again.

I noticed. I always do.

PUMPKIN LANE ROSE AHEAD, banners fluttering, planters defying the calendar, a carved jack-o'-lantern statue guarding the doors like it meant business.

Inside, the theater smelled of velvet and popcorn and old wood—the good kind, the kind that remembers applause.

Reed Chapman stood near the entrance, eyes bright. "Welcome everyone."

The lights dimmed. The first notes rose. The world tilted green.

The kids leaned forward as one.

Elphaba soared. Glinda sparkled. Jasper clutched his program like a map. Hank mouthed lyrics he didn't know he knew. Millie tracked costumes. Micah smiled toward the orchestra pit, hand moving in time. Ruby whispered acoustics facts until Stevie gently shushed her.

Intermission buzzed.

"I could do that," JJ said. "Not flying. But singing."

"We should start a theater group," Frankie said.

"I'll do lighting," Chase said.

"Costumes," Barbara added.

"I will be the director," Jasper said.

"No you won't dork, a teacher would do that," Hank replied.

"Ok I will build the stage, Gus would so hire me," Jasper said.

· · ·

I WAS MONITORING wrappers and restroom lines when the older kids clustered too tight near the vending machines. Teen whispers carry. They always do.

"The West Line," Paddy said.

"Started what," Wilder asked, no smile now.

"Tents," Paddy said. "Traps."

That word landed cold.

"You went alone?" Shep said.

"That's insane," Tucker added.

"That is crazy scary," Edie Claire said quietly.

"Don't," Paddy snapped. "Say. Anything."

I walked away like I'd heard nothing. Sometimes the fastest way to lose a truth is to grab it.

But the day had shifted.

The ride home was quieter. Not silent—just held. A hum here. A tap there. Arthur took the turn by the grain elevator and the windows rattled once.

My phone buzzed.

I waited until we stopped.

> Jasper: you know that wobbly belly thing can me and hank tell momma we gotta help you after school we can ride our bikes….. Kinda important

> Hank: we won't be in trouble right?

I didn't answer immediately. I watched them file off the bus, voices rising as the spell broke.

Then I typed:

> meet ya there in a few

They rode hard, dumped their bikes by the gate, took my porch steps two at a time.

They told me what they'd heard. Not much. Enough.

I listened. I promised only what I could.

"I won't rat you out," I said. "But I can't carry what I don't fully know."

They watched me, serious.

"You did right telling me," I said. "Now go home. Let me chew the fat a minute. You let it lie."

They nodded too fast.

"Okay?" I said.

"Okay," Jasper said. Hank echoed him.

I swatted their backsides, just enough. "I love you," I called, "but I do not want to get yelled at by your mean ol' momma."

They whooped and tore off down the road.

I stayed on the porch after the sound faded, holding what they'd handed me and knowing it wasn't mine to solve yet.

The light had gone low and gold across the yard.

Thursday, September 9

My brain had me thinking about being trusted; not told-everything. Sometimes it means being the place a kid can set something heavy down without watching it detonate. Sometimes it means knowing when not to move fast, and when not to turn the truth into a spectacle.

I did call Annie. Sometimes Yaya and Momma share a secret that doesn't look like a secret. Not to be sneaky, but to be careful. Annie was proud the boys came to me, and she gave me a "witches' honor," to hold our secret, which made me smile even while my stomach stayed tight.

Big Granny lives loud in our heads. We learned early that you can protect a child without announcing it.

Harvest Festival is next week. There are lists and pumpkins and carving kits and people who will absolutely show up late asking questions they could have asked two weeks ago.

Sturgill is my mowing companion, and tonight I cranked him up loud enough that my ears might file a complaint.

It didn't fix a thing but it gave my nerves something else to ride for a while.

Tonight's Listen: "Turtles All the Way Down" — Sturgill Simpson

To Do:
Touch base with Ross and Gladys on pumpkins
Unpack carving kits and count
Holler at Gus about firewood if needed

bumpy pumpkins and hayrides

WE GOT LUCKY THIS YEAR.

October in Oklahoma can't make up its mind, but this time it leaned merciful. Enough rain to take the edge off the heat. Enough cool evenings to remind us our skin could relax again. Not sweaters. Not scarves. Just relief.

Harvest Festival is how I know the season has shifted. School calendars, volunteer sign-ups, and grocery lists blur together until suddenly there are pumpkins on tables and hay bales lining fences, and the land itself seems to nod and say, yes, now.

Jordan's LAWHOMA STANDS TOGETHER shirts showed up all through the crowd. Hank tugged at his collar.

"It's itchy."

"That means it's official," Jasper said, already sprinting toward the hay bales.

Apples sat piled in bowls. A pot of cider simmered while I moved through the kitchen, scent threading its way into the evening. Outside, hay bales were set low enough to sit on, not climb. I am not breaking anybody's arm this year.

Pumpkins and gourds filled the long tables beneath the pecan trees. Tools were laid out. Paper towels stacked. Bowls set to catch seeds.

Adults hovered in that careful way—present, alert, trying not to steal the moment.

When carving started, the table quieted. Children bent over pumpkins like surgeons. Parents held lids or hands when needed, reminded fingers where they belonged.

Millie chose a pumpkin that was round and solid without being large. She turned it once, then again, inspecting it as a jeweler might.

"What are you carving?" I asked.

"A house," she said.

"For whom?"

"For the light," she replied.

I didn't interrupt after that.

Trip and Beck argued designs like it mattered to the state. Eleanor Ashe carved stars with steady patience. Spoons and paper towels traveled the table. Stories surfaced and drifted away. There is a peace that comes from making something with your hands alongside people you trust, and for a while the world felt small enough to hold.

Near the fence, Ross had stacked crates of pumpkins—ring-necked, warty, pale blue, deep orange. Jasper frowned at them.

"They don't look right."

"They grew right," Ross said. "These are heirlooms, grown for taste and for keeping."

He lifted one shaped like a squat lantern.

"They're harder but stronger from clay soil that fights them, and heat that scorches them. They deserve attention."

"Why grow the hard ones?" Jasper asked.

"Because they matter," Ross said. "And anything that lasts takes care."

Tally stepped closer. "My ancestors grew pumpkins like these," she said. "Some fed families, some saved seed, some became homes for birds. Each one had a purpose."

Hank considered that. "Are pumpkins assigned jobs like people?"

Tally smiled. "Not exactly but a bit like people."

.   .   .

AS THE SUN DROPPED, Ross nudged me toward the seat of my old International Harvester. The engine rumbled to life. Hay bales and blankets filled the flatbed. Families climbed aboard and sat close, knees touching, arms looped.

"All aboard," Pop called. "Scenic route. October edition."

I drove slowly down County Road 40, then turned onto Spruce Street. Porch lights blinked on. A few leaves let go and fell easy. The town softened in that light.

Jasper leaned toward Hank. "This is the part where Lolli says we're supposed to remember it forever."

Hank snorted, then watched the lights, the pace, the closeness. He bumped Jasper's arm once. They leaned back against Annie and Stetson without naming what they were holding.

When we returned, musicians gathered under the trees. Instruments tuned. Voices warmed.

Wilder Kate stepped forward, guitar slung low. Her voice rose clear and sure. Millie stood off to the side, hands clasped tight, watching as if unsure—and also certain.

When Wilder motioned her up, Millie hesitated only a beat. Then she stepped forward and found harmony.

They sang "Fantasy," nothing showy. Just right. The crowd went still. Even the leaves seemed to pause.

Millie held her place, steady and true. When the applause came, it came fast. She bowed toward Wilder, blushing. Wilder lifted her hand like she'd opened a door.

Lolli rushed in, hands to her face. Pop followed, pulling them both into a hug, holding Millie a second longer. No speeches. Real pride doesn't need them.

Later, the chili bubbled. Cornbread broke into waiting hands. S'mores were managed seriously and safely. Lanterns glowed, but the warmth came from the people themselves.

I stepped back and watched faces, carved pumpkins, tired children leaning into their people. That good kind of exhausted—the kind that means something happened worth keeping.

Once again, the land did what it has always done when given half a chance.

It gathered us.

boybands and backaches

THE LAWHOMA HILLS school gym has played every role a town can ask of a room. Exams and assemblies. Concerts and science fairs. Storm shelter. Late-night echoes of sneakers long after the last kid went home.

But on the Friday before Fall Break, it became a different kind of shelter.

The moment I walked in, I felt it—an older feeling in the air. Not dusty-old. Memory-old. Neon streamers draped reckless and bright from the ceiling. Glow sticks pulsed in the corners. A disco ball spun silver flecks across the floor like somebody cracked open a jar of stars. Giant cardboard cassette tapes leaned against the walls, nearly as tall as Juan Carlos, and a hand-painted banner from the Art Club stretched across the gym with grave sincerity:

TOTALLY RAD DANCE TONIGHT!

In the middle of it all stood Wilder Kate Everett in a denim jacket layered with iron-on patches, hair sprayed to heights that suggested commitment and possibly a small electrical incident. She held the microphone like it belonged to her.

"Welcome to the Throwback Dance!" she yelled. "We're starting with warm-ups from the eighties. Stretch your arms, stretch your legs, and stretch your dancing moves."

The gym erupted. Even the administrators looked like their inner children were trying to elbow free.

DJ Shia Goldberg didn't hesitate. "You Give Love a Bad Name" hit hard and fast, and the room responded like we'd been waiting for permission all week. Kids leapt without rhythm or shame. Adults swayed and rediscovered muscles they'd written off. Pop air-guitared with such enthusiasm he nearly clipped Lolli.

"Pop," she warned.

"I am expressing myself," he said, without apology.

Wilder Kate launched a medley from Bon Jovi to Bryan Adams to Journey, and Phil Collins—Tata fully reenacted the 80's accompanying him on "In The Air Tonight." Jasper, Hank, and Pop took turns holding her mic for the vocals and cheered her on through every drum beat. Trip Waddell tried to jump a folding chair during "Jump," misjudged, and laughed himself breathless. When "Don't Stop Believin'" hit, every hand went up, reaching for the same memory at once.

Then the decade shifted, and the room shifted with it.

Britney. Ricky Martin. TLC. A boy band mash-up that left the gym divided, confused, and fully committed. Two dads in work boots screamed "MMMBop" like it was their job. Mack Ashe attempted break-dancing, learned entirely online. Kolby Sweeney's moonwalk nearly counted. Gus Franklin joined a dance circle with Will and Mack that had clearly been rehearsed in secret.

I made a mental note to never ask questions.

Micah clapped perfectly in time, eyes shining, and my throat tightened the way it always does when joy reminds you how much there is to lose.

Hank, Jasper, and Millie attempted the Macarena three different ways at once. None were correct. None of them cared.

Pop joined the Running Man and nearly took out a cardboard boombox.

"Pop," Lolli cautioned again.

"I am still expressing myself," he said, adding a hip swivel that should be illegal in multiple counties.

I laughed hard enough my eyes watered, and for a few minutes I forgot the weight I'd been carrying like an extra purse.

. . .

THAT'S when I noticed the parents.

They were dancing, clapping, smiling—and clustering near the bleachers between songs, leaning in with that posture that means lower your voice.

I drifted close enough to catch the edges.

"We haven't heard back on the lawyer search," Dahlia murmured.

"Matty says don't promise anything yet."

"We've got festival money," Ricky said. "That's not legal money."

Annie's face stayed bright on purpose. Stetson stood beside her, hands in pockets, eyes tracking the room.

Annie caught my glance for half a second. Not tonight, it said.

So we didn't.

We danced anyway. We kept the music loud enough to drown the math. We smiled through it, which is both a terrible habit and a love language around here.

AS THE NIGHT WOUND DOWN, Shia dimmed the lights and cued "Kiss Me." Glow sticks sparkled. Adults swayed with children tucked into their shoulders. Friends rocked side to side as if the world were simpler. Wilder Kate sat on the edge of the stage, feet dangling, singing softly to herself, hair still defying gravity.

It felt like pulling on a sweater that still fits.

The final song was "Africa." Half the gym screamed at the opening notes. The other half invented choreography that never existed but felt required. Pop danced with abandon. Lolli stayed within rescue distance.

The floor shook with laughter and stomping feet.

When the doors finally opened, kids spilled into the cool night buzzing.

"That was the best dance ever!"

"They played all the jams!"

"I'm wearing neon forever!"

On the ride home, glow sticks flickered in the backseat, refusing to admit the night was over.

"I liked the slow songs," Millie said.

"I liked the fast ones," Hank said.

"I liked all the Lolli and Yaya jams," Jasper declared, rubbing his shin.

"Music does that," I told them. "It folds time."

As we drove under the stars, one hand on the wheel, I kept thinking about those quiet clusters by the bleachers.

The dance ended.

The math did not.

FRIDAY, OCTOBER 8

THE EIGHTIES GIRL IN ME HAD A REAL GOOD TIME. FOR A WHILE I FORGOT THE WORRY I'D TOSSED IN THE TRUCK BED, THE WAY I DO WHEN I TELL MYSELF I'LL DEAL WITH SOMETHING LATER AND HOPE IT LISTENS.

IT DIDN'T.

I WANT TO BE CAREFREE, FULL-VOLUME, NEON-BRIGHT, RAVE HAIRSPRAY, AND MADONNA.

THE KIND OF WOMAN WHOSE BIGGEST CONCERN IS WHETHER NSYNC OR BACKSTREET TAKES THE CROWN.

I ALSO WANT MY TOWN, OUR LAND, AND I WANT OUR CHILDREN TO KEEP BELIEVING THE GYM IS JUST A GYM—STICKY FLOORS, BAD ACOUSTICS, GOOD MUSIC—AND NOT THE PLACE WHERE GROWNUPS START WHISPERING ABOUT WHAT MIGHT BE LOST.

TONIGHT'S LISTEN: "WHAT'S UP?" - 4 NON BLONDES

To Do:

WED A.M./ CITY RUN WITH ANNIE FOR TRICK-OR-TREAT SUPPLIES

PICK UP APPLES FROM ROSS AND GLADYS

HAND PIES FRIDAY MORNING (LOLLI'S HOUSE PICKUP)

trick-or-treat espionage

HALLOWEEN FELL ON A WEEK NIGHT, so Lawhoma Hills softened the edges the Saturday before.

Lanterns in windows, string lights sagging between storefronts, children darting across the square like they'd been set loose by the moon itself.

I had my volunteer lanyard on, walkie-talkie clipped to my pocket, and a headcount running in my head like always.

Hank came dressed as a deer—quiet and careful in it. Pinned to his chest was a small badge that read Chairman, and he held himself, still figuring out what that meant. Jasper bounced beside him, bells stitched into his rodeo cowboy trim, so joy rang every time he moved. Millie trailed behind, a bushy fox tail swaying, toy microphone held just right, channeling Wilder Kate with such sincerity it made strangers smile.

I WAS HALFWAY through a mental roll call when I spotted the older kids.

They weren't doing anything wrong. Not yet. But they moved differently—circling, waiting, eyes sharp. Paddy. Jon Lucas. Wilder. Shep. Brick. Edie Claire. Whip. A quiet orbit.

As I passed the cider table, I caught a scrap of something—just the edge of a whisper.

"Now?"

"Give it a minute," Wilder said.

Paddy shifted his backpack. The strap squeaked, and he stilled it like the sound might give him away.

My stomach dropped just a little. Old nurse or suspicious mom instinct.

I didn't break the moment or pretend it was about safety, those instincts were really about control. I watched the space they left behind and turned back toward the littles, still pin-balling through the light.

I didn't know what the older kids were doing until later.

I only saw what it cost them when they came back.

They returned in pieces—one at a time, two together, trying too hard to look normal.

Hoodies pulled low. Breath fogging. Dirt where dirt didn't belong. Edie Claire kept tugging her sleeve down over her wrist. Paddy's hands stayed still—too still, like he didn't trust them not to shake.

They laughed too hard at things that weren't jokes.

Relief laughter. The kind that comes after fear burns off and leaves anger behind.

I kept my face easy. I passed cider. I asked about treat baskets. I made space.

But I started counting again.

WHEN THE PORCH lights dimmed and the square gave way to goodbyes, I got the younger kids home, hugged the necks I needed to and at home, I rinsed cider mugs in the sink, and tried not to think too hard.

My phone buzzed.

> Wilder Kate: are you up

> Jon Lucas: We need you. now. please don't call our parents

Paddy: at your place in five?

I typed the only thing I could afford to promise.

Come. Porch light will be on. Bring everyone.

RJ lifted her head before I even reached the switch. Beans pulled out his Chewbacca .

"They're coming," I told the dogs. "Be kind."

They arrived breathless, bikes dropped in the gravel like afterthoughts. They gathered on my porch the way finches do after the blue jay comes to the feeder.

I didn't ask questions outside.

"Come in," I said. "Shoes off if you can—never mind, just come in."

They piled into the kitchen. The light flicked on and every one of them flinched. I set water jars on the table. Pulled a blanket over Edie Claire's shoulders without a word.

"Okay," I said, voice steady, calm like triage. "Tell me the truth. Start from the part you can say without falling apart."

Paddy swallowed. "We went to the west line."

"And there were traps," Wilder said.

That was enough.

They told the rest in fragments. The dark. The metal. A prairie dog screaming without sound. A drone low enough to make them freeze. Hands shaking. Breaking what they could. Running when they had to.

When they finished, the room went still.

"You kids," I said, and my voice cracked before I caught it, "you could've been hurt."

"We know," Whip said.

"And you still did it."

Brick nodded. "We couldn't not help them."

I took a breath.

"First," I said, "nobody goes home alone."

A few protests rose. I stopped them with a look.

"Second, I'm calling your parents. Not to punish you. To protect you."

171

Paddy's shoulders dropped like something heavy had finally been set down.

"Third," I said, "I have to call Matty."

WHEN THE PARENTS ARRIVED, the house filled fast. Fear came first. Then anger. Then love.

Liam stood in my kitchen, arms crossed tight. "Why," he said, voice low, controlled, "did you come here instead of calling your mom or me?"

Before I could answer, Paddy did.

"Because Yaya listens," he said. "And we were scared."

Silence landed like a dropped plate.

Then Paddy glanced at me. Then at his mom. His voice got smaller.

"It's not the first time."

Caitlyn's head tilted—slight, sharp. "What?"

"I went to her before. A couple weeks ago. When I saw the tents the first time. She didn't tell anyone."

I didn't move. Didn't defend myself.

Caitlyn looked at me like she was trying to solve an equation that had suddenly stopped adding up.

"So this is the second time he came to you first. And you—what, you just kept it quiet?"

I nodded once. "I wasn't sure yet. I told myself I needed time."

"You had time," she snapped. "We didn't. Our kids didn't."

Her voice cracked, but it didn't soften.

"Do you know what it feels like to realize someone else has been keeping your son's secrets? To find out he was scared, and you weren't even in the room?"

Liam reached for her arm, but she pulled away.

"He's ours," she said. "He's a good kid. He does things right. And we should've been the ones he came to. We should've been told."

Paddy looked down. "I asked her not to."

"You don't get to carry that," she said, her voice gentler now, but still shaking. "That's not your job, sweetheart."

I stepped forward, slow and steady. "He trusted me. And I should've come to you anyway. I see that now."

Caitlyn swallowed hard. "I'm not angry that you love him. I'm angry that you left us out of it."

"You're right," I said. "You get to be angry. That part's yours."

She nodded—once, hard—and looked away.

The room froze again.

Liam turned toward her, voice quiet. "Cait—"

"No." Her voice broke, then steadied. "I'm not mad at him. I'm proud of him. But I'm standing here wondering—how did we become the backup plan?"

No one answered.

"I should've told you," I said, softer now. "I had doubts. I hesitated. That's on me. But when they came to my porch tonight, I wasn't thinking about roles. I was thinking about keeping them breathing and unbroken."

Caitlyn blinked. Her jaw clenched, then eased. She nodded—just once.

Liam exhaled and pulled Paddy into a long, wordless hug.

Matty arrived last. He didn't raise his voice or scold. He listened.

"You did what you thought was right," he told the kids. "Now the adults take it from here."

WHEN THE LAST truck rolled away and the porch light buzzed overhead, Matty and I stood side by side.

"We start building the plan," Matty said. "Quiet. Solid."

I nodded.

"We're not breaking," I said.

SATURDAY, OCTOBER 29
CHILDREN IN COSTUMES MADE OF PINECONES AND BURLAP AND CARDBOARD, RUNNING WITH THEIR WHOLE HEARTS.
I WAS HAPPY.
AND THEN THE NIGHT GOT LONGER.
I AM GRATEFUL THOSE OLDER KIDS TRUSTED ME.
I WANT TO BE THAT KIND OF ADULT—THE ONE THEY COME TO

WHEN FEAR OUTPACES AGE. THE ONE WHO CAN SIT STEADY AND NOT MAKE IT WORSE.

BUT MY HEART KEEPS SNAGGING ON SOMETHING ELSE.

PADDY CAME TO ME FIRST. WEEKS AGO. AND I WAITED. I TOLD MYSELF IT WAS TOO SOON TO SOUND THE ALARM, TOO SOON TO KNOW.

BUT MAYBE I JUST DIDN'T WANT TO SEE IT.

AND I CAN'T TAKE THAT BACK.

I HOPED HANK AND JASPER WOULD NEVER HAVE TO BE THAT BRAVE.

I WANT THEM BRAVE IN THE ORDINARY WAYS. BRAVE ENOUGH TO TRY SOMETHING NEW, BRAVE ENOUGH TO APOLOGIZE FIRST, BRAVE ENOUGH TO STAND UP FOR SOMEONE SMALLER, OR TELL THE TRUTH EVEN WHEN IT COSTS THEM.

NOT BRAVE IN THE DARK WITH METAL TEETH WAITING IN THE GROUND AND A HUMMING SKY OVERHEAD.

THERE ARE DAYS WHEN YOU DON'T KNOW WHETHER TO SAY THE ROSARY OR TAKE A SHOT OF WHISKEY.

BIG GRANNY ALWAYS SAID IT PLAIN:

WHISKEY-OR-ROSARY KIND OF DAY.

TONIGHT IS BOTH.

I NEEDED SOMETHING WITH A STOMP IN IT. SOMETHING THAT SAYS: WE'RE TIRED, BUT WE'RE STILL HERE.

TONIGHT'S LISTEN: "S.O.B." – NATHANIEL RATELIFF & THE NIGHT SWEATS
TO DO:
CHECK IN WITH MATTY
DOUBLE/ CHECK THE PORCH LIGHT BULB
NEXT TIME, SPEAK SOONER

form, figure, and dignity

ONE THING about Lawhoma is certain: our weekends stay booked like we're famous. But the morning of the Birch Creek Karate Tournament felt different, quieter, more deliberate. Even the air seemed to pause, graceful as Paul Chen on a mat.

Lolli and I rode over with Annie and the boys. Pop went up earlier to help set the gym in place.

Jasper and Barbara have struck up a real friendship, the kind grownups don't have to arrange. It probably helps that their mommas have been friends since they were thirteen or fourteen and never stopped.

Jasper was bubbling over with pride, worry, and excitement to watch his "kick butt and take names" bestie.

The gym was full of families seated in the bleachers, but the normal roar of weekend sports had been replaced by a serious, focused hum. Most voices stayed soft. Movement was intentional.

Mats had been laid out in rows across the floor, pale blue squares perfectly aligned. Behind the long tables sat the judges, clipboards ready, faces calm and attentive. Competitors warmed up in orderly lines, completing stretches and basic techniques with the seriousness of young martial artists who understand this space matters.

At the heart of it all stood the Chen family, steady and centered.

Kelly and Paul greeted attendees with formal bows to the side, palms down, eyes level. Nainai Chen-Lomai and Yeye XinLim sat nearby. Even retired, their postures held authority, and their attention stayed sharp, generous, and kind.

Their grandkids, Barbara, Lacey, and Kip, moved through warm-ups. Lacey dropped into a deep front stance, weight planted, spine straight. Kip worked straight punches, bringing each one back into guard with clean precision. Barbara, shorter but intense, ran her kata, her braid swaying with each transition.

"They look ready," Lolli whispered.

"They are," I said. But being ready doesn't mean it will be easy.

The Opening Ceremony

Judges asked competitors to line up by rank. At the signal, the room became still. A head judge stepped forward and bowed.

"This isn't a competition against each other," he said. "This is an evaluation of your discipline, focus, respect, and spirit. Compete with dignity."

Everyone bowed back.

Pop leaned toward me. "I like this sport," he whispered. "Very polite."

"That's the whole point," I whispered back.

Kip's Kata

Jasper leaned toward me, quiet and thrilled. "Kata is showing your best punches and kicks without anybody messing you up."

Kip bowed to the judges. Bowed to the mat. Closed his eyes as if he was shutting a door on the whole gym.

Then he began.

Every movement was sharp and clean. Rooted stances. Precise strikes. Smooth transitions.

Jasper whispered again, practically vibrating. "That snap right there is kime. Straight focus."

Kip finished and held still at the end, calm but ready.

"That's zanshin," Jasper said, proud as a commentator. "You're chill, but you're still aware."

I don't know if karate encourages applause, but Lawhoma does. The whole gym clapped like our hands had been waiting all morning.

Kip's scores came in high across the board. His face flushed, but he kept bowing steadily. Nainai and Yeye applauded quietly, pride contained but unmistakable.

Barbara's Turn

Next was Barbara.

She stepped onto the mat with intensity in her eyes, bowed, took a few seconds to center her breathing, then began. Powerful. Quick. Clean strikes. Correct footwork.

She was beautiful to watch. Jasper was even better, counting and breathing along with her from the bleachers, as if he could lend her steadiness from his seat.

Then, mid-turn, her foot slid on a faint dusting of chalk.

Not a fall. Just a fraction of hesitation.

Enough to nick the rhythm.

Her breathing hitched. Jasper's did too, his face dropping with worry. Barbara's face gave nothing away. She kept going, but the flow had been interrupted.

Jasper leaned close to me and tried to find the exact word for what he'd seen. "It's when your timing…fathered…no faltered," he whispered. "Barbara says it's like when the song skips."

She finished her kata. She bowed to the judges, bowed to the mat, then exited without rushing, without drama. Only a girl carrying disappointment with good posture.

Lacey hugged her. Nainai placed a hand between Barbara's shoulder blades. Kip offered her a water bottle with extreme seriousness.

Barbara watched the ground, then looked up and found Jasper. A sweet exchange of friends locking eyes in a sea of faces. Annie and I saw it. We both kept our own faces calm, because that's what mothers and grandmothers do when a child is holding herself together.

THE REST of the tournament continued, but my mind kept circling back to Barbara.

Lacey's Kumite

Next, Lacey competed in kumite. Jasper didn't have to explain this one. It was sparring, controlled and measured.

In this case, her partner was her daddy.

Lacey moved with lightness and speed. Footwork precise. Eyes alert. Strikes quick but controlled. Each point earned cleanly and respectfully. She never rushed. She never lost her balance. After her last point, she retreated and bowed.

The audience cheered loud. I've watched sports all my life, but this had real beauty in it.

Lacey bowed again, calm and collected. Proud, but humble.

While we waited for the awards ceremony, Jasper and I found Barbara sitting near the bleachers, swinging her legs slowly. Jasper offered her a handshake, the public-friendly kind twelve-year-olds use so they don't have to show feelings in front of God and everybody.

I sat beside her. "I once slipped during a school performance," I said gently. "Right in front of everyone."

She lifted her gaze. "You did?"

"Yes. And I finished anyway."

Barbara pressed her foot against the floor. "I messed up real bad."

I shook my head. "No, ma'am. You had two moments."

She tilted her head. "Two?"

"One was when you slipped," I said. "The other was when you finished." I leaned in just a little. "In any sport, that second moment is the real test. Today you proved your heart is bigger than the mistake."

Barbara took a deep breath, slow and deliberate. The kind of breath her grandparents taught her. Her shoulders loosened.

"I'm proud of you," I told her. "Your family is too."

She smiled, small but real.

AFTER THE JUDGES RETURNED, the room quieted again. Kip earned First Place in Kata. Lacey earned the highest honors in Kumite.

When Barbara's name was called, her eyes went wide, as if she hadn't known perseverance counted until it did. She looked straight at Jasper West.

Barbara blinked once, then bowed as if it hadn't touched her.

She earned a Special Recognition ribbon for Perseverance and Spirit.

Jasper leaned toward me, whispering with satisfaction. "See. Second moments."

The Chen family erupted in a chaotic display of cheering that absolutely exceeded the boundaries of decorum. Yeye blushed openly. Nainai tried to keep composure and failed with joy.

Outside, the afternoon air had a crisp edge to it. Leaves skittered across the parking lot, making their own little celebration.

The Chen family walked together, Kip holding his medal up where it could catch the light, Lacey waving her trophy, Barbara carrying her ribbon in both hands.

"That was a wonderful day," Lolli said.

"A truly wonderful day," I replied.

SUNDAY, OCTOBER 30

I LOVE THAT THESE BOYS HAVE A FRIEND GROUP NO ONE WOULD BELIEVE IF YOU TRIED TO DIAGRAM IT. THE RESPECT JASPER SHOWED BARBARA TODAY STAYED WITH ME. AND I DIDN'T HEAR ONE SINGLE BLIP OF WORRIED TALK ABOUT THE BIGGER CLOUD HANGING OVER US. EVERYONE HELD IT BACK AND LET THE KIDS HAVE THEIR DAY, AND I WAS GRATEFUL FOR THAT IN A WAY THAT SAT DEEP.

ANNIE CALLED ON THE DRIVE HOME. THE MOMS WITH SCHOOL-AGE KIDS ARE GOING TO DO A SHORT TALK, ON THEIR OWN TERMS, BEFORE THIS TURNS INTO HALLWAY CHATTER. NOT THE WHOLE STORY. JUST THE TRUTH THE KIDS NEED. GROWN-UPS ARE HANDLING THE MEETINGS. KIDS DON'T HAVE TO CARRY THE MATH. QUESTIONS COME TO US, NOT PASSED IN WHISPERS.

KELLY. JORDAN. MEGAN. LINDSAY. CONNIE. GINGER. EMMA MAE. BOOTSIE.

LOLLI AND I DON'T NEED TO BE THERE.

I SAID THANK YOU AND MEANT IT.

TONIGHT'S LISTEN: "BIGGEST PART OF ME"—AMBROSIA

To Do:
Call Rosemary and Shyra/ do they need help getting supplies here
What time do we start decorating and cooking
Ask Annie about outfits and yes paint faces or no?

lessons from abuelita shyra

COOL MORNINGS TURN into golden afternoons, and the smell of pecan leaves drifts over the fields—sweet and dry, gone as soon as you notice it. This is the time of year we prepare for one of our most important gatherings, Día de los Muertos, and we do it the way we do most things here: together, and under the steady guidance of Abuelita Shyra.

By late afternoon, the dining hall at Camp Run Amuck glowed marigold orange. Petals lined the walkway as if a small sunset had spilled onto the ground. Lanterns threw soft shadows. Papel picado dangled above the tables, swaying each time the door opened.

Helpers moved with purpose. Ruby placed candles carefully, counting under her breath as if the flame itself required respect. Juan Carlos added the final touches to sugar skulls, tongue pressed to the corner of his mouth in concentration. Shep and Brick tested the microphones and laughed when the speaker popped. Ranger strung extra lights while humming off-key, as if it were his offering to the universe. Beans and Rizzo Jane paced the room, supervising—an assignment they believed was sacred.

I had just set down a tray of pan dulce when I saw Annie at the doorway with the boys.

Hank Miller and Jasper West held tight to her hands as they took in the painted faces, the candlelight, the ofrenda filled with framed photographs and small treasures that belonged to people no longer walking around with us.

Jasper leaned in, voice low. "Momma… why are there people dressed like skeletons?"

Hank didn't look away. "Is this gonna be scary?"

Annie knelt so her face was level with theirs, lantern light warming her cheeks.

"Oh boys," she said, gentle and sure. "There's nothing to be afraid of here. Tonight, we're celebrating Big Granny. And Big Granny loved a party."

Jasper's shoulders eased first. Hank's followed.

Annie kissed the top of each head, smoothing their hair back the way she's done since they were small enough to fit under her chin.

"This isn't a pretend-to-be-dead celebration," she said. "It's the opposite. It's a celebration of the fact that love doesn't disappear. Not ever."

I watched the shift happen—that quiet moment when a child decides the world is safe enough to learn.

Abuelita Shyra called everyone closer. She didn't raise her voice. She didn't need to. The room settled around her the way a room does when it trusts the person standing in it.

"¡Feliz Día de los Muertos!"

"Día de los Muertos is not a day of fear," she said." "La muerte es una vida de recuerdos- Death is a life of memories, Que su luz nos guíe- May their light guide us."

Annie squeezed the boys' hands and whispered, "Big Granny liked bold colors, big laughter, and any reason for a meal you could taste for two days."

Both boys smiled.

The boys wandered to the ofrenda and studied the photographs. Hank paused at one and pointed.

"That's Doc."

"That's Doc," I said. "He held half this town together with tape and kindness."

Tata stood in front of the photo very still, her hand hovering near the frame as if tracing a doorway. She didn't cry. She didn't smile. She simply remembered.

The boys stopped next at a picture of Big Granny laughing, eyes crinkled in that way that meant she was fully tickled. Annie was seven in the photo, perched on Big Granny's lap in that red leather recliner, both of them wearing the same grin, like they were borrowing it from each other.

Annie's thumb brushed the frame, light and careful.

"When I was a teenager," she said, half-smiling at herself, "I used to tell Big Granny secrets I couldn't tell Yaya."

Jasper's eyes widened. "You had secrets from Ya?"

"Oh, honey," Annie said, and Big Granny lived again in her voice. "Plenty."

She glanced at me, then back to the boys. "There were nights I knocked on her window after I'd made not-so-smart choices. She'd let me in, no lecture first. She'd feed me biscuits and gravy to get me steady. Then we'd talk."

"That chair was my whole childhood," she said, voice holding firm. "I learned how to be brave by watching her be brave."

Jasper looked at Annie with new eyes, as if rearranging the picture of who his mother had always been.

"And you know something else," Annie added, softer. "Big Granny only got to meet you boys a couple of times when you were tiny, those pictures on the fridge. But she looked at you like she'd been waiting her whole life."

Hank frowned. "Why only two times?"

Annie took a breath. "Because her body was getting tired," she said plainly. "But her love still worked."

The boys stood quiet, building a new understanding brick by careful brick.

ABUELITA SHYRA STEPPED in just then, as if she knew the moment needed easing. "Come," she said, clapping her hands once. "We remember with music too."

Soon the hall filled with sound. Wilder Kate took the lead on guitar. Shep and Brick found the beat. Chase shook a maraca with fierce commitment, as if rhythm might solve everything. People laughed, feet tapped and bodies spun. The music wasn't sad. It was alive.

The music rose, covering us like a warm hand.

Hank grabbed Jasper's hand and pulled him into the dance. Any lingering hesitation disappeared as they stomped and twirled with the same joyful abandon Big Granny would have recognized immediately.

Pop danced past me and murmured, "Your mom would've made us all do the electric slide?" Then pretended he didn't have feelings and wandered off to steal Millie's empanada.

WHEN DINNER WAS FINISHED and the tables cleared, we moved outside. Gus Franklin had stretched a white sheet between two pecan trees. Blankets layered the grass. Beans curled beside Jasper in a warm coma. Rizzo Jane rested her head against Hank's legs.

The first notes of *Coco* drifted into the night, and the crowd softened into stillness.

I turned and found Annie. Her eyes were wet, but her mouth stayed steady. She didn't look like she was breaking, she looked like she was holding.

The boys leaned in close on either side of her, safe and calm, watching a story that told them what we'd been teaching all evening.

That remembering isn't scary.

That love doesn't die.

That family stays present even when you can't see them with your regular eyes.

When the movie ended, Hank whispered, "Big Granny would've danced with us."

Annie nodded. "She absolutely would have. With her cane and all." She smiled then, real and warm. "And what's beautiful is she still dances inside you."

Lanterns flickered. Marigolds glowed. Kids yawned and burrowed deeper into blankets. The hall behind us went quiet in that satisfied way a place gets after it has held something important.

I looked up at the night sky and spoke to my mother the way I still do.

Thank you for loving my daughter so loud we can still hear it.

TONIGHT WAS BEAUTIFUL. ABUELITA SHYRA HELD THAT ROOM WITH HER STEADY HANDS AND STEADY VOICE. ANNIE HELD IT TOO, IN HER OWN WAY. BIG GRANNY WAS HER PERSON. THICK AS THIEVES.

THEY HAD NO CHOICE. I HANDED MY NEWBORN TO BIG GRANNY EVERY MORNING SO I COULD FINISH THAT LAST YEAR OF NURSING SCHOOL. I DIDN'T HAVE A CHOICE MYSELF, IF WE WANTED LIGHTS AND GROCERIES, BUT LORD, IT WAS HARD. WE BECAME A TEAM—BOTTLES AND ROCKING ON ONE SIDE, RESEARCH PAPERS ON THE OTHER.

ANNIE TOLD THE BOYS ABOUT BEING A TEENAGER AND KNOCKING ON BIG GRANNY'S WINDOW AFTER SHE'D MADE NOT-SO-SMART CHOICES. BIG GRANNY LET HER IN ANYWAY. NO LECTURE, BISCUITS AND GRAVY THEN BED. THEY WERE SECRET KEEPERS, THE TWO OF THEM, A SMALL TEAM MOST OF THE TIME —AND YES, SOMETIMES I WAS THE ENEMY OF THEIR FUN.

AND STILL, IN THE MIDDLE OF ALL THAT LIGHT, I FELT THE OTHER WORLD HOVERING AT THE EDGE OF THE ROOM.

WHEN EVERYONE FINALLY WENT HOME AND THE HOUSE WENT QUIET, I RAN A BATH SO HOT IT TURNED MY SKIN PINK AND MY THOUGHTS SLOW. I NEEDED THE KIND OF QUIET WHERE YOU CAN HEAR YOUR OWN HEART AND DECIDE YOU'RE STILL HERE.

I HAD A CRY IN THE TUB. JUST A LEAK—THE WAY A FULL GLASS FINALLY GIVES UP ONE HONEST DROP.

GRIEF. I STACK IT YEAR AFTER YEAR AND PRETEND IT'S MANAGEABLE UNTIL A SONG COMES ON, OR A PHOTOGRAPH CATCHES THE LIGHT, OR I SMELL BISCUITS AND GRAVY AND SUDDENLY I'M STANDING IN EVERY LOSS I EVER CARRIED.

BUT, GRIEF ALSO DRAINS OUT OF US THROUGH LOVE. THROUGH FOUND FAMILY. THROUGH COMMUNITY. THROUGH CHILDREN

laughing under lanterns like the world hasn't hurt them yet.
I let the fear have its moment.
Then I let it go. I am not a what if girl anymore.

Tonight's Listen: "Lost Without You" — Freya Ridings

To Do:
This week is full again
Thank Abuelita Shyra
Check on Annie
Keep my backbone handy

gravity owes wyatt nothing

THE SIGNS APPEARED FIRST.

Handwritten posters taped to storefront windows. Cardboard placards staked into winter-hard soil. Flyers tucked under windshield wipers and slipped into library books. Some neat. Some crooked. All saying the same thing in different hands.

Protect Blue Creek. Volunteers Needed. Sign Here.

LAWHOMA STANDS TOGETHER

I saw them on my drive in, the town already awake in that half-lit way late-fall mornings bring. Folks stood in small groups near the square with clipboards out, breaths puffing, pens moving as if they were signing their names onto something with teeth. A few waved as I passed. A few lifted a hand mid-sentence and kept talking anyway.

BIRCH CREEK'S gym sat at the edge of it all, windows fogged from inside heat and early nerves. The parking lot filled fast. Cars backed in crooked. Trunks popped open. Gym bags thumped onto the pavement. That low hum of competition started before we even stepped through the doors.

Inside, the air was sharp with chalk and rubber mats. It grabbed the back of my throat the way hospital antiseptic used to. Not the same smell, but the same message: pay attention. Shoes squeaked. Ankles popped. Tape peeled back from fur or feathers and then stuck again. A coach barked a cue. A kid giggled too loud and got shushed with love.

I found our little crew and settled where I could see the bars.

Wyatt was already there, rolling her shoulders one at a time, jaw set. Raven-black hair pulled tight. Crow and magpie both in her family, but she was all crow—sharp-eyed, economical, nothing wasted. She kept her focus small, conserving it.

Her hands were already white with chalk.

Ronnie bounced beside her, all elbows and sunshine. "Did you sleep, sis?"

Wyatt gave her one glance. "Some."

"That's not an answer," Ronnie said, grinning, proud of herself for being irritating.

Wyatt's mouth twitched, just barely. "Enough."

Ronnie leaned closer. "You're going to rock this."

Wyatt exhaled through her nose. "I'm going to do my routine."

Her coach crouched in front of her, fingers pressing at her wrists, checking tape as if reading a map. "Hands?"

Wyatt didn't dramatize it. She never did. "They burn."

"That's good," the coach said. "Means you're awake."

Nearby, parents clustered with coffee cups and folded programs. Voices stayed low. Eyes followed their kids without apology. Daphne stood with her arms crossed, gaze steady, unreadable. Reed had his sketchbook out already, graphite moving fast, catching motion more than form. He paused, hovered, then kept going, as if he couldn't help himself.

Warm-ups were called. Music started and stopped. Vault thundered. Floor routines pulsed. Beam kids floated across four inches as if it was nothing, even when it was something. A Pine Valley gymnast slipped, froze, breathed, and finished strong. Applause came in uneven bursts, respectful and restrained.

Wyatt moved through it all without flourish. No show, no extra. Just watching, waiting, getting ready the way serious kids do. She didn't look fearless. She looked willing.

Uneven bars were last.

Her event.

WHEN THE ANNOUNCER called her name, the gym didn't go silent exactly, but the air tightened. The judges leaned forward. Ronnie stopped bouncing. Even Reed's pencil slowed.

Wyatt walked up, rubbed her palms together. Chalk ground into skin that looked too tender for what she was about to ask it to do. She shook her hands out once, twice. Her ankle popped as she stepped into place.

Her coach met her eyes. "Trust it."

Wyatt nodded. No smile. No hesitation. Just that small nod that says I'm here. I'm doing it.

She jumped.

And I watched the whole story happen at once.

Her body found the rhythm it knew. Swing. Cast. Turn. Legs snapped straight, clean lines. Shoulders held. The bars answered her, steady beneath her grip. I could see the strain even from the stands—that tremble that starts in the arms and tries to crawl into your confidence if you let it.

She did not let it.

Then came the release, the part that makes every adult's stomach drop even when you've seen it a hundred times. For a split second she was nothing but air and intention. The kind of moment where you remember gravity is a rule and also a dare.

She caught it.

Clean.

She finished strong. The dismount snapped into the mat, a period at the end of a sentence. Heels together. Knees locked. Chest lifted.

No wobble.

A breath released somewhere behind me in the crowd, loud enough I heard it. Ronnie shouted and clapped a hand over her mouth too late, and I loved her for it. The gym broke open with applause and whistles and that one dad who hollered like we were at a rodeo.

Wyatt blinked once, twice, and then her face softened. Not big. Not showy. Just a small, surprised smile, as if she couldn't quite believe her own body kept its promises.

Her coach's hand landed on her shoulder. Firm. Proud.

"You did it."

Wyatt nodded, swallowing hard. "I didn't fall."

"That's not why," the coach said, and even from the stands I felt that line land.

SCORES TOOK THEIR SWEET TIME. When they flashed, a ripple ran through the stands. Reed's pencil stopped mid-line. Daphne closed her eyes and opened them again, as if she needed one second to let pride hit without cracking.

Ronnie launched herself forward and nearly knocked Wyatt over. "You did so good," she said. "You really did crush it!"

Wyatt laughed, breathless, looking half-hurt and half-happy. "It hurt."

Ronnie grinned wider. "Hurt so good, like a boss?"

At the medals, Wyatt stood straight on that podium, gold heavy against her chest. She scanned the crowd, not searching, just seeing. Faces familiar, hopeful, tired and bright all at once. For one clean moment, she looked older than her age.

OUTSIDE, the snow started without asking permission. Fine and steady, soft as sifted flour. Cars idled. Breath hung in the air. Folks tucked programs into pockets and pulled hats down over their ears. A coach's clipboard snapped shut. At the edge of a parking spot, a volunteer sign flapped in the wind as if it was waving.

Ronnie reenacted the routine in boots, slipping on purpose and laughing. Wyatt's hands were wrapped now, the skin beneath tender and throbbing. Daphne touched the medal once, then again, testing whether it was real. Reed draped an arm around her and kissed his wife's cheek, and I pretended not to notice because that kind of tenderness deserves privacy even when it's public.

Wyatt ran up to me before she climbed into Reed's truck, eyes bright, cheeks pink from cold and triumph.

"Yaya," she said, then paused, like she was about to tell me the actual truth. "Did you see me on bars?"

"I saw you," I said. "Every second."

She nodded, satisfied, then leaned in. "Is it okay that I am really glad I did good?"

"Yes," I told her. "That part is yours and you can be glad when you worked so hard to do it."

Wyatt stared back toward the gym a moment, toward the doors and the lights and the people still milling. "I liked when I was up there," she said. "When I couldn't feel the floor."

I looked back toward town, toward those signs fluttering in the morning wind. Toward the work waiting with its own kind of nerves.

"Sometimes," I said, "being off the ground is the best part of it."

Wyatt considered that serious now. "It didn't feel safe," she said. "But it felt right."

I drove home slow, road slick and dim, headlights warm against the early dark. I thought about balance. About grip. About letting go when you must and catching what comes back.

None of us was fully on the ground right now.

Winter had begun to lean in.

To Do:
Check in with Dahlia/ Diwali anything else needed?
Order groceries for Thanksgiving (eggs, heavy cream, flour, sugar)
Make pie crusts
Check insurance selections and call if there's still time to change

diwali celebration

NOVEMBER IS BUSY. We just go-go-go. And the light in Lawhoma Hills starts acting different.

It doesn't leave yet, not really, but it leans. It lays itself long across fields and gravel roads as if it's thinking about what comes next. Even the lake looks as if it's holding its breath.

Late October, Dahlia Banerjee came up my porch steps.

She didn't knock right away. She stood there a beat, hands folded, like she was about to ask something important and didn't want to take up too much space doing it. Dahlia has that kind of presence. Quiet, steady. The sort of woman who can lead a crew into a storm and still remember everybody's name.

"Yaya," she said, smiling, then leaning in close for a hug. "You got a minute?"

"For you? Always."

She glanced back toward my driveway where Brick and Shep were waiting in the car, arguing about something without moving their mouths much. Boys can fuss in silence and treat it like sport.

Dahlia lowered her voice. "I wanted to ask before I asked."

That made me laugh. "Well, now you've got me curious."

She took a breath. "Diwali's coming. We've always done it at home. Small. A few friends. That's been enough."

I could tell she was choosing her words, not because she wasn't sure, but because she wanted them to land gentle.

"But this year," she continued, "with the council work and the meetings and…all of this," she said, tipping her chin toward the direction of Blue Creek Lake, "I think we need light. I think we need everybody."

I didn't answer too quick. I watched her face. She looked tired in the way volunteers get tired. Not worn out. Determined.

"You want a community celebration," I said.

Dahlia nodded. "If we can use the camp dining hall." Then, softer, "I know the dining hall is hosting Abuelita Shyra's celebration, but can we make room? The town needs light."

My mouth opened before my brain could get in the way. "Yes."

Her shoulders dropped, like she'd been holding them up for weeks.

"Dahlia," I said, reaching for her hands, "you've carried so much for this town. You've done the hard part. You don't have to do the light part alone."

That's when she smiled for real. "I was hoping you'd say that."

"Oh, honey. I'm not just saying it." I turned toward the house. "Come on. Sit. Let me text Arthur before you can talk yourself out of it."

She laughed. "He's already drafting a group text in his head. I can feel it."

She wasn't wrong.

Arthur Banerjee's group text hit the town not ten minutes later.

One group message. Simple.

> Arthur: Diwali at the Run Amuck dining hall. Community celebration. November 19th. 7pm. We need light this year. Who's in?

I barely had time to blink before the replies started.
Not polite little answers. Not one-at-a-time.
A flood.

> Papa Max: IN.

> Tally: Bring me recipes, I can cook.

Megan: You bet!

Lindsay: I've got folding tables if needed

Ricky: We can hang lights 🔌

Jordan: tell me what needs sewing on 🧵

Eugene: Shia got new speakers 🔊 🎤

Nanny/Hootie: We'll bring the candles

Lolli: Do we need marigolds because I know a
certain hoarder of craft boxes… 😏

I looked over at Dahlia, and she had her hand over her mouth, eyes shining.

"See?" I said. "Told you. This town loves to show up."

Dahlia wiped one tear quick as if it didn't count. "It's not an excuse," she whispered. "It's a gift."

TWO WEEKS LATER, my living room looked like a glittery explosion of gold, purple, and marigold-orange. We made garlands every spare minute. My house smelled of glue and flowers.

Manuel brought old Christmas lights from the town square, and I mean the old ones, the ones with a little crust on the plug that'll shock you if you get careless. Ricky promised to send two of his crew over to hang them.

"I'll make sure they don't die," Ricky said, as if that's a normal line to say about decorating.

Nanny and Hootie supplied candles. Enough candles to guide airplanes.

Stewart and Tallulah approached the menu with the seriousness of a mission. Tally had Dahlia's cookbooks marked with sticky notes and smudges.

Ginger and Caitlyn coordinated a fashion show.

Yes. A fashion show.

"In the dining hall?" I'd asked.

"In the dining hall," Ginger replied, like I was the one being dramatic.

Jordan sewed with the skill of a professional seamstress. Fabric came in from the theater company, thrift stores, Grandma Bertha's attic, and I am not asking questions about the attic because I do not want to know. Jordan made it all work.

BY THE TIME Diwali night arrived, Camp Run Amuck dining hall didn't look like itself.

It looked like a page out of a Bollywood movie.

Golds and purples draped across the rafters. Marigold garlands hung in loops across the room. Lights twinkled over the long tables, tender as a blessing. My sweet old barn looked lit from the inside out.

The buffet line smelled so good I almost cried. Rose lassi and watermelon juice, masala nuts, chicken tikka masala, lemon cauliflower rice, and basmati rice piled high. There were sweets I couldn't pronounce and a tater tots chaat nobody expected to work, but it did.

I walked in and saw Baby Beau asleep in his carrier like nothing on Earth could bother him. Bollywood music could've kicked down the door and he still would've snoozed.

Charlotte looked at me and whispered, "He's been out since the car."

I leaned down. "He's one precious angel, Charlotte. Y'all did good."

Then I looked up and found Millie.

Millie stood near the edge of the runway, yes, runway, hands to her face, trying to contain her excitement.

She was dressed up and sparkling. She was smiling so wide I thought her face might split.

"You look like a princess," I told her.

She whispered, "I feel like one."

Then she added, dead serious, "Do you think the lights will make me glow?"

I nodded. "Baby, you already glow."

Bridger Ashe tapped the microphone, and the room quieted in the way a room does when it respects a person.

"Alright, alright," he said, smiling like he'd been born to emcee a room full of food and glitter. "If y'all can hear me, raise your hand."

Hands shot up. A few people hollered for fun.

"If you cannot hear me," he continued, "raise your hand anyway and we'll pretend."

Laughter rippled across the tables.

Brick and Shep stood near the back, both in long jackets, sherwanis so sharp it made the whole room sit up straighter. Brick wore beaded ivory. Shep's was light blue with sequins that caught the light every time he moved. Both had tilak on their foreheads, that sacred red mark that makes even the loudest boys look a little holy.

When Shep turned, I saw a girl in the audience from Deer Creek fanning herself with a napkin, convincing herself she'd witnessed something sacred.

Lolli leaned over to me. "Is that her?"

"His girlfriend?"

Caitlyn chimed in, nodding. "She's been texting Ginger for fashion tips all week."

"Lord," I whispered. "Bless young love and Daddy's credit card."

The fashion show started with music that made my shoulders want to dance without asking my permission.

Models strutted, walked, glided down the dining hall runway like this was New York and not Lawhoma Hills. Folks were hooting and hollering, some standing on chairs and nobody pretending to be in charge of them. Trip Waddell came out in a mini mallard-sized sherwani and nearly took the roof off with how cute he was. The crowd lost its mind.

Goldie and Smith followed in matching turquoise saris, shining and proud, and I heard somebody whisper, "They wanted to match their Daddy's facial coloring." Everybody who heard it went AWW together.

Connie Franklin and Lindsay Sweeney walked together in their lehengas, both bright and meticulously repaired by Jordan. Connie was in sunflower yellow with iridescent sequins. Lindsay wore lavender with rhinestones that caught the light like dew.

When they reached the end of the runway, Connie did a dramatic spin and Lindsay pretended to faint.

Bridger leaned into the mic. "Dr. Bridget, get the smelling salts."

Then came the surprise.

The lights dimmed just a touch. The music changed.

Every grandmother in our community stepped onto that runway as if she was the reason it existed.

Because they were.

Abuelita Shyra wore a red sari that looked stunning on her. Grandma Bertha had on the tiniest bright purple sari and looked pleased as punch.

Nainai Lomai Chen walked in a Kelly-green pantsuit with seed pearls and a dupatta. At the end of the runway, she dipped into a bow-curtsy that made the whole room gasp and laugh.

And we heard Yeye XinLim give two big blows of his whistle as if the wrestling coach and the flirtatious young man were still living inside him.

"Yeye," Nainai called, not even turning around, "behave."

He whistled again.

Then Lolli and I walked together.

Lolli chose a rich burgundy with heavy beading, and I went pink, of course. I tried to beg my way into my pink Vans and got vetoed so fast it wasn't funny.

"Traditional footwear," Dahlia said, smiling sweet while crushing my dreams.

Pop whistled so loud I'm pretty sure he rattled a window.

And then the last two.

Papa Max escorted Tata.

Papa Max wore traditional male dress, standing tall and proud. He'd been waiting his whole life for this moment and only just now got invited. Tata wore the prettiest sari of all, rainbow colors, pinks, and golds. She looked like an Oklahoma fall sunset that refuses to be quiet.

When Tata hit the end of the runway, she lifted her chin and declared to the crowd, "If this isn't offensive, I think I would dress like this every day."

The room roared.

She looked down at her sari as if she couldn't believe it belonged to her. "I feel so pretty," she added, softer.

Papa Max squeezed her hand in agreement.

That moment right there, that was light.

When the applause died down, Arthur and Dahlia stepped up together.

Bridger adjusted the mic with care. He was passing over something sacred.

ARTHUR CLEARED his throat and started simple.

"Diwali is the festival of light," he said, "but not just because of candles."

Dahlia nodded. "Light is what you choose when there's darkness you can't control."

The room went still.

Arthur looked out at all of us, the whole messy bunch. "This year we have been talking about land in ways that make my head hurt. Land's possibilities for something other than our lives."

Dahlia's voice stayed calm, but it carried steel. "Those 163 acres on the west side of Blue Creek Lake belong to us, and we are here to say, we see it for what it is."

A voice near me murmured, "Amen."

Arthur continued, "For us, Diwali means we do not let fear have the final word."

Dahlia smiled small. "We light lamps anyway."

"And we do it together," Arthur said. "Not because we are pretending everything is fine."

"No," Dahlia agreed. "Because we are staying awake."

The room applauded again, softer this time.

Around the tables, conversations rose and fell like waves. I watched faces as people listened. Not scared faces. Awake faces.

BET SLID in beside me with her notebook pressed to her ribs like it was a secret she didn't want to spill on the tablecloth. "Ya," she whispered, "I got the confirmation back. It's solid. It supports what we've been saying, any luck with the attorney search?"

My shoulders tightened. My mind tried to sprint ahead, tried to turn candles into calendars and garlands into phone calls.

I leaned close to her ear. "Not tonight," I said. "Tonight is for the kids and the light. But Tuesday at the meeting, you bring every page you've got." I squeezed her hand. "I'm proud of the work you've done, girl. Truly." Then I nodded toward the kids spinning in sequins and joy. "But not tonight. I'm not putting you off Bet, just not letting land lawsuits steal Diwali. Tuesday, we talk business."

Bet nodded once, sharp. "Tuesday," she whispered back.

Across the room, Matty Benefield caught my eye and lifted his cup just slightly, a silent message I understood without words. We were moving. We were getting organized. We were not letting the lamps be the only thing we lit.

At some point, Jordan set a small stack of LAWHOMA STANDS TOGETHER ball caps on the end of a table, as casual as if they'd always been part of our parties. Ten sold before anybody could blink, cash folded and slipped to her without fanfare. Later, when the music shifted and folks started milling, one of those caps became the hat. It made a quiet circle through the room and came back heavier. Bridger lifted it once, eyes widening just a touch.

"Alright then," he said. "That's for LAWHOMA STANDS TOGETHER."

The cheer that rose up wasn't loud because we were showing off. It was loud because giving feels like agency when you've been waiting on a call back.

DANCING SPREAD across the dining hall in waves. Kids and adults tried to keep up. Millie spun in her princess feeling until she nearly toppled into my hip.

"You okay?" I asked.

She nodded, breathless. "I'm perfect."

Baby Beau slept through all of it. Jingles and drums never rustled him.

Somewhere between songs, the subject shifted the way it always does in small towns, serious to practical without making a speech out of it. Adults leaned close in quick clusters, then pulled apart again when a kid ran up laughing or somebody needed a refill. Arthur and Dahlia moved through the room, hugging people, listening, holding steady. Bet's notebook stayed tucked to her ribs. We were warm, we were loud, we were pretending nothing could touch us for one night, even while we kept one hand on the work waiting for Tuesday.

Tonight, nothing was wished for-we already had it.

SATURDAY, NOVEMBER 19
I USED TO JOKE I PEAKED IN 1987. TRUTH IS, IT REALLY WAS A GOOD YEAR. HOMECOMING. THAT DANCE. MUSIC SO LOUD IT MADE A SMALL SHIELD AROUND YOU. NOTHING BAD COULD GET A GRIP WHILE YOU WERE MOVING
TONIGHT CAME CLOSE ENOUGH TO THAT TO CATCH ME OFF GUARD.
MY FEET ACHED IN THE FAMILIAR WAY, AND I DIDN'T MIND IT. THAT ACHE CAME FROM STANDING TOO LONG, DANCING A LITTLE, AND BEING SURROUNDED BY PEOPLE WHO MATTERED. FROM STAYING PRESENT INSTEAD OF BRACING FOR WHAT COMES NEXT.
I KEEP SEEING THE GRANDMOTHERS ON THAT RUNWAY, STEP-PING OUT LIKE THEY OWNED THE VERY IDEA OF CELEBRATION. MARIGOLDS AND CANDLELIGHT. BRICK AND SHEP STANDING THERE LOOKING SHARP AND JUST A LITTLE HOLY. BABY BEAU ASLEEP THROUGH DRUMS AND GLITTER LIKE PEACE IS HIS DEFAULT SETTING
"MONY MONY" FELT EXACTLY RIGHT. KIDS, GO ASK YOUR GRANDPARENTS WHAT RIDICULOUS THINGS WE SCREAMED TO THAT BEAT. OR DON'T. SOME THINGS ARE BETTER LEFT UNEXAMINED.
IN '87, AT LEAST, I GOT TO KEEP MY STINKING VANS ON.

Tub, extra scoop of Epsom salt and bed are the plan tonight.
And Tuesday, we stop whispering.

Tonight's Listen: "Mony Mony" - Billy Idol

To Do:
Clean/ Then clean again. The dining hall needs a scrub.
Tuesday/ town meeting. Pray. Cuss. Pray again.

the line is drawn

THE MEETING DIDN'T START with a gavel.

It started with boots scraping the floor, coats slung over chair backs, Lindsay setting a crock pot a little too close to the edge of a folding table. People arrived in twos and threes, most still in work clothes, some smelling faintly of hay or copier toner, some carrying notebooks they hadn't opened since the Obama administration.

The community room filled the way Lawhoma Hills always fills when something matters. Slowly. On purpose. Like nobody wanted to startle the truth.

Bet Sinclair stood near the front, flipping through a folder thick with paper. She'd arranged the chairs in a loose semicircle instead of rows. This wasn't a lecture. It was going to be a reckoning.

Matty Benefield leaned against the wall, arms crossed, nodding as people came in. Rosemary Rodriguez set a cardboard box on the table and began pulling out laminated maps, their corners soft from use. Dahlia Banerjee moved through small clusters, touching shoulders, murmuring hellos, counting heads without looking like she was counting.

I took a seat close enough to hear, far enough to watch. My usual place.

Paddy Quinn sat near the aisle, knees bouncing, hands clasped like he didn't trust them loose. His parents sat tight on either side of him. He didn't pull away. He looked like a boy who'd done something brave and only afterward learned bravery comes with paperwork.

When the door finally clicked shut, Bet cleared her throat.

"Thank you for coming," she said. "I know it's late. I know it's cold. And I know we all thought we had more time."

A few heads nodded. Yeye XinLim sighed. Pop's stomach growled, loud and unapologetic.

"We don't," Bet continued. "So we're going to talk about what we know, what we've found, and what we can still do."

She looked to Matty.

Matty pushed off the wall. He didn't raise his voice. He didn't need to. He has that turtle calm that makes you believe steady work still counts.

"The development company has moved forward without completing required notification steps," he said. "They've marked land. They've brought in equipment. They've done preliminary disturbance work."

A murmur moved through the room.

"They're counting on us not noticing," he added. "Or noticing too late."

Rosemary stepped forward and unrolled a map across the table, weighing the corners with coffee mugs and her keys.

"This section here," she said, pointing to the southwest edge of Blue Creek Lake. "Earleaf false foxglove. Skinner's foxglove. Both documented. Both protected."

She slid photographs across the table—leaves, stems, bloom patterns —each labeled in careful handwriting.

"They grow where they grow because the soil, the water, and the light agree," Rosemary said. "You break that agreement, you lose them."

"And once lost," Dahlia said quietly, "they don't come back."

Bet turned a page in her folder.

"I was down in the creek bed," she said. "South corner. Low water. Clear day."

She passed around photos of small, dark shells clinging to submerged wood.

"Winged maple leaf mussels," Bet said. "Alive. Filtering. Doing their work."

Lolli leaned closer. Nanny whispered, "I thought those were gone."

"They nearly are," Bet said. "Which makes this population even more significant."

That shifted the room. Protected species do that. You can argue opinions, but you can't argue a living thing the law already recognizes as needing help.

Matty tapped the map again. "There's a pond here. Easy to miss."

"I didn't miss it," Tata said from the back.

Matty smiled. "That's because you know how to look."

"We've documented chicken turtles," he continued. "Nesting behavior. Tracks. Shell markings."

The room went still—not silent, just attentive. We were no longer talking about land as acreage. We were talking about a body.

DAHLIA GLANCED TOWARD PADDY. "Do you want to tell them?"

Paddy stood. He stared at the map, like he needed something solid to look at.

"I didn't mean to find things," he said. "I was just…curious."

"I saw the markers," he continued. "Traps. Prairie dog burrows. They were setting them right over the holes."

A sharp inhale moved through the room.

"We opened them," he said. "The dogs ran. We broke the traps so they wouldn't work again."

Silence stretched—not judgmental, just heavy.

"That matters," Dahlia said. "Prairie dogs are a keystone species. That strengthens our case."

Matty lifted a hand. "Let's be clear. What these kids did was brave. It was also not the plan going forward."

Paddy nodded. "I know."

"We don't put kids in the middle of this," Matty said. "We document. We report. We stay clean."

Paddy swallowed. "There's one more thing."

"When we were out there," he said, "a drone came over us."

"How low?" Matty asked.

"Low enough to hear it change pitch."

That did it. Power math replaced fear.

"From here on out," Matty said, "no one under eighteen goes out there alone. Or at all. We handle this the right way."

Bet stepped forward again. "This land qualifies. Multiple protected species. Waterway impact. Habitat continuity."

She paused. "What we need now is legal structure."

"And money," Carter added, hating both the sentence and the truth.

ANNIE SPOKE UP. "We moved the donations into a real account. Farmers & Ranchers Credit Union in Oklahoma City. Multiple signees. Current balance is $11,987.75."

"Enough to make a call," Bet said. "Not enough to hesitate."

"And the attorney search?" someone asked.

Lolli exhaled. "Conflicts. Booked. No call backs. All over the state."

A bitter laugh rippled. "Aperture must own them all."

TATA SLAPPED LOLLI'S ARM. Hard.

"Ow! What?"

"Debbie Kay," Tata said, using the full government name like a gavel. "That boy you went to school with at OU. Tall. Late to everything. Tommy something."

Lolli froze. Then her eyes lit.

"Tommy Dale Whitehorse?"

"That's him," Tata said. "Environmental law. Native land protections. Saw him on the news last week, fighting wind turbines down in Stephens County."

Matty nodded. "I know him."

Bet closed her folder. "Then we call him."

A SHIFT MOVED through the room. Pens came out. Pages turned.

"501(c)(3)," someone said.

"Conservation easement, non profit for unity and long term protection."

"I can walk doors."

"I'll bring soup."

"I'll watch kids."

Purpose settled in—not loud, not flashy. Certain.

Paddy finally sat back, his knee still.

When the meeting ended, nobody rushed to leave. The chairs got folded. Papers stacked. Plans whispered.

Outside, the wind moved through the trees the way it always had.

Inside, Lawhoma Hills stood up.

TUESDAY, NOVEMBER 22
I'VE SAT THROUGH A LOT OF MEETINGS, BUT THIS ONE STARTED WITH NO FLUFF AND GETTING STRAIGHT TO BUSINESS.
I DROVE HOME THE LONG WAY, PAST PRESTON FARM, SOMETHING WAS NOT SITTING RIGHT IN ME. ROSS AND GLADYS....I DON'T KNOW—BUT THEY ARE NOT AROUND MUCH, GLADYS DOES NOT RETURN MY CALLS. I KNOCKED ON THE HOUSE DOOR TWICE NOW TO NO ONE. I KEEP TROUBLING MYSELF. ONE OF THEM MUST BE ILL? RANGER AND OZZY HAVEN'T MENTIONED IT. "DON'T BEAT A DEAD HORSE." PAPA J HAS SAID THAT TO ME A MILLION TIMES.

TONIGHT'S LISTEN: "BIG YELLOW TAXI" - JONI MITCHELL

TO DO:
LOOK UP CHICKEN TURTLES AND WINGED MAPLE LEAF MUSSELS
LAUNDER WINTER BLANKETS

PART FOUR

winter

WINTER ROLLS INTO OKLAHOMA LIKE KIN WHO NEVER SENDS WORD AHEAD. YOU WAKE TO A POND SEALED OVER WITH A THIN GRAY SKIN, BREATH CUTTING SHARP IN YOUR CHEST, AND RJ FROZEN AT THE EDGE OF THE PORCH, PAWS BRACED, STARING AT THE YARD AS THOUGH IT OWES HER AN APOLOGY. FORTY EIGHT HOURS LATER THE SUN SLIDES BACK OUT, GRINNING, AND I STAND IN THAT SAME SPOT SHEDDING LAYERS I DUG FROM THE CLOSET TWO MORNINGS BEFORE.

IN LAWHOMA HILLS, WINTER DOES NOT HALT US. IT DRAWS US INWARD. KITCHENS CROWD WITH STEAM AND TALK. CAMP HALLS KEEP THEIR LIGHTS BURNING PAST THE HOUR WE PROMISED TO LEAVE. CASSEROLE DISHES TRAVEL ARM TO ARM INSTEAD OF NEIGHBORS LINGERING ON PORCHES. SUGAR DISAPPEARS FROM ONE SHELF AND RETURNS IN A POT OF SOUP CARRIED ACROSS THE ROAD. WE GATHER CHILDREN IN CLUSTERS, KEEP AN EYE ON MITTENS AND TEMPERS. WE LEARN THE SHAPES OF ONE ANOTHER'S HOLIDAYS, THE CANDLES, THE SONGS, THE PLATES SET OUT FOR REMEMBRANCE, AND WE NOD AS THOUGH IT TAKES NO EFFORT AT ALL, THOUGH THE TRUTH RESTS PLAIN. LIGHT MATTERS MORE WHEN DARKNESS STRETCHES LONG.

This winter the land holds itself in a new posture. The ground has not shifted. The creek still bends where it always has. The sky spreads wide overhead, humbling in a way that steadies me. Yet something presses up from below. I feel it under my boots when I walk the dogs along the creek line. I feel it standing at the sink, water running hotter than needed, steam rising to the window while my mind drifts elsewhere.

Folks keep smiling. Music drifts from house steps and school stages. Flyers tack up straight for the next supper, the next meeting, the next reason to gather. From the road everything looks unchanged. Lawns trimmed. Mailboxes upright.

The ground, though, keeps its own memory. It hears the figures spoken over it. It senses the tape stretched tight from stake to stake. It absorbs words uttered in rooms where our names never enter the air.

Winter teaches through exposure. Cold lays a hand on what endures and what cracks. We will find out which is which.

No-Skip Albums for Winter:

Elton John – Madman Across the Water
Prince – Purple Rain
Fleetwood Mac – Rumours
Sturgill Simpson– Metamodern Sounds in Country Music
In These Silent Days– Brandi Carlile
Caamp – Caamp
I'm With Her– Wild and Clear and Blue

porch signs and hard truths

PHONE LINES STARTED IT. Not the kind strung on poles. The kind that lights up in your hand when Larry texts.

Larry: Y'all seen this?

and your stomach drops before you even open the picture.
A flyer.
A groundbreaking ceremony.

TWO WEEKS earlier we'd sat in a circle and agreed the line existed. Since then, we'd been documenting what we could, learning the shape of the fight, stacking proof the way you stack sandbags—steady, measured, hoping it holds before the water comes.

Lolli called Tommy Dale Whitehorse the morning after that meeting.

"Listen, I'm not above flirting for justice. I will bat my eyelashes, I will bake, and I will pledge my blood to OU if you come help us."

Tommy laughed once, then went quiet.

"Send me what you've got, Debbie Kay, and don't bleed on the paperwork."

By Friday, we had him. $5000.00 retainer pulled out and paid.

Papers filed. Receipts saved.

LAWHOMA HILLS FOLKS were going to be there, yes—but not to clap. Not to smile. Not to bless a thing that hadn't asked permission from the dirt.

Snow came in loose pieces, skittering sideways, melting as fast as it landed. Roads went shiny and gray. By midafternoon the podium and makeshift steps were wet, the grass trampled down to dark mats, and the air smelled faintly of diesel and wool.

They set the podium early, before the crowd arrived. Two microphones. Cords taped down with black gaffer tape. A banner snapping in the wind, corners curling inward like it wanted to fold itself up and leave. A man in a too-clean coat kept trying to flatten it with his palms. Step back. Squint. Step forward. Repeat.

The letters were straight enough.

Everything else was crooked.

BY THE TIME PEOPLE GATHERED, the ground was already marked. Footprints layered over footprints. A stroller track pressed deep near the curb. A pair of boots had slid, leaving a crescent-shaped skid that Lolli stepped into by accident. She corrected herself immediately, because even her missteps preferred order.

Orange cones sat in a neat line. Folding chairs were stacked in the back of a box truck. A white tent stood half-raised, optimistic in a way that felt personal. It looked like a ceremony. Like they believed standing in front of a thing could finish it.

Our signs were not uniform. Thank the Lord.

Poster board with bent corners. Plywood with rushed brushstrokes. One printed at home and taped to a yardstick. Abuelita Shyra used a snow shovel handle, which I respected deeply. If you can shovel a driveway, you can shovel your opinion right up where it belongs.

People came layered. Parkas and hoodies. Scarves pulled over mouths. Knit hats tugged low. Gloves that had lost their mates years ago.

Folks stamped their feet, trading places with kids who wanted to see. Babies bundled so tight you could only see their eyes and their judgment.

KSW7 was already there, parked at an angle that blocked nothing and everything. The reporter had her coat unzipped like she was daring the cold. Hair pinned back tight. Practicing her opening line under her breath. Start. Stop. Start again. The red light blinked on, off.

And then we saw it.

The bulldozer at the edge of the lot.

Idle. Blade streaked with dried mud. Tracks still packed from morning work. The kind of machine that doesn't care if you cry. The kind that waits.

Tata reached it before anyone thought to stop her.

She wore a puffy coat that made her look rounder than she is, scarf looped twice, boots worn and sensible. She placed one foot on the metal step like she was testing a porch stair, then looked back over her shoulder, checking whether any of us had the nerve to tell her no.

Nick laughed. Harry yelled her name. Stewart reached out too late.

Tata hauled herself up slow and deliberate, hands tight on the cold rail. She stood steady, peering into the cab as if she might start it herself and drive it straight back to wherever foolishness breeds.

The crowd surged half a step, then stopped. We didn't know whether to cheer or intervene. That's the thing about elders. They remind you they're still here.

Tata turned toward us and lifted her fist.

"YOU CAN'T HAVE OUR LAND," she shouted.

We answered her.

The sound didn't come out polite. It came out alive.

The camera swung toward Tata. The reporter's voice pitched up, surprised, then corrected itself. The operator shifted his stance, boots sliding, and caught himself.

Pop and Lolli ran like Tata was a toddler on a countertop.

Tata climbed down on her own. Boots hit the ground clean. She adjusted her scarf, nodded once at Lolli—"I'm fine!" She disappeared back into the bodies, leaving the bulldozer looking smaller. Less certain. Like it had just been corrected by a woman five feet tall.

·   ·   ·

AFTER THAT, the podium speech never found its footing.

Words were said. A ribbon was held. But the moving crowd, the signs lifting and lowering, the chant breaking and reforming—it swallowed the ceremony whole and kept what mattered.

Snow picked up just enough to cling to shoulders and hats, softening edges. It made the whole thing look like a photograph someone would find later and say, They showed up.

That night, Papa Max called.

"You seen the six o'clock?" he asked.

"No, rubbing my hands by the stove. "Still thawing my toes."

"Turn on seven." I could hear the smile in his voice. "They got Tata."

"Tata climbing the dozer?"

He laughed, sharp and delighted. "Baby, she climbed that bulldozer like it owed her money."

We watched together, the way old folks watch hard things—with dinner and a phone line between them. His voice came through steady. Mine did too, until they showed Tata.

From the camera angle, the crowd looked bigger than it felt standing in it. The reporter's voiceover ran smooth. Developers. Ribbon cutting. Community opposition. Legal proceedings ongoing. Words pressed flat.

Papa Max muttered, "Could've said that better." Then, "Didn't need to sound like that."

But the footage didn't belong to the reporter.

It belonged to us.

The next morning, the field sat empty again. Footprints frozen mid-step. Banner gone. Only the faint tracks of the bulldozer remained, leading nowhere.

The sound stayed.

In kitchens. In living rooms. In the way people stood straighter when they asked, "What's next?"

The ribbon lay somewhere, cut and useless.

Winter had taken its place.

THURSDAY, DECEMBER 1
GROUNDBREAKING THEY SAID, AS IF THE GROUND'S BEEN

sitting around waiting on a stranger to put a shovel in it.

I stood there in my coat and watched people with money try to make something ordinary sound inevitable.

Then Tata climbed up on that bulldozer.

I don't know what kept her strong all these years. Whatever it was, it held. She raised her fist and the sound that came back to her didn't hesitate. It felt like the town remembering it still had a mouth.

I came home wet-cold, cheeks stinging. Later, Papa Max and I watched the news together, my jaw set so tight it turned into a headache. Hearing the reporter say legal proceedings like it was a weather update made my hands curl. Seeing Tata on the screen made me laugh anyway. Anger and relief crossing paths. That's the truest mix I know.

Tonight's Listen: "The Harvest" — Tyler Childers

To Do:
Text Ginger about the Open House
Ask Annie about Saturday's shopping trip / who's driving
Order seed starting mix
Inventory seed box

sugar, spice, and gingersnaps

THERE IS COZY, and then there's Gingersnaps cozy—the kind that hits the second the bell rings and your glasses fog from the warm air and spice. Lawhoma was hungry for normal. Folks weren't rushing, not even the ones who usually do, lingering by the sample table with warm cups in their hands, taking one more minute before stepping back into the cold.

Cinnamon and pine. Cardamom and orange peel. Peppermint tucked underneath like a secret. It wasn't a holiday smell so much as winter itself, dressed and fed and invited in, the way folks do when the dark starts getting ideas.

Hank Miller and Jasper West made a clean break for the glitter, shoulders set, already competing with themselves. Millie followed with purpose—she does not wander, she selects. Pop held the door for a family of hedgehogs who insisted on single file, then drifted toward the sample table, drawn by whatever was warm and free. Lolli headed straight for the ornaments, that look on her face that means the house is about to be rearranged around a feeling.

I lingered. Gingersnaps never feels like a sale. It feels personal, the way Ginger Everett throws open the doors and says, alright then, come in and be warm in here.

Christmas Corner sat up front with a small spruce dressed in hand-made ornaments. Instrumental carols hummed low. Stockings hung across a pretend mantle. Little Santas and elves smiled from the shelves. It was postcard-perfect, yes, but the kind that still smells faintly of somebody's kitchen.

Jordan had a pop-up tucked beside the tree. Folding table. Red-and-green cloth weighted down with stacks of LAWHOMA STANDS TOGETHER shirts so the door-draft wouldn't flip them. Mugs lined up clean. Coasters tied with twine. Stickers fanned like playing cards. Jordan stood behind it in a knit beanie, antennas loose, turning her head so her earrings caught the light. She talked with her hands, laughed quick, leaned in to read a size tag, then fluttered back to the next neighbor. The whole operation ran on momentum and trust. A small card reader blinked patient beside the cash box.

"I'm not taking donations," clocking me immediately. "It's merch now. We're official."

"Official," I nodded, and picked up a mug that sat solid in my palm, lettering clean and brave. I added a set of coasters. If we were going to worry, we could at least set our coffee down on something that meant we knew each other.

Jordan slipped a sticker into my bag like a benediction and was already greeting the next person.

Around the bend was Hanukkah Haven—blues and silvers, cedar tucked in. The Goldberg family had painted menorahs with tiny forest scenes. Dreidels waited in bowls for warm hands. Ophelia's recipe cards stood stacked neat as hymnals: applesauce for latkes, each labeled A Family Tradition.

Past that, the Banerjee table glowed. Brass oil lamps, marigold garlands, silk ribbons, trays of sweets. Bright without being loud. Dahlia leaned down to a knot of kids and said, "This is about knowledge returning. Light in the mind, not just the room."

Tally's corner was quieter. Natural materials. Woven pieces. Simple signs that didn't push. Winter storytelling season. Respect for ancestors. Preparation for what comes back around. It felt good just standing there, listening with your whole body.

Bootsie Howard had built the solstice table—beeswax candles, herbal tea, small cards explaining the longest night and the turn back toward light. Even the animals know it, if you watch close enough.

At the back, the Rodriguez family had turned hospitality into practice. Spices and citrus. Cinnamon sticks snapped in half. Recipe cards passed hand to hand. Food offered open, without instruction. Faith was there, sure, but softly—in the feeding, in the welcome.

MILLIE SLIPPED her hand into mine. "Why do we have so many celebrations?"

I watched her take it all in.

"Because winter asks a lot, people answer in the ways they know."

Jasper tilted his head, sorting. "So they're all… okay?"

"They're okay, of course!" "Different can mean someone learned another way from their family and their own roots."

Hank nodded once, satisfied. "We're sharing winter."

"Yes," I told him. "We are."

We looped back through slower. Eugene choosing candles. Dahlia showing a fox kit how an oil lamp sits steady. Tally talking about stories that belong only to winter. Juan Carlos argued cinnamon versus cloves like the town depended on it.

All under one roof.

When we stepped outside, the snow had settled into itself, clean and steady, the kind that doesn't sting—just chooses you. The storefront windows glowed behind us.

FRIDAY, DECEMBER 9
THE BOYS LEFT WITH LOLLI AND POP FOR A CHRISTMAS MOVIE MARATHON WITH MILLIE. I HANDED OUT ALL MY HUGS AND CAME HOME TO THE DOGS.
CHRISTMAS KEEPS TURNING ITSELF INTO A MACHINE. I FALL FOR IT SOMETIMES. TOO MUCH SPENT ON GIFTS AND DETAILS. MATCHING PAPER AND BOWS. TRYING TO MAKE IT LOOK RIGHT WHEN WHAT I'M REALLY REACHING FOR IS SAFE.
NOBODY CARES ABOUT THE PAPER.
WHAT STAYED WITH ME WAS WHAT WASN'T THERE. NO PRESTON

family apple cider. No Gladys potpourri doing its quiet work in the corners. I noticed it the way you notice a missing tooth with your tongue—without meaning to.

So I called her.

She answered on the second ring. Her voice was a little too bright. I pictured her in the middle of her kitchen, one hand on the counter, holding herself upright.

"Hey, I just got home and realized I never smelled your potpourri tonight. I kept waiting for it to announce itself."

A pause. Then a small laugh. Something clinked—a spoon in a mug, maybe.

"I didn't make it, I wasn't feeling… domestic."

"Well, I missed it. The cider too. The Prestons don't get to disappear from winter."

That earned another laugh, quieter. She said she'd been tired. She said everything was fine. She said it three times, which told me enough.

I didn't push. I let my voice stay with her for a minute, warm and steady.

Tonight's Listen: "South Dakota" — GAVN!

To Do:
0500 alarm
City shopping with Annie
Comfy shoes
Crossbody
Take your list

hands off our shelves

WINTER PRESSED in as we edged toward the holiday break. Snow hadn't committed, but ice rimmed the parking lot and turned every step into a decision. Breath showed when you talked. The doors at Lawhoma schools stuck unless you leaned your shoulder into them.

I wasn't at the school board meeting. I was home with the dogs and a sink full of something that had needed soaking since Tuesday morning. I told myself I'd earned one quiet night.

Lawhoma Hills does not reward that kind of thinking.

My phone rang a little after nine. Kelly Chen's name lit the screen, and I knew before I answered this wasn't a potluck call.

"Yaya," voice tight and courteous—the sound of someone already angry but keeping her hands steady. "You got a minute?"

"For you? Always."

"Good." She'd allowed herself one breath. Then, "They kept the list."

My stomach dropped. "What list?"

"The banned books for schools," she said, and the fact she had to say it out loud landed between us. "They voted. They kept it."

I leaned my hip against the counter, fingers whitening around the phone.

"What'd they put on it?"

Kelly didn't dramatize. She never did. She just named them, steady and furious.

The Outsiders. To Kill a Mockingbird. Bridge to Terabithia. Judy Blume. Roald Dahl. And more.

It's strange how a title can hit you like a slammed door. How your body remembers the exact age a book saved you, even if nobody else knew it was happening.

"What did Arthur say," I asked, already half knowing.

"He told them we're not going to stop teaching kids to read. We'll just do it somewhere else."

I closed my eyes.

Lower now: "We're not fighting the district from the podium. But we can outgrow it."

"What do you need?"

There was a pause—not uncertainty, just surprise that the answer might be simple.

"Space, somewhere that isn't the school. Somewhere kids can come without asking permission."

I didn't hesitate. "Camp's open."

On the other end, she exhaled. Not relief exactly. More the sound of a latch turning.

"Thank you, Lolli's starting a phone tree. Bridger and Paul are in. Rosemary and Ophelia are next."

"I'll host meetings or help Rosemary at Spruce Street. And if anyone asks, we're not doing anything wrong. We're reading."

Kelly made a sound that might've been a laugh if she hadn't been so angry.

"That's the problem."

After we hung up, the house felt too quiet. Beans lifted his head. RJ sighed, already informed. I stood there a long minute, looking at my own shelves and seeing logistics instead of spines.

The kids found out the next day. News travels through a town the way woodsmoke does—quiet, fast, unavoidable.

By the time I drove into town, Spruce Street Books looked gently overtaken. Butcher paper across the table. Marker caps rolling free. Wes's coat flung over a chair. Serious work underway.

Wilder Kate had her phone propped against a stack of paperbacks, adjusting the angle like she was filming something that needed witnesses.

"Bigger," Tucker leaned over Whip's shoulder. "If it's banned, it should shout."

Whip held his marker like he hadn't decided whether it was a tool or a weapon.

One of the Flanagan girls traced a jacket outline. "What if the shirts look like greaser jackets."

"Stay Gold," Chase suggested, grinning.

They wrote it uneven on purpose. Tucker added a prairie dog near the hem, because even in trouble we still draw the land we love.

"That's gonna get us in trouble," Whip declared—not scared. Awake.

"Reading already did," Tucker said, and the table laughed.

Rosemary watched from behind the counter, calm as only a bookseller can be. She didn't quiet them. She slid titles closer, one at a time, feeding the moment.

Hank and Jasper hovered, pretending to browse. Hank held the Bridge to Terabithia. Jasper kept glancing between the butcher paper and me, deciding what category this fell into.

Wilder Kate lifted her chin toward the phone. "Short reviews, plain talk."

"You keep it honest," I told her.

She nodded. "Always."

As I turned to leave, Edie Claire asked, softer, "So what do we do when we meet. If we did."

No one answered right away.

Then, Tucker puffed his chest forward, "We don't need permission to read."

Whip added, "We just need a plan."

I didn't turn around, but the words landed all the same.

A FEW DAYS LATER, Lolli and I met for lunch. Even in a crisis, Lawhoma still eats.

She slid into the booth, hair piled high, eyes bright with that mix of exhaustion and purpose that makes her effective.

"You should see my call log!" "Oh, and Arthur deposited another chunk. Tommy got his third payment."

"That sentence lets a body breathe."

"The what ifs are still a worry to me."

"Good," she replied. "Means you're awake."

SHE RECAPPED THE STORY, only breathing twice.

The teacher's lounge version. Arthur's coat still on. Kelly shutting off the blender. Bridger's joke that landed wrong. Paul saying they could outgrow the district. Kelly calling Lolli because she needed motion, not permission.

When she finished, Lolli reached across the table and squeezed my hand.

"You saying yes helps."

"Sometimes all I know how to do is open a door and serve some sweet tea."

She smiled, tired enough to mean it.

Outside, the day stayed gray and sharp-edged. Inside me, something steadied.

MONDAY, DECEMBER 12

AFTER THAT CALL FROM KELLY, THEN LUNCH WITH LOLLI, AND MY OWN OPINION SITTING ON MY CHEST ALL DAY—I HAD THOUGHTS.

I HAD A RULE WHEN MY KIDS WERE GROWING UP: ART DIDN'T GET CENSORED IN MY HOUSE. MUSIC. PAINTINGS. SCULPTURE. ESPECIALLY BOOKS. BOOKS WERE WHERE KIDS WENT TO PRACTICE BEING HUMAN BEFORE LIFE ASKED THEM TO DO IT OUT LOUD.

ELIJAH WAS A READER THE WAY SOME KIDS ARE RUNNERS—ALWAYS MOVING, NEVER SATISFIED. I STILL REMEMBER HIS

third-grade teacher calling to ask if he could read
Lord of the Flies. Her voice carried that careful tone,
like she was handing me something live. I told her yes. He
read it. Then we had the kind of dinner-table talks that
stretch long and honest, the kind that make you think
maybe you didn't ruin everything as a parent.
Calling that kind of thing protection has never made
sense to me.
Tonight, Hank and Jasper sprawled on my living room
floor, legs tangled, arguing over whose turn it was to
read the dialogue. Hank kept correcting a word
Jasper hadn't met yet. Jasper kept insisting the char-
acter meant it another way. They laughed, louder than
necessary. But I saw it—the learning fire, the one that
hardens into backbone if you don't put it out too early.
And I was mad. The kind of mad that makes your jaw
ache.
I heard Junie B. Jones had landed in the bad influence
pile, and I nearly drove to the school in my slippers. Yes,
she's sassy. That's the point. She's honest about being
little. Let kids be little. Let them read it while
they are.
The boys finally settled, noses back in the book, voices
lowering as the story took over. I watched them a
minute longer than I needed to.
Books don't make children reckless.
They make them ready.

Tonight's Listen: "Jet Airliner" — Steve Miller Band

To Do:
Get the boys every book on the banned list
Call Rosemary, she hosting or me?
Start lisianthus seeds
Check greenhouse heater and grow lights

the night everything shifted

THE CHAIRS WERE SET CLOSER TOGETHER.

Camp Run Amuck's dining hall had been used so many times lately that nobody questioned it anymore. Tables shoved back. Coffee urns at each end. People filled the room fast and stayed standing longer than usual, coats still on, conversations half-finished. The volunteer group asked for the space because it held bodies well. Because it felt neutral. Because when something needed deciding in Lawhoma Hills, this was where voices landed.

MATTY BENEFIELD STOOD near the front with a folder tucked under his arm. He waited until the door closed and the scrape of chairs slowed.

"We'll keep this moving. We've got a full room."

A murmur answered him.

The 501(c)(3) had taken weeks of drafting, revising, and waiting. Tonight was the last piece.

"The invitations went out," Matty said. "And we've heard back."

Arthur Banerjee lifted his hand slightly, already smiling. "Yes, I'll serve."

Applause broke out, quick and warm.

"Larry Brewster."

Larry nodded once. "Yes."

Casey Jo whistled, unable to help herself.

"Charlotte Windsor."

"Yes," Charlotte, quickly responded, steady as a fence post.

"Ophelia Goldberg."

"Yes!" Her voice carrying clear to the back.

"Tallu-"

"Absolutely," Tallulah Sweetstripe cut in, already half-standing. "I wouldn't miss it."

The room exhaled together. The chairs shifted. People leaned toward each other, the way you do when you can finally feel a plan turn solid in your hands.

"One thing we still don't have," Matty continued, tapping the folder, "is a clean ownership record. What's on file doesn't match what's happening on the ground."

"All approaches at the Aperture site, and their office got us know where."

"Tommy says since it's inside city limits, we can file under a protective nonprofit," he added. "It buys time. Until he can find the who, what, and, where. That's all."

"We'll finalize paperwork this week," Matty said. "The structure is in place."

He glanced down at his notes, then back up.

"Before we close."

Ross Preston stood.

He didn't hurry. He set both hands on the chair in front of him and waited until the room found its quiet. Gladys rose beside him, close enough their shoulders nearly touched, two people bracing the same weight.

"We asked for the floor," Ross said. His voice carried, but it sounded thin. "Thank you for giving it…." Clearing his throat, hands wringing back and forth. "Time we gave y'all some of those answers."

The room turned fully. Chairs creaked. A boot scraped. That particular stillness settled, the one that means a town can feel a shift coming.

"We've owned those 163 acres a long time," Ross said. "Long before any of this."

He swallowed once.

"I need y'all to understand something. It wasn't just mine."

Gladys nodded, eyes forward.

"My daddy left that land to all us kids," Ross said. "Two brothers and a sister. Shared ownership. On paper."

A few faces changed. Folks know what inheritance can do.

"They don't live here now," Ross continued. "Arkansas. Texas. They built lives elsewhere. I'm the one who stayed on the Preston homestead. I'm the one who kept it from falling in."

His jaw worked like he was chewing something bitter.

"When Aperture first came around," Ross said, "I listened."

Gladys's fingers tightened on the chair back.

"It sounded like growth," Ross continued. "It sounded like helping the town. It sounded like maybe we could make sure Ranger and Ozzy had a future here that didn't depend on luck of the year's apple crop."

Gladys spoke then, steady and plain. "We weren't trying to sell anybody out. We thought we were protecting our family. Our town."

Ross nodded, grateful and wrecked at the same time.

"And then we started seeing things."

"Markers. Equipment. Work that looked too bold for a company still calling it 'early steps.'"

He took a breath that didn't fill all the way.

"We asked for the soil and water reports," Gladys said. "We would not have moved forward without them."

Ross nodded. "They brought us test results."

He looked down at his hands, then back up.

"And we told my siblings," he said. "Because if there's going to be a decision about land, it ought to be made by the people who own it."

His voice roughened.

"But when we told them Aperture was already digging, and when those reports started not adding up, my siblings said, we need the money. We're done waiting."

Gladys's mouth tightened. She didn't interrupt. She didn't have to.

"They weren't evil," Ross said. "They were distant. They saw money for their kids."

Gladys's voice went softer, which is always when I listen harder.

"So we did the hard thing. "We bought them out."

Ross nodded once. "Checks written. Shares signed over. Certified envelopes. Signatures from two states away."

He looked around like he wanted everybody to hear the point of it.

"We couldn't stand up in public with the deed split," he said. "We couldn't fight this if the paperwork could still be used against us."

"And once we owned it outright," Gladys said, "we thought, alright. Now we can finally tell everybody the truth. Now we can stop carrying it by ourselves."

Ross let out a sound that wasn't quite a laugh.

"But Aperture didn't care."

The air tightened.

"They didn't care whose name was on the deed," Ross said. "They didn't care, we cleaned up the ownership. They didn't care, we said no."

Gladys lifted her chin. Her anger had posture.

"They smiled and laughed at us trying to pull out. Just…smiled. Like we were adorable rednecks."

Ross nodded, eyes bright now.

"They reminded us they had more power and money than we ever would," he said. "They acted like this is how it always goes. Folks like us get tired. Folks like them keep walking."

A chair creaked. Somebody swore under their breath. The room held it in, but the room heard it.

"We're old, but we're not stupid."

He pressed his palm flat on the chair back.

"That's why we're standing here," he said. "We know how to work the land. We know how to hold a family together. But this…this is a different kind of fight. And we don't know how to do it alone and…. Our absence from all of you was not in hiding, we just don't know what to do now."

He took a breath, and his voice thinned on the exhale.

"And the worst part is," Ross said, "the reports they gave us…"

Gladys finished it, clear as a bell.

"They don't add up, I know how much water is there, and I know the prairie from the hills–I worked it from the time I was knee high."

Something moved through the room, not quite a gasp, not quite a voice. Quick as grief standing up and grabbing its keys.

Ross lifted his hands, palms open, trying to show sincerity the way you show empty pockets.

"We didn't know," he said, too fast. "We didn't know how to stop them until it was too late."

His face changed before anybody could move.

One hand went to his chest, pressing hard.

Gladys turned toward him. "Ross?"

He tried to answer. The chair tipped. His knees buckled.

The room surged forward at once, bodies moving on instinct, the way they do when something is falling and you can't let it hit.

"Clear space," I said firm and quick, already moving. My body chose my job before my heart could catch up.

Eli caught the chair. Carly shouted his name.

"Lay him flat," I said. "On his back. Now."

Hands obeyed without question.

I dropped to my knees beside him. Pale under fluorescent light. Sweat beading at the hairline. The air tasting like old coffee and winter coats and that sharp metal fear that rises in your mouth when you know what you're looking at.

"Call it in," I hollered to anyone. "Cardiac arrest. Camp Run Amuck dining hall."

Larry was already on the phone.

I checked for a pulse.

Nothing.

"Starting compressions," I said.

My hands found the center of his chest. I began.

The silence came then. A working silence.

"Count with me," I spoke out-loud to no one. "One. Two. Three."

Dr. Bridget was there before I even looked up, already kneeling opposite me, summoned by the sound of my voice the way some people get summoned by a siren.

"I'm here."

Foster slid in beside us, all focus.

"No AED?" Bridget asked.

"No AED," I said. "We're it."

"Keep going," she said, and her voice didn't shake.

Gladys was pulled back gently by Ranger and Ozzy, both holding her upright as her body tried to fold.

"No," she kept saying. "No, no, no."

"Stay with us, stay with us, please."

"Ross," Gladys cried. "Please."

My arms burned. I kept counting anyway. I kept going until time stopped being something you could measure.

Bridget leaned in, checked the airway, nodded. "Again!"

We worked without talking much after that. Only what was necessary.

"Get Carter with the flight team now," Bridget ordered, sharp. "We're not waiting."

Annie lifted her phone, and Stetson, reading his wife's urgency, ran for the doors. Time stood still, no sensation of the minutes, only

OUTSIDE, I heard rotors before I saw them. That sound turns your stomach even when it's bringing help.

When they lifted Ross, his weight surprised me. How heavy a life feels when it's not holding itself up.

"Careful," I said.

They moved fast and steady, the way people do when there is no room for error. The doors blew open. Cold rushed in.

Gladys broke loose then, reaching for him until Ozzy caught her again.

"I'm going with him."

"You will," Bridget told her. "We'll get you there."

The doors closed.

The rotors faded, a buzzing light being pulled away from the valley by force.

Nobody spoke at first.

Lolli shut the dining hall doors at last, the latch clicking too loud in the quiet. Gladys's chair was still tipped where it had fallen. Bridger set it upright without comment. Hands hung at people's sides, useless now that the work had moved out of the room.

"I didn't know," Bet Sinclair said finally. It wasn't aimed at anybody. It was just the truth falling out.

"None of us did," someone answered.

Matty stayed near the front, hands braced on the table. His face had gone pale under the fluorescent lights.

"They didn't do this out of greed," Charlotte Windsor said. "They were trying to help."

"Yes," Tallulah said immediately. "That was clear."

Arthur nodded. "They thought they were protecting the future of the town."

A murmur of agreement moved through the room.

"What gets me," Ophelia said quietly, "is that they held it alone."

That landed.

"They must not have felt safe enough to tell," Dahlia said.

"To ask," Arthur followed.

"To question," Rosemary whispered.

People looked around then, as if seeing the room differently. As if realizing the worst part wasn't the mistake. It was the silence around it.

"They trusted the reports," Larry Brewster said. "They trusted people who were supposed to know better."

"And when they found out," Matty said, his voice rough now, "they still came. They still told us."

That mattered. It settled something in the room that had been hovering unnamed.

No one spoke of blame again.

Megan reached for Gladys's abandoned coat and folded it carefully over the chair. Tenderness offered without speeches.

Then the town did what it always does after a crisis.

It organized.

"I'll start a call list," Kelly said, already typing.

"I can cook," Shyra offered.

"Freezer space," Ophelia said.

"I'll take tomorrow morning," Liam said near the door. "Cleaning, errands, whatever."

It didn't need a leader. It didn't need a microphone. It happened because we've practiced, again and again, in smaller emergencies.

LATE THAT NIGHT, a message came through.

Ozzy: He made it through surgery.

Three-vessel bypass.

ICU.

Phones lit up across the valley. Replies stacked fast.

Caitlyn: Thank goodness 🙏

Annie: Tell her we're here 🖤

Bridger: We've got them.

Only then did some people sit down.

By morning, Ross and Gladys's house was full of quiet movement.

Shoes lined up by the door. Music low. Windows cracked just long enough to change the air. Laundry folded. Counters wiped. Trash taken out.

A calendar appeared on the refrigerator.

Names filled the squares.

Soup. Casserole. Bread. Fruit.

No one signed up for everything. No one signed up for nothing.

Tata left a note on the counter:

Eat what you can. We'll handle the rest.

The next morning, I sat at my kitchen table with a cup of coffee warming my hands.

The pond on the west side of the property was still, a thin skin of ice catching the light. Beyond it, the Preston land lay quiet, fields pale and waiting.

My phone buzzed on the table.

A group text.

SATURDAY, DECEMBER 17

I CAN STILL FEEL THE PAIN IN MY WRISTS.

ROSS TRIED TO REVEAL THE TRUTH, BUT HIS BODY GAVE OUT MID-SENTENCE.

THE LIGHTS WERE SO HARSH. I HAD NEVER LOOKED AT THE DINING HALL LIGHTS BEFORE.

I CAN'T STOP PICTURING GLADYS'S FACE AS SHE SPOKE THOSE WORDS. HER POSTURE DROOPED, AND A BLANK LOOK SETTLED ON HER SWEET FACE. RIGHT AT THAT MOMENT, THE PERSON WHO SAID THAT TURNS INTO A BLANK FRAME. MY DEAR FRIENDS.

A COMPANY MIGHT SEEM FRIENDLY BUT HAVE MALICIOUS INTENTIONS. APERTURE'S APPROACH TOWARDS US; FARMERS, OLD FOLKS, AND SIMPLE MINDS TO PAT AND WAIT OUT.

TONIGHT'S LISTEN: "PYRO" — KINGS OF LEON

To Do:
TEXT GLADYS
LEAVE A CASSEROLE FOR OZZY
THANK DR. BRIDGET
PRICE AN AED
THANK CARTER

the show must go on

AFTER THE NIGHT WITH ROSS, after the helicopter sounds and the hush that followed, the weeks between Christmas and New Year felt heavier, a cart you push with your whole body.

When the days started feeling too long and the nights too quiet, the community did exactly what it always does when winter tries to turn us inward.

We staged a play.

Every December, without exception, our town devotes itself to the beautiful madness of a full production. It follows the same pattern each year. Mr. Ashe stands up at Spruce Street Books the week after Thanksgiving, clears his throat, and tells us what we're doing whether we're ready or not.

This year his smile was bigger than normal, the kind he can't quite hide when he's pleased with himself.

"The Music Man," he said.

The whole place groaned. Then laughed. Then clapped.

"Of course it is," Chase muttered, and somehow that explained everything.

Mr. Ashe didn't even blink.

Auditions and work nights came fast after that. The town got drafted without anybody calling it that.

Some people showed up confident as a rooster. Some trembled like they'd been asked to speak at their own funeral. Most arrived because their neighbor told them to and they trust Lawhoma more than their own comfort.

Once the cast list went up, time stopped belonging to anyone individually.

Tuesday nights disappeared. Most weekends got swallowed whole.

Gus and Liam took possession of the stage wing at Birch Creek and started building sets piece by piece. Sawdust covered the floor. Paint took forever to dry in the cold air. Ricky climbed up and down a ladder giving lighting directions while cables snaked above the stage, curious black vines in the dark.

Jordan laid out big tables with sketches and fabric swatches and then, with that steady hand of hers, turned drawings into real costumes you could touch. Ginger brought donations from the beauty counter, and on makeup nights she and her helpers walked in with purpose and made worried faces look like characters who knew what they were doing.

Down in the orchestra pit, the high school band sat with polished instruments and music stands lined up in rank, soldier-straight. Two hundred seats waited in the dark, patient as winter itself.

Ozzy Preston stepped into Harold Hill with a surprising kind of ease. The fast-talking fit him. The timing fit him–he needed it this year, and when he sang, conversation stopped. Even the fidgety kids went still, eyes lifted toward the stage like something had tied a string to their chins.

Shay Brewster came to rehearsal some nights straight from nursing school, still in scrubs, doing that practical thing young women do when they're running on grit. She looked tired in a brave way. She never missed.

She played Marian Paroo like solid ground. Thoughtful. Steady. A clear voice you could lean on.

Watching those two together, there was something warm in the air that had nothing to do with the stage lights. Not fireworks. Not a show. Just two people finding the same rhythm and not stepping away from it.

"I wonder if that's chemistry," Lolli whispered one night, "or if I'm just projecting because I want romance in this cold season."

"I think it's real," I whispered back. "Or at least promising."

Bridger watched from the aisle with that big grin on his face, pleased as a man who'd managed to trick a whole town into healing.

The rest of the roles filled in quick. Kids learned choreography and forgot it and laughed and learned it again. Adults took their places as townspeople, barbers, parents, students, whoever the script needed. They lent their bodies and voices to the story until the stage felt crowded and alive.

Costumes hung in neat rows, props got labeled, cues were called, mistakes were made, they were corrected, and hats were lost at least once.

By the final week, everybody was tired.

And everybody was proud.

PERFORMANCE NIGHT CAME and the house packed in tight. Two hundred people sat down with coats folded on laps and programs held. The stage curtain hung still. The orchestra waited, bows poised.

Mr. Ashe walked out with his script in his hand and that calm face he saves for two things: opening nights and emergencies.

"Before we start," he said, and the room settled in a way I felt in my teeth. "We've had a hard stretch. We've got folks in this town carrying worries they didn't ask for."

He cleared his throat once, softer now.

"If you're the praying kind, I'm going to ask you to pray for healing. For Ross. For Gladys. For anyone in this room who needs it and doesn't know how to say so out loud."

He looked out over us like he could see the shape of every family.

The theater went quiet.

Then Mr. Ashe nodded to the pit.

The lights dimmed. The orchestra started.

And the show went off smooth, with energy and precision and a couple of perfect little moments of confusion that made it even more ours.

Ozzy shined. Shay glowed. The band played their hearts out. The town cheered not because it was flawless, but because it belonged to us.

When the last curtain call finished, the audience erupted. Applause went on so long it echoed through Birch Creek, thunder trapped indoors. People stood up. Whistles cut through the noise. Kids bowed too far and nearly toppled. Adults wiped tears and tried to hide it like they were embarrassed to be caught loving something.

BACK IN THE GREENROOM, laughter and relief ran wild. Smudged makeup, loose costumes, and lingering hugs.

Annie and I made our way through and gave most of those hugs.

In the wings, I saw Ozzy and Shay talking soft and smiling free, the kind of smile you don't put on for an audience. Ozzy held a program in his hand like he'd forgotten it was paper. Shay's shoulders dropped, just a little, hard not to notice a bit of softness in her eyes. Maybe nothing comes of it. Maybe something does.

Either way, the play did what it came to do.

It cinched us back into one room. It gave winter a pulse, and reminded us that even in the coldest stretch of the year, creativity still shows up and insists on dancing.

MONDAY, DECEMBER 26

THIS WEEK, BETWEEN EXTRA FOOD, PICTURES, AND PULLING MYSELF TOGETHER MORE OFTEN THAN USUAL, THERE HASN'T BEEN ENOUGH HOT WATER IN MY TANK TO SOAK THE WAY THESE MUSCLES WOULD LIKE. I THOUGHT MORE THAN ONCE ABOUT MARCHING UP TO THE HOSPITAL AND ASKING FOR A FULL REPORT ON ROSS. INSTEAD, I KEPT MY NOSE WHERE IT BELONGED AND TEXTED CARLY TO SEE WHAT SHE, RANGER, AND OZZY NEEDED.

THAT SHOW ALWAYS LANDS ON DECEMBER 26. EVERY YEAR. A STUBBORN LITTLE ANCHOR IN THE DULL STRETCH BETWEEN CHRISTMAS AND NEW YEAR'S.

TONIGHT, AS ANNIE AND I LEFT THE GREENROOM, I SAW IT ALL UP CLOSE. SMUDGED MAKEUP ON CHEEKS THAT HAD BEEN BRAVE

All month, bobby pins clinging to sweaters, costume hems dragging like tired tongues, grown folks laughing too loud, then hugging hard; trying to stitch each other back together before stepping back out into the cold.

And I thought—our applause isn't going anywhere.

Tonight's Listen: "Famous Blue Raincoat" — Jennifer Warnes

To Do:
Call Ozzy and tell him how wonderful he was!
Call Annie
Make sure Stetson put parental controls on the boys' new phones

new year, same valley

SOME NIGHTS TURN their own pages.

After the fundraising push and parents stretched thin with kids on break, the valley was ready to move again. Ready to stand shoulder to shoulder and remember what that feels like.

By late afternoon, the town square had started to glow under white lanterns swaying in the cold. Snow dusted roofs and rails. The old clock tower wore a crooked scarf of twinkling lights that Ginger Everett talked Ricky's crew into hanging.

"New year, new sparkle," she'd said.

I could live with that.

Annie, Stetson, Addie, and Silas came with Pop, Lolli, and the kids. Hank Miller, Jasper West, and Millie kept tugging my coat sleeves as we walked toward Pumpkin Lane Entertainment Center, where the indoor farmer's market was already humming.

The wind hit our noses hard, but the smell of cocoa pulled us forward.

When the doors opened, heat wrapped around us so fast my shoulders dropped without asking. String lights stretched from the upper balconies, making a canopy over the floor. Booths lined the aisles, busy and bright, every table offering somebody's version of comfort.

Gingersnaps ran a hot cocoa station—extra whipped cream, no judgment. Running Waters Café laid out spiced cookies in neat rows. Bootsie Howard poured winter herbal tea that smelled of mint and something older. Nanny and Hootie's beeswax candles glowed in clean lines. Abuelita Shyra stood at a corner table with tamales, steam rising steady around her hands.

"It looks like the inside of a snow globe," Millie whispered.

Pop and Lolli stationed themselves near the candles with Eugene and Ophelia Goldberg.

"I'm trying every scent, scientifically."

"They're all good," Ophelia said, already amused.

"He's tried twenty-seven," Lolli added.

Near the entrance, Wilder Kate sang into a vintage microphone with Shep and Brick backing her up. Her voice moved through the room easy and sure. Kids wandered. Parents leaned. Even the cold outside seemed to pause.

For a minute, the year loosened.

We drifted from booth to booth, tasting things, hugging neighbors, letting the room do its work.

"Yaya," Jasper asked, "Why is new year such a big deal?"

"It's opening a new chapter. You look forward to what is to come."

Millie held that thought carefully. "My chapter will have singing and STEM club."

Hank grinned. "Mine will be adventures."

Jasper nodded. "Mine will have adventures too bub, without getting grounded."

"That sounds ambitious," I laughed, and ran my fingers through his hair.

LATER, families gathered around the Wish board under the lanterns. A chalkboard with one simple instruction:

WRITE A WISH FOR THE NEW YEAR

Some wishes came out bold. Some careful. Some stayed blank, honest as anything else.

At eight o'clock, we did Kid Midnight, because Lawhoma knows its limits.

The town pressed close beneath the lights, snow falling soft and steady. Cups passed hand to hand. Kids bounced. Parents held on.

Ginger stepped up to the microphone.

"Lawhoma Hills, thank you for the kindness you carried this year. Keep it moving."

The clock tower rang.

"Ten… nine…"

"Three… two… one!"

Confetti lifted. Paper snowflakes drifted down. Pop kissed Lolli on the cheek and gave her fanny a quick pat. Annie and Stetson shared a fast peck, and both boys did the finger-down-the-throat gag gesture so dramatic I thought they might topple right over. We laughed so hard we couldn't help it.

ON THE WALK HOME, snow brushed our coats. The kids surged ahead, leaving three wide paths of footprints.

"Yaya?" Hank called back. "What's your wish?"

I looked at the lit windows across the valley, the lantern glow still hanging in the air.

"My wish already came true, I am here with you all."

SATURDAY, DECEMBER 31

I HEARD THE SONG IN MY HEAD BEFORE WE EVEN GOT OUR COATS OFF. IT CAME IN SIDEWAYS, THE WAY MUSIC DOES WHEN IT'S TIED TO A DAY YOU CAN STILL FEEL IN YOUR BONES.

ANNIE WALKED DOWN THE AISLE TO IT. I REMEMBER THINKING, THERE GOES MY BABY, AND THERE GOES MY WHOLE HEART—IN A WHITE DRESS. STETSON LOOKED STEADY, BUT HIS EYES TOLD THE TRUTH. AND ANNIE—MY GIRL—LOOKED BRAVE AND TENDER AT THE SAME TIME, THE WAY WOMEN DO WHEN THEY CHOOSE THEIR LIVES ON PURPOSE.

TONIGHT, WATCHING HER LAUGH WITH THE KIDS, WATCHING

Stetson lift a cup and smile at Pop's foolishness, pride settled in me so deep it startled me. Love does that.

I wish Papa J lived closer to Lawhoma. Some nights the distance feels physical—a stretch of road that doesn't shorten no matter how often I picture it.

My mind is already moving ahead. Valentine's Day will be here before we notice. I need to gather the small love-things. Notes. Treats. Plans that say we're still soft, even while we're holding a line.

New year. Same valley. Same people I'd walk through hell for.

Tonight's Listen: "Lifetime" — Justin Bieber

To Do:
Breathe

prn shift comes calling

EVERY WINTER, Lawhoma Hills hits that stretch where the season presses harder than it needs to. Gray days stack. The cold settles deep. Sunlight skims low and leaves early.

We were still easing out of New Year's sweetness, still half-listening for trouble out at Blue Creek Lake, when the sniffles showed up.

A sneeze in math class. A cough in the grocery aisle. A kid in gym who didn't bounce back.

Nothing dramatic. Just enough for every mother and grandmother to say it together, tired and resigned.

Here it comes.

My phone rang while I stood at the sink pretending the dishes mattered. Foster's name lit the screen.

"Can you help triage?" he asked. Behind his voice I heard it—the winter clinic sound I still carry in my chest. Phones. Printers. Parents holding it together. "We're covered up. Two nurses out."

"And Bridget?" I asked.

"She keeps you first in her rolodex."

"Give me ten minutes."

Scrubs. Hokas. Hair up. Hands washed until my knuckles felt thin. The mirror showed me the version of myself that knows what to do when people are sick.

At the hospital, the printer ran nonstop. Foster slid electrolyte cups across the counter with that gentle firmness he uses on everyone.

"Hydrate," he said. "Yes, even if you're mad about it."

Dr. Bridget moved room to room—ears, lungs, throats, skin tone, hydration. Calm without being distant.

"Rest is not negotiable," she told one family, and the dad blinked like she'd cursed.

Down the hall, Lindsay Sweeney and the lab team worked steady behind glass. Samples rotated. Names stacked up—Quinn, Sweetstripe, Waddell, Rodriguez. Even Sweeney, twice.

BY MIDWEEK THE PICTURE SHARPENED. A familiar virus. Mean but manageable. Fluids. Time. Staying home longer than anyone wanted.

"We've identified it," Lindsay told Bridget. "Now we manage."

Outside the hospital, the town didn't wait for instructions.

Bootsie set a jar of winter wellness tea on her porch.

"Bring it back empty or not, I'll refill it."

The Sweetstripe sisters delivered soup to elders who would've tried to power through. Pop and Lolli and Annie and Stetson made daily rounds—blankets, thermometers, better snacks.

At the Quinn house, Micah lay on the couch while Jon Lucas read comics, as comics might be medicine. Paddy measured tea precise as a lab tech. Caitlyn whispered updates. "He's better today."

Micah lifted a hand in greeting, eyes bright inside his pale face. Annie sat and read, and for a few minutes the house felt held.

At school, teachers cracked windows. Kids carried tissues. The Chen grandparents handed out sanitizer with solemn purpose.

The Science Club turned it into a project.

HOW GERMS TRAVEL AND HOW WE CAN STOP THEM

By week's end, coughs softened. Eyes cleared. The fog lifted thin and slow.

Sunday brought a small mercy—sunlight, warm and steady. The kids played again. Bootsie collected jars and teased folks for returning them too clean.

At the clinic, Bridget leaned back in a rare quiet pocket.

"We did good work."

"You always do," I told her, handing over a jar of honey tea.

"We have a strong town."

By Monday, life edged toward normal.

Hank and Jasper burst into my kitchen, voices clear, energy back online.

"Everyone's getting better!" Hank announced.

"Finally," Jasper said, proud as anything.

They fist bumped. "Teamwork."

I hugged their stubborn little necks.

FRIDAY, JANUARY 13

DECEMBER FLEW BY, AND NOW WE'RE WELL INTO JANUARY, AND I AM OFFICIALLY BEHIND ON WINTER SOWING FOR SPRING FLOWERS. I'LL CATCH UP BETWEEN COUNCIL MEETINGS AND READING THE FIRST BANNED BOOK, BECAUSE REST REMAINS A RUMOR AND I CONTINUE TO BELIEVE.

WE USUALLY MARK LUNAR NEW YEAR EARLY, BUT WITH THE COUGHS STILL MOVING THROUGH TOWN, YEYE XIN LIM AND NAINAI LOMAI DECIDED TO CANCEL AND RESCHEDULE. EVEN IF THE NEW DATE LANDS CROOKED. THAT'S HOW WE DO THINGS HERE. IF IT'S FOR LEARNING—FOR KIDS—WE ADJUST AND KEEP GOING.

I LOVED THE WEEK IN THE TRENCHES AT THE CLINIC. I DON'T SAY THAT LIGHTLY. DR. BRIDGET IS THE KIND OF PHYSICIAN I WISH EXISTED EVERYWHERE—CALM HANDS, SHARP MIND, NO PATIENCE FOR NONSENSE, PLENTY FOR PEOPLE.

MY BACK IS SORE AS ALL GET OUT. I WROTE MYSELF A NOTE ABOUT CORE STRENGTH AND TAPED IT TO THE FRIDGE. THE NOTE MADE ME FEEL BRIEFLY CAPABLE, AND THAT COUNTS.

THIS WEEK I NEED TO CLEAN THE DINING HALL AND GET READY FOR VALENTINE'S DAY AND BOOK CLUB. NAPS COME FIRST. THEY ALWAYS DO.

Tonight's Listen: "The Banjo Song" — Mumford & Sons

To Do:
Clean dining hall
Start seeds: tomatoes, and peppers
Inventory seed box; order what's missing (Johnny's, Baker Creek)
Check Farmer Bailey plugs and allow shortcuts
Restock Epsom soak

rugelach and views

THE COUGHS finally loosened their grip on Lawhoma Hills, Blue Creek plans were out of our hands, and our kids were busy reading, so…

We got busy.

Wilder Kate and her crew set the first meeting the way they'd set a concert date. Most folks finished the book while we were sick and stuck inside with tissues and soup. And once the committee text thread started, it didn't stay quiet for long.

Rosemary: Spruce Street Books confirmed. Saturday. After lunch. Discussion: The Absolutely True Diary of a Part-Time Indian by Sherman Alexie.

Connie: Tell me what to bring.

Arthur: I'll be there early to help set up.

Ophelia: Bringing rugelach.

Caitlyn: Do we need to bring our copy?

Wilder Kate: Only if you took notes.

BY MEETING DAY, Wilder Kate had read it twice, once fast and once slow with a pencil dragging the margins. Corners folded. Pages bristling with notes. One paragraph starred so hard the paper looked bruised.

She arrived at Spruce Street Books early anyway.

The bell over the door rang, then kept ringing, because cold kept coming in on shoulders and cuffs. The shop smelled of paper, old glue, and coffee that had been good an hour ago. Boxes of used books waited under tables, titles written in marker, labeled careful in a hurry, meant to get handled later.

A sign was taped crooked inside the front window:

BANNED BOOK CLUB

Wilder Kate fixed the corner without asking, stretched up on her toes, and pressed the tape until it held.

Rosemary watched her from behind the counter. "You're filming this?"

"It's an educational playlist for my YouTube," Wilder Kate said, checking her battery, preparing to go to war.

Micah rolled in careful, front wheels catching the edge of the rug before he adjusted and pushed through. Arthur Banerjee followed, hand hovering behind the chair without touching.

Micah's device said, "I've got it," calm as a weather report.

Arthur smiled. "I know."

Annie and I came in with the boys and a gust of snow on our sleeves. Hank immediately kicked Jasper's heel, not hard, just enough to be Hank.

"You brought snacks?" Hank asked.

Jasper held up a bag. "Yes."

Hank peered inside. "That is trail mix if trail mix hated people."

Annie didn't look at him. She just said, "Try reading first, outlaw."

Ronnie came in next, feathers in a top knot half loose, cheeks pink from the cold, Joey right behind her already talking. Eleanor slipped in quiet and hovered near the graphic novels, her library cover peeling at one corner. Shep and Brick arrived together, Brick with a pencil tucked behind his ear, Shep with sticky notes already crawling out of his book like little flags.

Shia Goldberg came in with Ophelia, who set a foil-wrapped plate on the counter.

"Rugelach," Ophelia said. "For stamina."

"That is a love language," I told her.

WILDER KATE STARTED RECORDING before she meant to.

"Okay," she whispered into the phone. "Spruce Street Books. First meeting. Banned Book Club. I'm Wilder Kate and I'm not nervous."

Ronnie leaned into frame. "She's nervous."

Wilder Kate stopped recording, glared, then restarted like she could wrestle the truth into behaving.

"What book do you recommend," she asked the camera, "the one people said kids shouldn't read?"

She stopped again, frustrated.

Rosemary touched her shoulder. "Start with the one you read."

Wilder Kate nodded once, set the phone on a stack of atlases, and climbed onto the low stool by the reading nook.

"Okay, we're starting."

Kids settled into a loose circle of chairs and floor. Micah angled his chair forward, screen lit and ready. Hank sprawled like he was on my living room carpet. Jasper sat straighter than he meant to. Parents stayed near the edges like respectful furniture. I cradled my mug in both hands and watched the way a room changes when kids realize they're allowed to speak.

WILDER KATE HELD up the book.

"*The Absolutely True Diary of a Part-Time Indian* by Sherman Alexie."

She didn't pull out discussion questions like a worksheet. She looked around at all those faces and said, "First: what does it mean to feel red on the inside and white on the outside? Second: what stereotypes does this book smash, and what does it show instead? Third: poverty, addiction, and how a kid survives with humor. These are hard. I know. But we're not here for easy."

Ronnie raised her hand. "Why do people ban it?"

"Because it doesn't lie politely," Joey said.

Wilder Kate nodded. "It talks about hard things in a real way. And some grownups don't want kids thinking about real life."

She looked toward Sasha Sweetstripe, cross-legged near Tallulah.

"Sasha," Wilder Kate said. "Do you want to go first?"

Sasha nodded slow.

"People think Native means one thing, a picture. Or a story that has already ended."

She held up the book, thumb pressed hard on the cover.

"This kid is just… a kid. And that messes with people."

She swallowed. "In some places, being Native is a lesson. Not a life."

The room went still.

Hank's grin slipped off his face, it simply forgot how to stay. He stared at the book, then at Sasha, then down at his hands, as if he was trying to understand something he'd never had to notice.

Jasper said, quiet, "I didn't know people did that."

"They do," Sasha said.

Micah tapped his screen.

Micah (AAC): People stare like they are deciding something.

Eleanor nodded hard. "The part, where he's always choosing where to sit. Where his body goes."

Micah tapped again.

Micah (AAC): Always looking for his space.

Joey leaned forward. "Yes. Like you're bracing."

Shia waited for space, then spoke, voice careful.

"I related to Junior," he said, "but from the side of being Jewish as different."

In Lawhoma, Shia had air to breathe. In other places, he said, he felt like a question mark people wanted to solve.

"Questions that sound friendly but aren't," Shia said. "Assuming we're just... a version of something else."

Shep nodded. "Other schools don't understand Hinduism either. They think it's mythology instead of religion."

Brick frowned. "It's wild."

Hank scratched his jaw. "Here, nobody really gets left out."

Jasper nodded. "That's true."

And that's when Will, near the door, shifted like something pinched him.

"I didn't understand the 'white dude' thing," Will said. "Because here you just show up and you're in."

Mack added, "Then you go to the city or a rival school and it's not that at all."

Hank's voice went quieter. "You don't notice what you don't have to notice."

Micah tapped again.

Micah (AAC): Noticing is work.

My mouth moved before I could overthink it. "And reading is practice."

That landed. You can hear a room shift when a truth finds its place.

Jasper nodded once, slow. "So it's... you building brain muscle?"

Hank muttered, "I'd rather build the snack table muscle."

Jasper didn't even look at him. "We are being serious Hank."

Wilder Kate adjusted her phone and kept recording, quieter now. Not her face. Hands holding books. Micah's screen lighting up. Sasha's fingers pressing the page edge. Brick's pencil tapping like a heartbeat.

Adults didn't take over. We let the kids work through the hard parts in their own words, skipping what they weren't ready to say and circling back when they were. That is the point of a circle. You can come around again.

When the conversation finally softened, Rosemary cleared her throat.

"This," she said, looking at the kids, "is why books matter."

Then she turned to Wilder Kate. "Do we need to add this to the monthly calendar?"

The yeses came so loud they sounded like a hymn.

Rosemary smiled so proud, she'd been waiting on that answer her whole life.

"If you could recommend one book for the next meeting," she asked, "what would it be?"

Hands shot up. Titles spilled out. Arguments started immediately.

"No, that one's boring."

"It's not boring, you just skimmed."

"I did not skim."

Micah tapped.

Micah (AAC): Pick book that makes Hank uncomfortable.

Hank pointed. "Rude."

Micah's screen blinked.

Micah (AAC): Friends tell truth.

Ronnie made a sound that was half laugh, half gasp. "Micah just roasted you."

Laughter loosened the room, rising like a breeze from an opened window.

WHEN THE MEETING ENDED, nobody rushed out. Folks lingered, voices low. Shia packed his book careful.

"Don't cut what I said," he told Wilder Kate. "Even if someone complains."

She nodded. "I won't."

Two days later, Wilder Kate posted the first clip.

And that's when Annie called me from the car, laughing as if she was half proud and half terrified.

"Yaya," she said, "the boys say they might be famous."

. . .

WILDER KATE HAD STOOD in the school hallway outside the library, phone tucked low like a secret. She caught Joey first.

"Look."

Joey leaned in. "What is that?"

"Views."

Micah rolled up beside them. Jasper and Hank crowded in. Ronnie pretended not to care. Eleanor watched from one step back, careful but hungry for it.

Wilder Kate turned the screen.

12,456 views. 312 comments.

BANNED BOOKS PLAYLIST #1

Hank made a sound between awe and panic. "That's… people."

Jasper leaned closer. "What are they saying?"

Wilder Kate scrolled, eyes darting. "Some just say they read it too, and some liked we made a group."

Hank swallowed. "Okay well… I am not reading comments. Comments are where joy goes to get punched."

Micah tapped.

Micah (AAC): Hallway is not the whole world.

Wilder Kate smiled so hard it looked like it hurt.

The comments kept coming. People liked it. Some wanted in, even from far away.

"Next meeting," Wilder Kate said, "we pick the next book."

"And bring more kids," Jasper added.

"And better snacks," Hank said, suddenly running the logistics.

Micah angled toward the library doors.

Micah (AAC): Keep talking.

They moved together down the hallway, not in a straight line, but with purpose, testing how far the space would hold now that they knew it existed.

SATURDAY, JANUARY 21

I FINALLY CAUGHT UP ON CHORES, AND THE GREENHOUSE IS GLOWING, HOLDING A LITTLE SECRET SPRING INSIDE.

Annie's call thrilled me—not just because the kids held their own in that book talk, but because our small circle reached twelve thousand other minds. That still startles me when I say it slow.

I use YouTube for things I'm unsure about. How to change a furnace filter. Why my sourdough is angry? I am now officially a Wilder Kate subscriber and I better not miss an upload.

Life stays full. Meetings. Valentine plans. The next vote for the next book. Worry still tries to elbow its way in, acting like she runs the place. Not much word on Ross or the plan for the 163 acres, trying to be patient but Lord knows—not my greatest strength.

Tonight's Listen: "Work Song" – Hozier

To Do:
Finish Valentine cards
Bake cookies and brownies
Water seed trays
Turn off heat mats/ remove domes on peppers

seeds of love

IN OKLAHOMA, we start hoping it's time to leave winter behind when February rolls in.

The year keeps moving, but the mornings stay dark and my old wood floors stay cold. This winter sits heavy—buffalo-hide thick, pressing breath low. Ross still laid up. Gladys running on fumes. 163 acres west of Blue Creek Lake waiting on a hearing and a roomful of people who don't know the land's real name.

Kids burrow in February. They bargain. They build nests out of pillows and promises and ask for five more minutes. Adults negotiate blankets like diplomats. Boots disappear. Gloves multiply. Everyone's looking for something ahead that isn't worry.

That was the Valentine's party at Camp Run Amuck. A little sappy; yes, maybe, but we don't claim that, we call it necessary.

ONCE ROSS MADE it through surgery and we had a steady rotation for Gladys, we started planning. We met when we could that week—dyeing cloths, braiding branches, stringing dried flowers. Some afternoons passed in near silence. Other days a Bluetooth speaker carried seventies country while our hands kept moving.

We were making tenderness on purpose.

Long tables ran the length of the hall, dressed in tablecloths dyed a soft rose from amaranth I'd saved in the fall. Dried zinnias and strawflowers hung in loose wreaths above the beams. Two terra-cotta planters near the door held possum haw holly heavy with red berries. Braids of nine bark lined the runners, more patience than I personally possess, which tells you it was a group effort. Winter jasmine twisted through callicarpa, pale purple berries catching the light like small moons.

A chalkboard near the entry announced the theme:

SEEDS OF LOVE

Under it, a small sprout pushed through illustrated dirt, stubborn as truth.

People arrived with arms full and cheeks pink from the cold. The Chen grandparents brought two pots of soup—one for "comfort," one for "bravery." Annie and Stetson came in with loaves of Lolli's chocolate bread, the smell doing what good bread always does. Lolli brought chicken-and-wild-rice soup and garlic knots that vanished on contact. Dahlia carried curried lentils. Liam and Caitlyn brought veggie soup cradled in one of Liam's walnut bowls, dark as turned soil.

We ate close. Plates on laps. Elbows bumping. Stories trading places with seconds. The cold stayed outside.

AFTER DINNER, Wilder Kate lifted her guitar and the band gathered under the lights. Millie hovered near the microphones, trying not to beam. They started with songs you don't have to rehearse to survive. Folks sang soft at first, then louder. Bodies swayed. The kids watched the adults, learning a language without needing every word.

When "Isn't She Lovely" started, Pop and Lolli were on the floor in seconds, laughing like they'd been waiting all winter for permission. Something loosened. February gave a little.

Each table held a handmade card. Butter wrote every one. Each card carried a Sauk phrase—belonging, care, kinship. Wilder called her up, and Butter spoke quiet and steady about the Yellow Earth people within her Sac and Fox heritage.

"It made me love my stripe."

People read slowly. Fingers traced the words. A calm settled, the good kind.

THAT'S when Ranger and Carly stepped forward.

Ranger cleared his throat, looking down and shifting his weight left to right.

"Carly and I thought tonight felt right," he mumbled. "I umm, talked with my daddy in his hospital room last week, and he said, you better marry that girl and make a life."

He swallowed. Held Carly's hand up like a lantern.

"We went to see Tommy Dale Whitehorse, y'all know him as the lawyer fighting for our town." "He can also marry folks, and well umm…"

"So he did. Yesterday afternoon."

"So, uh—here's my WIFE!"

The room blew open. Joy rushed in. People cried without asking permission. Hugs stacked up. Plans started forming out loud.

We danced. We sang. We went back for seconds. For a little while, everyone felt renewed—even knowing tomorrow was still waiting.

When the night wound down, coats went on and dishes stacked. Kids leaned heavy against their parents, half-asleep and warm with music. The hall held that deep, earned hush.

I stood by the door and watched families step back into the cold, arms full. Breath rose white. Boots crunched. The camp lights cast a soft halo as each one passed through.

Winter wasn't finished. The hearing wasn't here yet.

But something had taken root.

Love got shared. Culture got spoken aloud. And underneath the laughter was the quiet promise we keep making in Lawhoma Hills: even in winter, growth is already happening.

SATURDAY, FEBRUARY 7

TONIGHT I CHECKED MY PHONE ONE MORE TIME BEFORE

closing the house down. Gladys had sent a picture earlier—Ross's hand with the IV taped in place, those small plates along his knuckles catching the hospital light. His wedding band still there. That ring looked stubborn. I appreciated that.

We have a rotation now. Meals. Rides. Visits. Lolli goes tomorrow. I'm sending soup and love.

The hearing is coming. The date sits on the calendar like a stone. The 163 acres on the west side of Blue Creek Lake are still out there in the dark, doing what land does—holding steady while humans work themselves into knots.

Tonight's Listen: "Pushing Up Daisies" — Brothers Osborne

To Do:
Water the greenhouse first thing
Check seed trays / start a new flat
Order new hoses before the old ones split
Order The Outsiders for Hank and Jasper

the night the lights went out

WINTER WEATHER in Oklahoma doesn't always announce itself. Some storms arrive quiet, no spectacle, just a steady test of whatever you left exposed.

That afternoon, snow fell gentle. The boys tipped their heads back, trying to catch flakes before they vanished. Cars moved easily. Smoke rose straight from chimneys, the air behaving for once.

Jasper, Hank, and Millie were staying the night with me and the dogs. Their parents were out with Lolli and Pop, doing a city shopping thing. Supper started the usual way. I cooked. Millie set the table with her natural order. The boys carried dishes as seriously as bankers. Beans and RJ supervised from underfoot.

I tried not to show my worry. The news had been on. The weather had been creeping. The court stuff sat in my chest, that stone you forget about until you bend wrong.

I called Annie. She answered with grocery noise and said, "We're headed back to Lawhoma, Mom," she knew that's what I needed. I didn't tell her I'd been holding my breath.

THEN THE AIR SHIFTED.

The wind didn't build. It arrived. Trees bent into sudden stillness.

Snow lifted and came back sharp. Ice followed, ticking against glass and siding.

The forest went quiet.

A low electrical hum.

A dull thunk.

The lights went out.

Not just my house. You could feel it—furnaces shutting down mid-cycle, clocks blinking away, refrigerators clicking once and going dead. Darkness moved room to room. Winter walked the valley turning off switches.

Millie's voice went careful. "Yaya. Is it everywhere?"

Through the frosted window, the hillside answered. Lights vanished one by one, stars erased.

"It looks like it," I said. "Winter wants us to change plans."

My phone lit up.

> Daphne: Wood-stove on?

People don't waste words in a crisis.

Millie became my secretary without being asked. She sat at the table, answering calls, responding to texts, in her small, steady way.

> "Yes ma'am. Stove's going."

> "Yes sir. Bring blankets."

> "We'll make room."

The boys and I crossed the yard into the storm to unlock the Camp Run Amuck dining hall. The wind slapped the door from my hand and I caught it hard enough to ache.

Inside smelled of old wood and memory. We lit the stove. Turned on propane lanterns. The room warmed slow, she had been waiting.

CARS CAME ONE AT A TIME, then pairs, then steady. Boots

knocked. Steam rose from coats. Lanterns settled on tables, benches, along walls. Shadows stretched and shifted.

Soup arrived. Chicken. Lentil. Spicy. Gus fed the stove. Ophelia labeled pots with tape and scraps of paper.

Kids found a Monopoly board.

"Who's banker?"

"Not you."

"You cheated last time."

Dice scattered. Laughter cut through the cold.

Karaoke started the way it always does here—by accident. Winnie climbed onto a bench and sang like she'd been waiting for permission. Groans turned into clapping. Voices joined in, loud and wrong and perfect.

Abuelita Shyra worked the fire, turning tortillas patient and sure.

"They'll tell you when they're ready," correcting a hovering hand.

Later the door opened again. Cold rushed in. Lolli and Pop. Annie and Stetson. Tata in the middle, small and regal.

"Well," Tata said, surveying the room, "I see I missed nothing."

Someone handed her a mug of hot tea. She sipped, nodded.

"Anybody need a chant? "I could go for one and a tiny sip of Disarrono."

Laughter rolled through everyone.

The kids settled on the floor near the stove. Millie tucked a blanket around a huddle of ducklings like she'd decided they were hers.

"It's so loud in here now," Jasper whispered.

"It's family," I reminded him.

Time stretched. The storm worked itself out beyond the walls. The hall held.

AT 4:12 A.M., the building changed.

A low hum. Heat kicked on. Lights blinked, steadied.

For a moment nobody trusted it.

Then Trip jumped up. "It's back!"

Cheers broke loose. Kids slumped. Adults hugged.

By sunrise, snow lay smooth and pale. People gathered their things slow. Blankets folded. Promises made.

RICKY CAME in with snow on his shoulders and that wired look of a man who's been fixing something that mattered. He didn't take his boots off.

"I was on the southwest feed."

"In the dark….and it wasn't just weather."

He slid his phone across the table.

Ground torn back. Gravel scattered wrong. Insulation ripped and exposed.

"When the wind hit," he told us, "ice built straight onto the bare line. The breaker shut us down before something worse happened."

Nobody needed that spelled out.

"I documented everything as best I could," he said. "Timestamps. Measurements. Close and wide."

"I can't say who or why, but this didn't happen clean."

Matty's jaw set.

TWO DAYS LATER, Matty sat across from Tommy Dale Whitehorse. Photos spread between them.

"They were careless with main lines for the whole town," Tommy said.

"One storm shut down the whole town," Matty replied.

Tommy stacked the pages. "I agree with Ricky's evaluation, this isn't weather damage."

"This is compromised infrastructure."

Outside, sunlight hit the snowbanks hard enough to sting.

"That's not inconvenience, that's liability. We'll present this at the hearing. They don't get to call it an accident."

When we all heard that, something in me settled.

The lights had gone out.

What caused it wasn't hidden anymore.

And the town was ready to carry that into court.

Sunday, February 22

I didn't journal for two days.

While I scrubbed and folded and put things back where they belong, I felt a lot of thankfulness working its way through my tired bones. I said some of it out loud. RJ tilted her head and gave me that slow, steady look that says she's listening. Maybe even understanding, the way she always has.

No matter how long I get to live in this little village, it won't be enough. This place has given me more than it ever promised.

Now. Here's the part I won't say out loud in public, because I do try to keep my halo shiny.

I cussed like a sailor while I cleaned.

Not at the mud or the dishes or the soup spills. At the people who endangered this family, this town, this whole valley, by tearing back what should have stayed protected. Careless. Reckless. Acting like we're all just background characters in their money story.

Blankety blank blanks.

I did my best impression of Papa Mike doing any kind of work—the kind where you only catch half the sentence and the rest is pure spirit. "Son of a—well, you know the rest." It helped. Sometimes righteous anger needs a vocabulary.

Tonight's Listen: "Sleeping on the Blacktop" — Colter Wall

To Do:
Return borrowed lanterns and propane tanks
Wash and fold camp blankets (again)
Restock batteries and matches at Camp Run Amuck
Text Ricky thank you
Check on Gladys tomorrow

o captain, my wheels

OUR ANNUAL OVERNIGHT lock-in lands on the Sunday that kicks off the kids' week out of school for spring break. A silly little night, usually fueled by popcorn, squeals, and lost socks. We needed it this year more than ever. With the hearing sitting heavy in all of us, a night that belonged only to the kids felt necessary, not optional.

Monday was coming fast. None of us were going to sleep much anyway, so we kept the tradition and showed up to skate the night away, as if joy was a job and we intended to do it well.

The sign outside Whippoorwill Wheels buzzed on one letter. The W flickered, tired of holding itself together. The parking lot glowed orange under tall lights that hummed faintly, cars pulled in crooked, doors slamming, voices carrying farther than they meant to in the cold.

INSIDE, the music hit before the door closed.

Bass thumped through the walls. Neon shapes collided underfoot, jagged lightning bolts and teal grids that belonged on an old arcade screen. The air smelled of popcorn, soda syrup, and rubber wheels.

Skates clattered onto the counter.

"Sizes," Wes called, snapping gum. "And don't lie."

Kids lined up in a loose snake, shoes already half off, arguments starting early.

Micah rolled up beside the bench, front wheels catching the carpet seam before he adjusted. His AAC screen lit.

[AAC: loud but good]

Hank laughed. "That's the slogan."

The lights dimmed without warning.

A cheer rose instantly.

The disco ball spun to life, scattering dots across the walls as the music switched tracks.

"CONGA!" DJ Shia shouted.

Arthur and Liam crouched beside Micah's chair, hands light and practiced.

"Ready?" Arthur asked.

Micah tapped once.

[AAC: yes]

They tipped the chair carefully and helped him onto the rink, legs folded easy beneath him. The wheels stayed close. No one moved them away. No one treated his joy like something fragile.

Wes watched, shrugged. "Owners won't care."

"It's wheels," Whip shrugged his shoulders.

Micah reached for the nearest shoulder, grinning.

The conga line re-formed, looser now, bending to follow him. Skates rolled careful around the edge. Kids hopped on and off, laughter breaking loose when somebody missed a beat.

No one hurried Micah.

No one needed to.

WHEN THE MUSIC SLOWED, the room stayed loud a little longer, not ready to let go.

Near the far wall, the older kids claimed the pool tables. Balls cracked sharp and clean. Green felt glowed under swinging lamps.

I watched them with my heart doing that foolish time-skip, seeing Hank and Jasper there before I'd even learned to miss who they are now.

Lolli nudged me. "Look at Paddy."

Paddy stood with his notebook out, the group gathered close.

"Well," he said, rubbing the back of his neck, "I got confirmation today. My Eagle Scout Challenge. I just wanted to tell y'all… you helped me with the courage and service sections."

"You did the work," Ronnie said.

"We just let you talk us into it, but we did what you did what needed done," JJ added. "Even if we all got grounded for a month, it was so worth it." Wilder piped in.

Paddy smiled despite himself.

Then Tucker climbed onto the middle table like a preacher about to start a sermon.

"O Captain, my Captain!" He recited, dead serious.

Whip slid in behind him. "O Captain, my Captain!"

Voices joined. Laughter followed. Paddy shook his head, blushing hard, that extra bit of confidence settling into his shoulders whether he wanted it or not.

"Y'all are idiots."

"Respectfully," Tucker replied, hopping down, "Mr. Whitman says, we are cultured idiots."

THE MUSIC SHIFTED SLOWER. Purple and gold slid across the rink.

"How low can you go?" DJ Shia shouted.

The limbo pole came out.

Micah tapped his screen.

[AAC: lower]

The bar dipped.

Hank wiped out spectacularly. Applause erupted anyway. Brick cleared it clean. Sasha brushed the floor and grinned. Jasper collapsed laughing halfway through and accepted his fate.

Then the lights snapped red.

Then yellow.

Then opening piano notes came straight from the halls of East High Wildcats.

A collective groan.

Parents froze.

Then they sang.

Full voices. Wrong harmonies. Absolute commitment.

Phones appeared, half-hidden, recording.

Micah watched, delighted.

[AAC: they know every word]

By the time the song ended, nobody pretended to hate it anymore.

Skates came off. Socks went damp. Kids sprawled in sleeping bags, sugar crashing. Parents checked phones more often now. Conversations lowered.

WE FINISHED the night with a movie marathon. *High School Musical* 1, 2, and 3. Annie would have had it no other way.

At sunrise, the disco ball dimmed. Coats were gathered slow. Sleeping bags rolled messy. People lingered, reluctant to break the bubble.

Outside, the cold hit sharp and clean.

By seven, engines started. Heaters cranked. We lined up.

The road to the city waited.

TUESDAY (MORNING), MARCH 4

I CAME HOME FROM WHIPPOORWILL WHEELS AT DAWN.

WE NEEDED ONE NIGHT WHERE THE SOUNDTRACK WAS LOUDER THAN THE FEAR.

I WILL COME BACK TONIGHT, HOPEFULLY WITH GOOD NEWS TO PUT ON PAPER.

TONIGHT'S (MORNING) LISTEN: "THE WATER IS WIDE" – JAMES TAYLOR

To Do:
COFFEE THERMOS
CHARGERS
SNACKS, GUM

the hearing

NO ONE DROVE ALONE.

Cars lined up before nine, engines idling, headlights cutting through the dark. Thermoses passed through windows. Ricky knocked twice on a hood before pulling away—half superstition, half blessing. We formed a line without planning it, a quiet procession heading toward the city.

We rode together where we could. Even the older kids came, pressed into back seats, earbuds dangling but unused. They watched the sky lighten ahead, as if the day itself was trying not to startle us.

The courthouse parking lot filled fast.

Inside, the building already felt awake. Shoes echoed on the tile. Security bins clattered. Belts came off and went back on. Arthur dropped his keys and scooped them up so fast you'd think they were on fire. No one joked.

The courtroom was packed. Our work boots and Aperture's high heels both present.

People filled the benches, coats folded careful over laps. A few stood along the back wall. The air smelled faintly of old paper and burnt coffee.

Gladys sat in the front row, hands clasped tight, knuckles white. Ranger sat on one side of her, Ozzy on the other. They didn't let her drift. Ross's absence sat among us, spoken without words.

. . .

AT EXACTLY 11:00, the judge entered.

He didn't hurry. He took his seat, adjusted his glasses, and looked straight ahead.

"Be seated."

The room complied.

Tommy Dale Whitehorse stood first. He placed his folder on the table, opened it, then closed it again.

"Your Honor," he said, "this is a straightforward request for an order to stop work while the court reviews the facts."

The defense shifted. Chairs creaked.

"We'll keep this simple," Tommy said. "A brief opening, then the key evidence."

The judge nodded once.

"This case concerns 163 acres on the west side of Blue Creek Lake, land held for decades. Farmed lightly. Left largely intact."

A pen scratched.

"The plaintiffs are not opposed to change, your honor."

"They are opposed to harm."

He let that sentence stand.

"The defendants, Aperture Development, LLC, began work relying on land and water reports produced by their own science team, without meeting the requirements of applicable federal and state statutes."

A murmur moved through the room and died.

"We will show that those reports led to physical damage and a safety risk to shared infrastructure."

Then Tommy paused.

The Aperture attorney rose quickly.

"This is an overreaction—"

"Counsel," the judge said, lifting one hand. "You'll have your turn. Keep it concise."

Tommy began again. "We'll show the lack of communication to the city board and the electrical incident causing a power failure for all residents and businesses."

Ricky Howard took the stand.

He wore his work jacket. His hands stayed still on the rail. He looked at the judge the way you look at someone you expect to understand plain facts.

Tommy's questions came steadily.

"What is your role in the valley?"

"I am a chief lineman for Lawhoma Power, power-line maintenance and response."

"Did you inspect the electrical feed after the outage?"

"Yes."

"What did you find?"

Ricky described the exposed line, the torn insulation, the way weather stressed what was already compromised. He explained the breaker doing its job because something upstream had failed.

Photographs were admitted.

The screen lit. The room leaned forward. Fabric tightened over knees. Someone sniffed quietly behind me.

On cross, the defense pressed.

"Winter storms cause outages, do they not?"

"Winter can cause outages," Ricky responded. "Not in this case, the lines were crushed, exposed, and left open to the weather."

Tommy returned for one question.

"What did the breaker do?"

"It shut the system down to prevent a larger failure; fire, sparks, maybe worse."

NEXT CAME THE LAND ASSESSMENT.

Maps unrolled. Boundaries named. Soil disruption described with chart-level precision. The judge leaned forward.

"This report?" He asked tapping the page. "You're telling me it was falsified?"

"Yes, Your Honor," Tommy said. "We have the corrected assessment regarding the discrepancy."

The defense objected.

"Overruled," the judge said. "Proceed."

. . .

APERTURE'S legal team presented their case, but confidence frayed. Answers stretched. One voice rose.

The gavel came down once.

"This is not theater," the judge firmly stated.

Tommy's closing was brief.

"This land cannot be developed, with the evidence shown today of landmark species in both water and prairie sections. Only now by stopping the work and beginning restoration can this native land be correctly maintained."

The defense spoke longer. Faster. Less careful–words blurred together: economy, growth, financial, phase one…..none of it was Lawhoma.

THE JUDGE REMOVED his glasses and sat still for a moment, eyes on the file.

"I've heard enough," he said.

The room stilled.

"This development is ordered to cease immediately.

Quite frankly, I do not need to remind you, but I will: the federal Endangered Species Act of 1973 and Oklahoma Statute Title 29 apply here. Aperture failed to complete proper mitigation and obtain the required permits prior to commencing work. All equipment is to be removed within twenty-four hours."

A breath broke loose, then sobbing, laughter, hands finding hands.

"And let me be clear," the judge continued, looking directly at the developers. "If this order is ignored, delayed, or undermined, do I need to send Metro Police to ensure compliance?"

"No, Your Honor," Aperture's attorney said.

"See that I don't," the judge replied.

The gavel struck.

FOR A MOMENT, no one moved.

Then the room broke open.

Gladys covered her mouth, shoulders shaking. Ranger and Ozzy pulled her close. Papa Max laughed and startled himself with the sound.

The kids grinned, trying to look grown.

In the hallway, the air felt thinner. People leaned against walls, coats half-on, unsure what to do with their hands. No one quite knew where to put themselves now that the holding was over.

Gladys stood near a bench, one palm flat to the wall. Upright. Present.

"He comes home tomorrow," she said.

Tomorrow.

TALLY SWEETSTRIPE APPEARED the way she always does when a room needs redirecting, the little bell in her apron pocket ringing like common sense.

"Well," she said, clapping once, "this is not a moment to skip lunch. Running Waters is open, and I've already got bison burgers thawed."

Stewart nodded beside her. "Three sisters. And mulberry pie."

That settled it.

LATER, at Running Waters, tables were pushed together. Jackets hung off chair backs. The grill flared. People toasted with coffee, water, and one brave soda.

WHEN THE AFTERNOON THINNED, my phone rang.

It was Gladys.

"We're setting it up," she said. "A trust. All 163 acres."

"To the nonprofit," she continued. "Permanent."

Outside, the afternoon light slid across the pond. The fields rested.

Tuesday, (evening) March 4
The judge's voice is still in my ears, calm as a man who

HAS SEEN EVERY KIND OF HUMAN MESS AND REFUSES TO BE
IMPRESSED BY IT. I WATCHED GLADYS HOLD HERSELF TOGETHER
WITH HER OWN TWO HANDS UNTIL THE RULING CAME DOWN, AND
THEN SHE FINALLY LET GO AND LET PEOPLE CATCH HER.
ROSS COMES HOME TOMORROW.
THE HEARING IS OVER.

TONIGHT'S LISTEN: "SISTER CHRISTIAN" – NIGHT RANGER

To Do:
GET THE STUFF FOR H&J CAKES
CALL ANNIE
CHECK ON ROSS AND GLADYS

what the years give back

MARCH BRINGS me back to the porch.

Rain settled in the night and left its mark. The morning air smells heavy of petrichor—thick and low, and the boards under my feet hold the damp. I wrap both hands around my mug and let the heat press into my palms. The journal lies open beside me. Music hums soft from the speaker near the swing. The hills sit quiet, listening among themselves, deciding when to send the sun over the ridge.

Twenty six years since I signed my name and took this farm in my hands.

Twenty six years since I stepped onto this land with a heart that paced and would not lie down.

Twenty six years since Lawhoma took hold of my collar and kept me upright.

THIRTEEN YEARS since the boys first filled my arms.

They came in March, on the day my Daddy would have turned ninety. I marked it in ink and in bone. I stood in that hospital room and felt the old and the new crowd together. I did not argue with it. I whispered my father's name into their soft ears and let the past braid itself into the present.

The valley moves inside my chest. Water travels somewhere out of sight. My morning stands on its own two feet.

BY MIDDAY we gather at Blue Creek Lake.

March water doesn't pretend to be warm. Sunlight skims across the surface and throws back a bright lie, but the shade under the sycamores keeps its chill. The cable stretches from bank to bank and hums low, steady and patient. Folks arrive in small clusters. Tata in her scarf. The Banerjees. The Brewsters. The Flanagans. The Sweetstripes. The Ashes. The Goldbergs. The Quinns, every face of my Lawhoma family. Faces drift in and settle. Not a crowd. A holding.

The boys stand at the edge with their boards, toes near the lip of the dock, fingers dragging through the cold water. Thirteen shifts a spine. Hank squares his shoulders and stares out across the lake, storing the line of trees, the dip of light, the shape of this hour. Jasper tosses a rock and watches it skip. He reaches for his brothers arm, one squeeze and a grin that curls at his edges.

Lolli watches without blinking.

Millie circles them, bossy and tender, waving a bottle of sunscreen nobody reaches for.

Kolby takes a run and the spray leaps into the air, bright and clean, and the crowd answers with a shout that breaks sharp in the cold.

THEN STETSON STEPS onto the dock, board under his arm, and does not move toward the edge. He moves toward Micah.

This work began weeks back. Calls made. Measurements taken. Practice done in quiet. Gus and Pop built a wheelchair platform level with the dock, wide and steady. The chair rolls forward and stops clean at the edge.

Stetson kneels first. He speaks to Micah soft and low. He shows him where to place his hands, where the pull will come from, when to lean. Arthur and Liam stand ready. They lift Micah in one smooth motion. Stetson takes his weight and settles him onto the board. The chair waits close, respectful.

"Ready?" Stetson asks.

Micah claps once.

The cable catches and draws them forward with a steady tug. No jerk. No scramble. Water rises and parts. They slide out from the dock and into the open stretch. Balance finds them. The line carries them clean across the surface.

Micah's laugh flies back over the water, full and bright. It skips across the lake and lands in our chests.

My knees soften. I sit down hard on the dock and let the tears come. Lolli presses a hand to her mouth and does not hide her shaking. Pop draws Tata into his side. Annie buries her face against Hank and Jasper, and the boys hold her, startled by the weight of what stands in front of them.

Stetson circles once and brings Micah back in. When the board meets wood, the crowd exhales together.

LATER, the boards lean against tree trunks. Towels pass from hand to hand. Millie wraps a blanket around Micah's shoulders. He nods once, then taps his device.

[AAC: again someday]

"Yes," Stetson says, quick and firm. "Again."

Cakes appear from coolers and boxes. Three of them. Red velvet. German chocolate. Carrot. Plates travel. Forks scrape soft against paper. Nobody rushes. We have learned to sit with a thing when it arrives.

We sing. The notes wobble and drift and find one another anyway. Hank stands straight, hands at his sides, holding himself still. Jasper smiles wide through the song, then swipes at his eye and squints toward the sun.

THAT IS WHEN GLADYS ARRIVES. She does not come alone.

Ross walks beside her.

Ranger, Carly, and Ozzy flank them the way family does when a body is recovering, close enough to steady, careful not to crowd. For a second, the lake holds its breath.

Then people move.

Hands reach. Wade laughs through tears he tries to hide. Charlotte says his name like a question and a prayer at the same time.

Ross looks thinner. Paler. Alive.

Gladys squeezes his hand once before letting go.

"We didn't want to interrupt," she says. "But we didn't want to miss it either."

"You didn't," I tell her, and my voice does that thing where it tries to stay steady and fails.

WE OPEN the circle without fuss. Folks shift coolers. Children scoot over on blankets. Space widens.

After cake, after plates are stacked and we finally sit down, Ross clears his throat.

"We've been busy," he says, the small smile on his face telling the truth. "While I was recovering, we worked with Tommy Dale Whitehorse."

Gladys nods. "As soon as the nonprofit was legally in place, the papers were drawn."

Ross takes a breath. "We're donating it. All of it."

The 163 acres on the west side of Blue Creek Lake.

The land.

And the money set aside to care for it.

No one speaks for a moment. Not because we don't understand, but because we do.

Ranger steps forward. "We will tend it," he says. "We have a list of ideas from a monarch station to a nature preserve with protected conservation trails."

Ozzy folds his arms and nods once. "We will teach from it and make it something for all of our futures."

Gladys looks at the boys, at the water, at the trees bending along the bank. "We want to hand over this land to our community," she says.

A low sound moves through the crowd. Not loud. Not wild. Deep. Hands find hands. Some of us sit because our legs remember their age.

.   .   .

THE CABLE HUMS ABOVE US. Kolby takes another run. Spray rises, catches the sun, and falls back into the lake.

This day does not shout. It roots.

THAT EVENING I walk back up the drive, gravel crunching under my shoes. The pink front door waits at the top of the steps. I climb onto my little porch and sit down in the same chair from morning. The soil still carries rain. The hills hold their shape in the fading light. I set my journal on my lap and let the quiet come in.

SUNDAY, MARCH 23

BEANS AND RIZZO JANE GREET ME AS IF I'VE BEEN GONE A YEAR—OFFENDED AND RELIEVED ALL AT ONCE. THE AIR STILL SMELLS OF WET DIRT. THE WARMER SEASONS ARE CLOSER NOW, CLOSE ENOUGH TO FEEL IF YOU STAND STILL LONG ENOUGH.

I OPEN MY JOURNAL BECAUSE I DON'T WANT THIS DAY TO SLIP AWAY.

WHEN I BOUGHT THIS FARM, I WAS GROWN—MID-LIFE GROWN—BUT LORD, I WAS STILL CARRYING A LITTLE GIRL INSIDE ME, SPLINTERED FOR YEARS. AND I WAS CARRYING THE WOMAN I'D TURNED INTO BECAUSE OF IT. I KNEW HER WELL. SHE WAS THE ONE WHO CALLED BRACING STRENGTH. I WORE IT AS ARMOR AND NAMED IT SURVIVAL. I CUT PEOPLE FIRST AND TOLD MYSELF IT WAS DEFENSE. THE TRUTH IS, I WAS SCARED THAT IF ANYBODY GOT CLOSE ENOUGH, THEY'D SEE THE SOFT PARTS, AND I WOULDN'T BE ABLE TO STAND THE SHAME OF IT.

IF I GET PRACTICAL ABOUT HOW I ENDED UP ON THIS FARM, IT WAS A TINY BUDGET, A BANKER WITH A STUBBORN STREAK, AND A WOMAN WITH A CREDIT SCORE THAT HAD SEEN BETTER DAYS. HE FINANCED ME ANYWAY. A NUT—SO, HE PROBABLY CALLED ME WHEN HE WENT HOME.

IF I GET MYSTICAL ABOUT IT, I THINK SOMETHING STEADY GUIDED

me here. The kind of something that does not flinch at broken things, or act surprised by them.

Either way, I found this land. And then I found this uncommon family—human and animal—and the love showed up so steadily it finally wore my fear down.

Today, watching the boys in their thirteen-year-old bodies, watching Stetson's gentleness with Micah, watching Ross walk up alive beside Gladys and then give away what most people would cling to, I felt a peace I never believed I'd have in my lifetime.

Lawhoma Hills gave me a life I only dreamt of. It reached right through me so I could keep giving that love to these boys—my wild, kind, ornery, big-hearted, curious rascals.

Whatever God you choose to thank, please thank Him, or Her, or the holy mystery of mercy, on behalf of this Yaya.

And maybe a baby sister or brother or two, if the Lord and the parents are feeling brave. Lawhoma Hills has so many new adventures in store for all of us.

Here's to another thirteen years.

Tonight's Listen: "Matilda" – Harry Styles

To Do:

Help the boys write thank-you cards

Research how nature preserves are run

Inventory spring seeds

Update the camp calendar for summer

Try a few new veg ideas (eggplant, yellow cukes, purple pole beans, rutabaga, new Swiss chard varieties)

YOU BETTER NOT PROCRASTINATE because warm weather doesn't wait

THE PRESTON ARMADILLOS

Ross and Gladys Preston steward a farm rooted in soil health, patience, and care. Founders of the Farmers Market alongside Yaya, their work anchors the land itself. They have a prolific apple orchard with their sons Ranger and Ozzy working to continue that legacy—Ranger through goat education and Ozzy through beeswax candles and quiet craftsmanship.

THE BREWSTER BEARS

Larry is Lawhoma Hills' barber—keeper of stories, hairlines, and birthdays—while his wife Casey Jo works steady nursing shifts at Willow Creek Care Center. Papa Max, Larry's father and a retired KSW7 newsman, anchors the town with memory and unmatched bear hugs. Their children move easily through the valley: Shay follows her mother into nursing, Tucker runs with the Flanagan girls like one of their own, and Stevie bikes through Lawhoma Hills with fearless speed.

THE EVERETT FOXES

The Everetts add style to Lawhoma Hills the way sunrise adds color. Ginger draws crowds into Gingersnaps with her window displays alone, while Eli works remotely for Dr. Bridget's healthcare tech team, grounding the household with quiet steadiness. Their children carry momentum: Chase makes leadership in STEM look effortless, and Wilder Kate's voice threads through markets, Camp Run Amuck, and anywhere music is needed.

THE WADDELL DUCKS

The Waddells live near Blue Creek Lake in an eco-home that feels grown from the cattails. Wade runs the canoe and kayak shop, greeting visitors from the dock, while Darla guides planes from the airport tower and volunteers with local climate groups. Their children; Trip, Smith, and Goldie—move through the world in close formation, equal parts curiosity and confidence.

THE WINDSOR BEAVERS

Harry and Charlotte Windsor are still building their dam for baby Beau Charles. Harry runs Willow Ridge Garden Center with reverence for every tree, while Charlotte designs forest trails and playground structures with engineer's precision. They are generous guides to anyone learning how to grow or build something that lasts.

THE SIMMONS SNAKES

The Simmons family coils their lives around enthusiasm. Carter flies commercial routes for Lawhoma Regional and serves as captain of the county's emergency helicopter service, the one called when minutes narrow and the sky becomes a road. When he is home, he chases motion with the same steady focus he carries into the air. Megan writes code and keeps the household balanced. Their sons, Wesley and Whip, work at the skating rink and volunteer with younger athletes at Birch Creek, bringing discipline and heart in equal measure.

THE RODRIGUEZ RACCOONS

The Rodriguez home hums with ideas. Rosemary studies plants as a botanist and owns Spruce Street Books, while Manuel keeps Pumpkin Lane calm through even the busiest seasons. Ruby is a STEM standout, Juan Carlos helps Abuelita Shyra at the Farmers Market, and the family plays a central role in celebrating Cinco de Mayo and Día de los Muertos with the whole town.

THE CHEN RABBITS

The Chen household moves at joyful speed. Kelly teaches dance at Wiggle Worm, Paul teaches karate at Birch Creek, both teach at the school. Grandparents Xin Lim and Lomai pass down quiet wisdom. Their children Barbara, Lacey, and Kip—balance school, dance, and tournaments with disciplined grace, shaped by both movement and tradition.

THE GOLDBERG OWLS

Ophelia Levy-Goldberg, PhD, curates art at MONA with an eye for hidden stories, while Eugene owns Red Foods, greeting customers after returning home a wounded Veteran. Their son Shia balances school, field hockey, and part-time DJ work. The family offers steady education and openness around Jewish life in Lawhoma Hills.

THE SWEETSTRIPE SKUNKS

The Sweetstripe home smells like flowers and fresh bread. Stewart runs the floral shop, and Tallulah—Tally to most—owns Running Waters Café, where her Sac and Fox heritage flavors every dish. Their children, Butter and Sasha, read to kids at Spruce Street Books and help keep Camp Run Amuck running with minimal glitter casualties.

THE ASHE-FRANKLIN FROGS

This blended family moves like a choir, different voices, same song. Bridger Ashe, Connie Franklin's former husband, teaches music, theater, and band at the school. Connie works as a physical therapist and is now married to Gus Franklin, who owns Augustus Construction. Their households sit near one another, close enough for bikes to pass back and forth and for supper plates to cross porches. Together they are raising Ellie and Mack Ashe and Will Franklin, who refuse to divide themselves into halves and prefer to say they belong to the whole. Between sports fields, rehearsal rooms, and Birch Creek, their lives overlap more than they separate.

THE SWEENEY BEETLES

The Sweeneys buzz with motion. Lindsay works as a lab tech at the medical center, Nick works in tech sales, and their sons Boone and Kolby split time between football, soccer, and wakeboarding at Blue Creek Lake. Grandma Bertha watches it all with satisfied pride.

THE CHAPMAN CROWS

The Chapmans are known for contrast and brilliance. Reed, of magpie heritage, helps develop striking art at MONA, while Daphne serves as Lawhoma Hills' postmaster, keeping messages—and people—moving. Their girls Wyatt and Ronnie, balance athletics, pageants, and creative focus with sharp determination.

THE QUINN PORCUPINES

The Quinns are busy in the best way. Liam builds custom furniture with Gus Franklin, while Caitlyn designs clothing at Gingersnaps. Their sons —Jon Lucas, Paddy, and Micah—carry music, service, and quiet brilliance. Liam's sister Carly lives nearby with Ranger, running goat yoga, farm classes, and the You-Pick flower booth.

THE FLANAGAN COYOTES

The Flanagan girls are known for speed and grit. Foster works as Dr. Bridget's Physician Assistant, Emma Mae volunteers at Spruce Street Books, and their daughters—Frankie, Edie Claire, Joey, and JJ—are accomplished runners who now help coach younger kids.

THE HILL HONEY BEES

Jordan sews recital costumes for Wiggle Worm after a long dance career, while Pete coordinates sports at Birch Creek with easy confidence. Their children, Clover, Sage, and Beck, teach and play with joyful precision, while grandparents Nanny and Hootie run the town apiary. They host honey and bee education classes at Camp Run Amuck.

THE HOWARD BUTTERFLIES

Bootsie teaches herb gardening and tincture-making with quiet grace, while Ricky keeps the power running across Lawhoma Hills. Their daughters, Jessi, Winnie, and Avery, combine dance, music, and motion, inheriting both their mother's calm and their father's electricity.

THE BANERJEE DEERS

Arthur Banerjee serves as both superintendent and school bus driver, while Dahlia represents Lawhoma Hills as a Forest Ranger. Their twin sons, Shep and Brick, are talented musicians who frequently back up any musical performance. The family shares Hindu traditions with generosity and ease.

THE SINCLAIR-BENEFIELD TURTLES

Dr. Bridget Sinclair is Lawhoma Hills' beloved family physician. Dr. Bridget trained under Lawhoma's longtime physician Doc before he retired. Her partner, Matty Benefield, a biologist studies water quality at the Nature Center, together they are educators and leaders in the community. Bridget's sister Bet completed her PhD on environmental systems affecting local waterways. Bet works alongside Matty at the Nature Center.

THE HUMAN FAMILY

Yaya is the journal-keeper of Lawhoma Hills Woodland. Her daughter Annie and son-in-law Stetson live nearby with twin boys, Henry Miller and Jasper West. Extended family—Lolli, Pop, and Tata; circle close, anchoring Camp Run Amuck and daily life. Millie, Stetson's niece keeps Hank and Jasper in line, and her parents Silas and Addie come once in a while. Rizzo Jane and Beans, Yaya's dogs, serve as constant companions and unofficial greeters. You will hear about family far away—Elijah, Yaya's son, Papa J, Yaya's ex-husband. You will all get to know Tommy Dale Whitehorse too.

RETAIL AND FOOD

Larry's Cuts – East Maple St.

Town barber shop

Larry Brewster

Gingersnaps Department Store – West Sycamore St.
Retail shopping

Ginger Everett, Caitlyn Quinn

Red Foods Grocery – West Sycamore St.

Grocery store

Eugene Goldberg, Shia Goldberg

Sweetstripe Floral – West Sycamore St.

Floral shop

Stewart Sweetstripe

Running Waters Café – West Sycamore St.

Restaurant

Tallulah "Tally" Sweetstripe

Pumpkin Lane Shoppes – Town Center

Retail complex

Manuel Rodriguez

Spruce Street Books - South Spruce Street

Independent bookstore and event space

Rosemary Rodriguez

ARTS, CULTURE & COMMUNITY SPACES

MONA (Museum of Natural Arts) – West Chestnut St.

Museum and gallery

Ophelia Levy-Goldberg, Reed Chapman

Pumpkin Lane Entertainment Theater – Town Center

Movies, shows, performances

Town Square – Town Center

Public gathering space and events

Summer Concert Stage – Town Square

Seasonal outdoor music venue

HEALTH, WELLNESS & CARE

Lawhoma Regional Medical Center – East Oak St.

Hospital and clinics

Dr. Bridget Sinclair, Connie Franklin, Foster Flanagan, Lindsay Sweeney

Willow Creek Assisted Living Facility – East Oak St.

Elder care residence

Casey Jo Brewster, Tata

EDUCATION, YOUTH
SPORTS AND EVENTS

Lawhoma Hills School – East Willow St.

K–12 public school

Arthur Banerjee, Kelly Chen, Paul Chen, Bridger Ashe

Wiggle Worm Dance Studio – South Spruce St.

Dance education

Kelly Chen, Jordan Hill, Annie

Birch Creek Sports Complex – West Birch St.

Athletics and recreation

Whippoorwill Wheels – South Spruce St.

Roller skating rink

Whip Simmons, Wesley Simmons

NATURE, LAND & UTILITIES

Blue Creek Lake Boat Shop – West Pine St.

Canoe and kayak rentals

Wade Waddell

Lawhoma Nature Center – West Birch St.

Research and environmental education

Bet Sinclair, Matty Benefield

Lawhoma Power & Light – West Chestnut St.

Utilities provider

Ricky Howard

Post Office – East Maple St.

Mail and town communications

Daphne Chapman

Airport – East Oak St.

Regional transport

Carter Simmons, Darla Waddell

FARMS, CAMPS & OUTDOOR PROGRAMS

Camp Run Amuck – Southeast County Road 40

Campsite and community hub.

Yaya, Lolli & Pop, volunteers

Yaya's Farm – Southeast County Road 40

Farm, gardens, community space

Yaya

Goat Yoga Pavilion -Southeast County Road 40

Wellness and farm programs

Carly, Ranger

Farmers Market – Town Center

Seasonal market

OTHER COMMUNITY BUSINESSES

Willow Ridge Garden Center – East Willow St.

Garden supply and nursery

Harry Windsor

Augustus Homes – East Willow St.

Construction company

Gus Franklin

KSW7- West Chestnut St.

Local News and Weather Station

MUSIC FROM THE VALLEY

These are the records and songs woven through the year. Some are played straight through, others arrive one at a time and stay longer than expected.

Find Lawhoma Hills Playlists on Spotify

YAYA'S NO SKIP ALBUMS

Spring
Tracy Chapman — Tracy Chapman
Bon Jovi — Slippery When Wet
Taylor Swift — Folklore
The Chicks — Fly
The Story— Brandi Carlile
Tyler Childers — Bottles and Bibles

Summer
Harry Styles — Harry Styles

Brothers Osborne — Port Saint Joe
Ed Sheeran— Divide
Eric Church — 61 Days of Church, Volumes 1–5
Kings of Leon — Come Around Sundown
Ashley McBryde — Ashley McBryde Presents: Lindeville

Fall
10,000 Maniacs — Our Time in Eden
Pearl Jam — Ten
Sturgill Simpson—The Ballad of Dood & Juanita
Tyler Childers — Live on Red Barn Radio I and II
AC/DC — Back in Black
*Taylor Swift — The Tortured Poets Department: The
     Anthology*

Winter
Elton John — Madman Across the Water
Prince — Purple Rain
Fleetwood Mac — Rumours
Sturgill Simpson— Metamodern Sounds in Country Music
In These Silent Days— Brandi Carlile
Caamp — Caamp
I'm With Her— Wild and Clear and Blue

SONGS FOR EVERY DAY

"Past Life" — Maggie Rogers
"Vagabond" — Caamp
"She's Got Her Ticket" — Tracy Chapman
"Sunday Mornin' Comin' Down" — Willie Nelson
"Hand in My Pocket" — Alanis Morissette
"It's a Great Day to Be Alive" — Travis Tritt
"And I Love Her" — Passenger
"Golden" — Harry Styles
"Keep Lookin' Up" — Kacey Musgraves

"Faith" — George Michael
"Strange Magic" — Electric Light Orchestra
"Jingle and Go" — Ryan Bingham
"Wildflowers" — Tom Petty
"Carry On Wayward Son" — Kansas
"Never Grow Up" — Taylor Swift TV
"Shine" — Collective Soul
"Hard Sun" — Eddie Vedder
"Celebration" — Kool and the Gang
*"Morning Comes Wearing Diamonds" — Ray
    LaMontagne*
"Back Down South" — Kings of Leon
"Turn the Page" — Bob Seger
"Rose Colored Glasses" — John Conlee
"At Last" — Etta James
"Famous in a Small Town" — Miranda Lambert
"Bonfire at Tina's" — Ashley McBryde
"Tough Little Boys" — Gary Allan
"Give a Little Bit" — Supertramp
"You're on Your Own, Kid" — Taylor Swift
"Revelry" — Kings of Leon
"Barton Hollow" — The Civil Wars
"Dog Days Are Over" — Florence and the Machine
"Little Bird" — Annie Lennox
"Broken Horses" — Brandi Carlile
"Rock Salt and Nails" — Tyler Childers
"Turtles All the Way Down" — Sturgill Simpson
"Sleep on the Floor" — The Lumineers
"What's Up" — 4 Non Blondes
"S.O.B." — Nathaniel Rateliff and the Night Sweats
"Biggest Part of Me" — Ambrosia
"Lost Without You" — Freya Ridings
"Mony Mony" — Billy Idol
"Big Yellow Taxi" — Joni Mitchell
"Make It a Good One" — Brothers Osborne
"The Harvest" — Tyler Childers

"South Dakota" — gavn!
"Jet Airliner" — Steve Miller Band
"Sleeping on the Blacktop" — Colter Wall
"Famous Blue Raincoat" — Jennifer Warnes
"Lifetime" — Justin Bieber
"The Banjo Song" — Mumford & Sons
"Work Song" — Hozier
"Pyro" — Kings of Leon
"Pushing Up Daisies" — Brothers Osborne
"The Water Is Wide" — James Taylor
"Sister Christian" — Night Ranger
"Matilda" — Harry Styles

MUSIC INSIDE CHAPTERS

"Fantasy"- Mariah Carey
"Isn't She Lovely"- Stevie Wonder
"Gentle on My Mind" — Glen Campbell
"Rhinestone Cowboy" — Glen Campbell
"Wichita Lineman" — Glen Campbell
"Purple Rain" — Prince
"I Would Die 4 U" — Prince
"Let's Go Crazy" — Prince
"Sh-Boom" — The Chords
"Blue Moon" — Frank Sinatra
"Earth Angel" — The Penguins
"Popular" — Stephen Schwartz-Kristin Chenoweth
    (Wicked on Broadway Original Cast)
"Defying Gravity" — Stephen Schwartz- Kristin
    Chenoweth & Idina Menzel (Wicked on Broadway
    Original Cast)
"You Give Love a Bad Name" — Bon Jovi
"In The Air Tonight"- Phil Collins
"Jump" — Van Halen
"MMMBop" — Hanson

"Don't Stop Believin'" — *Journey*

"Summer of '69" — *Bryan Adams*

"Kiss Me" — *Sixpence None the Richer*

"Africa" — *Toto*

"Seventy-Six Trombones" — *Robert Preston(The Music Man on Broadway)*

"Iowa Stubborn" — *Meredith Wilson (The Music Man on Broadway)*

"We're All in This Together" — *High School Musical Cast*

"Gotta Go My Own Way" — *High School Musical 2 Cast*

"Breaking Free" — *High School Musical Cast*

"Jersey Giant" — *Elle King*

"Foggy Mountain Breakdown" — *Flat & Scruggs*

"Wildwood Flower" — *The Carter Family*

"Good Hearted Woman" — *Waylon Jennings and Willie Nelson*

"Will the Circle Be Unbroken" — *Nitty Gritty Dirt Band*

"Cotton Eyed Joe" — *Asleep at the Wheel*

"Hound Dog" — *Big Mama Thornton*

"Okie Dokie Stomp" — *Clarence Gatemouth Brown*

<h1 style="text-align: center">bibliography</h1>

RESEARCH AND REFERENCES

I have always believed the heart of a family beats strongest in the way it teaches its children. In Lawhoma, we learn at kitchen tables, on creek banks, in 4H barns, in classrooms, and in the middle of town meetings where somebody brings a folding chair and a question.

The pages of this book hold stories, but those stories rest on real soil. I read about prairie dogs and turtles and easements. I studied youth camps and conservation plans. I learned how fireflies glow and how wetlands heal. I listened to the language of tribes who were here long before any pink door stood upright on a porch.

When our children ask why the tornados come, or why a field matters, or how a goat gets tied at a rodeo, I believe we owe them more than a shrug. We owe them the right answers, or at least the honest search for them. From farming practices to wildlife protection, from cultural celebrations to climate conversations, I wanted Lawhoma to stand on something sturdy.

We read so our children know there is room for them. We read so a porcupine who speaks with his hands and a device is not left standing at the edge of the playground. We read so Diwali lights and Cinco de Mayo music and Sabbath candles are not foreign words but familiar tables with extra chairs pulled close.

I have known what it feels like to sit outside the circle. Books were the first place I found welcome. In Lawhoma Hills, we pass that welcome forward. We learn the names of plants and rivers. We learn the history of the land—the animals and people who came before us. We learn how to listen when someone speaks in a different way. That is the heart of our town. That is why these pages hold more than facts. They hold belonging.

———

Autism Speaks. "Augmentative Communication Road Map." Autism Speaks,
www.autismspeaks.org/sites/default/files/2018-08/Augmentative%20Communications%20Road%20Map%20%281%29.pdf
Referenced in relation to Micah's use of AAC communication tools and family education.

Autism Speaks. "Technology and Autism." Autism Speaks,
www.autismspeaks.org/technology-and-autism.
Supports discussion of assistive communication and adaptive technology in Micah's storyline.

Boy Scouts of America. *Eagle Scout Service Project Workbook.* Boy Scouts of America,
https://filestore.scouting.org/filestore/boyscouts/pdf/542-900.pdf
Referenced in Paddy Lucas's Eagle Scout challenge and leadership development.

Daggett County. "Junior Goat Tying Rules." Daggett County,
www.daggettcounty.gov/DocumentCenter/View/4588/2013-CCJR-rules.

Background material for junior goat tying involving Jasper and Ranger.

Fortier, Jacques. "Heterochromia." Jacques Fortier Art, 27 Feb. 2025, jacquesfortierart.com/2025/02/27/heterochromia/
Research reference for Beans and JJ Flanagan's heterochromia.

Goat Yoga by Lainey Morse. "Origins of Goat Yoga." Goat Yoga, goatyoga.net/lainey-morse/.
Historical background for the goat yoga at Camp Run Amuck with Ranger and Carly.

Indian Association of Oklahoma. Indian Association of Oklahoma, www.iaok.org/page-18260.
Referenced in connection with the Banerjee family and Diwali celebration.

National Geographic Kids. "Cinco de Mayo." National Geographic Kids, kids.nationalgeographic.com/history/article/cinco-de-mayo.
Used in Granny Shyra's explanation of Cinco de Mayo traditions.

National Geographic Kids. "What Is Climate Change?" National Geographic Kids, www.natgeokids.com/au/discover/geography/general-geography/what-is-climate-change/.
Referenced in youth discussions of climate change during drought and wildfire concerns.

Oklahoma Conservation Commission. "Economics of Conservation." Oklahoma Conservation Commission, conservation.ok.gov/wp-content/uploads/2021/07/20-10-minute-guide-economics-conservation.pdf.
Supports the volunteer group's conservation advocacy efforts.

Oklahoma Conservation Commission. "Legislator Guide to Conservation." Oklahoma Conservation Commission, https://conservation.ok.gov/wp-content/uploads/2021/07/29-20-minute-legislators.pdf

Background for civic engagement and legislative outreach within the conservation storyline.

Oklahoma Department of Wildlife Conservation. "Chicken Turtle." Oklahoma Department of Wildlife Conservation,
www.wildlifedepartment.com/sites/default/files/fedaid/T-75.pdf.

Research reference for Matty Benefield's chicken turtle conservation work.

Oklahoma Department of Wildlife Conservation. "Field Guide." Oklahoma Department of Wildlife Conservation,
www.wildlifedepartment.com/wildlife/field-guide.

Primary reference for recurring Oklahoma wildlife throughout the series.

Oklahoma Department of Wildlife Conservation. "Wildlife Youth Camp." Oklahoma Department of Wildlife Conservation,
www.wildlifedepartment.com/education/youth-opp/wildlife-youth-camp.

Inspiration for Camp Run Amuck and youth conservation programming.

Oklahoma Department of Wildlife Conservation. "Winged Mapleleaf." Oklahoma Department of Wildlife Conservation,
www.wildlifedepartment.com/wildlife/field-guide/invertebrates/winged-mapleleaf.

Referenced in Bet Sinclair's environmental research for at risk species in Oklahoma.

Oklahoma Historical Society. "Sac and Fox Nation." *Encyclopedia of Oklahoma History and Culture*,
www.okhistory.org/publications/enc/entry?entry=SA001.

Historical background for Tallulah Sweetstripe and tribal context.

Oklahoma State University Extension. "An Introduction to Fireflies." Oklahoma State University Extension,
https://extension.okstate.edu/fact-sheets/an-introduction-to-fire flies.html
Scientific background for Oklahoma presence of fireflies.

Oklahoma State University Extension. "Gardening and Lawn Care in Oklahoma." Oklahoma State University Extension,
extension.okstate.edu/topics/plants-and-animals/gardening-and-lawn-care/
Referenced in Yaya's gardening practices and seasonal planting discussions.

Oklahoma State University Extension. "Prairie Dog Ecology and Management in Oklahoma." Oklahoma State University Extension,
extension.okstate.edu/fact-sheets/prairie-dog-ecology-and-manage-ment-in-oklahoma.html.
Background for keystone species discussions in youth education scenes.

Oklahoma State University Extension. "Protecting Open Lands Through Conservation Easements." Oklahoma State University Extension,
https://extension.okstate.edu/fact-sheets/protecting-open-lands-in-farms-and-ranches-from-development-through-conservation-easements. html#how-is-the-value-of-a-conservation-easem
Research support for the land trust and conservation easement storyline.

ReNEW Wetlands Program. "Guidelines FY26." Oklahoma Water Resources Board,
wetlands.ok.gov/wp-content/uploads/2025/11/1.-Guidelines_Re NEW_Program_FY26-11-24-2025.pdf.
Referenced in Matty, Bet, and volunteer wetland restoration efforts.

Sac and Fox Nation. "Talk Sauk." Sac and Fox Nation,
www.sacandfoxnation-nsn.gov/talk-sauk/

Cultural language reference for Tallulah Sweetstripe and Butter Sweetstripe's cards.

Smithsonian Latino Center. "Day of the Dead Resources." Smithsonian Latino Center,
    https://latino.si.edu/learn/teaching-and-learning-resources/day-dead-resources
    Referenced in Granny Shyra's discussion of Día de los Muertos traditions.

Texas Oklahoma Regional Consortium of Herbaria (TORCH). TORCH,
    https://portal.torcherbaria.org/portal/index.php
    Referenced by Rosemary Rodriguez in her work as a botanist.

YouTube. -Next Level Ride- Wakeboarding- Video YouTube,
    www.youtube.com/watch?v=6LLWPiF1r_o.
    Visual reference for Stetson, Kolby, and Micah wakeboarding with the overhead cable system at Blue Creek Lake. .

acknowledgments

I grew up running in a track field made from an empty prairie pasture in a tiny map-dot town in Oklahoma. I ran every morning with the high school girls' track team coached by my Daddy. I can vividly remember the smell of spring soil coming to life, the sensation of my lungs burning after each lap, and the sound of my four-year-old feet hitting the dry ground in hand-me-down shoes that were a size too big and covered in mud from the big brother who wore them first. I got to go back home and have a cup of coffee on the red bench with my oldest brother, who always made it the perfect milky white with creamer. These are the mornings of my childhood I will forever romanticize, because so many others did not start or end with the happiness of running into my Daddy's arms. These were the days that shaped me, at least the ones I keep tucked in my back pocket, so for those mornings I am grateful until my last breath.

How do I acknowledge two little gulf fritillary butterflies that came to me that summer the boys were growing inside my baby? I do not know how, other than to look up at Mother Nature and acknowledge that she sent them to me for reassurance, and the same sensation of my four-year-old happiness on the dirty track field returned to me, a comfort I had not felt in many years.

I am nothing in my days without the constant companionship of Rizzo Jane and Beans, so to my dogs, thank you for lying at my feet and beside me in the bed for every keystroke I hit while I ignored walks and hikes to put this together. RJ, you can keep the pillows at the top, and Beanzee boy, you are always welcome under my covers.

To my other half in this lifetime, in one house or miles apart, Papa J, you are my everything, you old grouch bag. No one else could say, "What the hell, Crazy Woman," and have it simply mean you love me.

To my children, no words I can type will ever explain that this book comes from me getting to be your Momma. The deep catch of my breath when I even think of your faces is all I need in my days. To Tullahoma and Lawton, the birthplaces of my babies; that together, named Lawhoma for me.

For BDP—You and your family spread a giant canopy of love and shelter that comes with a full tank of laughter and chaos, all in the best forms. Thank you for loving my kid and for sharing them all with her and me despite my constant attempts at distance. I am overwhelmed by seeing the husband and Daddy you are.

For Ross and Gladys, our neighbors on 44th. Thank you for teaching me about a garden—how to get used to the sticky itch from picking okra, for sharing the mimosa tree on our property line, and most of all for letting me use the honeysuckle vines on our fence row as my first set of hurdles.

To my parents, I choose to believe those cardinals I see every day are you letting me know you are together again, but this time it is peaceful and loving for both of you. I know you are holding tight to your sons and grandson there with you and sending them my love each time we speak near the feeders.

Now, over the mushy stuff.

Thank you to each one of my beta readers who gave me thoughtful feedback and helped a nurse with a journal write a better book.

To my writing and editing coach, my answer when I asked a million times, "How do I write this smell or that feeling," or "How do I set up a website," or "What is better, Scrivener or Google Docs," or "Should I buy Vellum?" Every question I asked, you answered. You never once yelled at my overuse of metaphors and similes. Best of all you taught me find and replace in Scrivener! Vivienne, you are worth every cent.

To a magical librarian in another map-dot Oklahoma town, Maggie, I am so glad I walked in and started a conversation. Endless thank you for the encouragement to include a bibliography in a fiction book. The day you said, "A story like this can help raise readers, and we need more folks raising readers."

To my real job work family, you did not know I would borrow names from you or your children and grandchildren seen in our Slack channels —or create a fox that runs a remote nursing team while managing their equipment. I am proud of stealing inspiration from what we do each day to truly love our patients and from each of you in the trenches of work-from-home life across the country alongside me.

To Paul at the print shop in yet another map-dot Oklahoma town, thank you—sir, for teaching me how to take my photos and turn them into my watercolor illustrations. Thank you for helping take my wackadoodle vision of Lawhoma's world of characters and their businesses, drawn in my chicken scratch with pencil and pastels, and making them into the digital copies good enough, despite the art, to put in print.

Melinda, thank you for the videos, Zooms, the text screenshots, and the no panic when I wanted to cuss at Adobe InDesign, and for knowing when to make me tell myself it is good enough, that a millimeter of color is going to be okay.

To every Gen X reader, please know that if there are two spaces after a period in one spot and not in another, or an overuse of the Oxford comma, twenty-seven edits later and eyes rolled at me directly by my much younger editing crew, I left them in for us. Because if we grew up buying a goat named Munchie at a flea market, then rode home in the back of a truck with said goat, drank from the water hose barefoot on red dirt in 100-degree weather, well—we are tough enough to stand for the things that gave us our spine and old enough to know it was time to stop letting others edit us.

For PDP—Danielle Marie at Pink Door Publishing, thank you most of all.

COMING SOON

Blue Creek Lake Recipes

A companion collection from the tables of Lawhoma Hills

Coming Next in the Lawhoma Hills Series

Book Two

Lawhoma Hills: When the Rain Did Not Come

Summer settles hard over Lawhoma. The rain holds back. Wells sink lower. Pastures thin beneath a white sky. Burn bans stretch across the county while the nature preserve rises board by board on the west side of Blue Creek Lake.

The Banned Book Club finds its footing and its voice, gathering momentum far beyond Spruce Street Books through Wilder Kate Everett's growing channel. Big doors crack open for some of Lawhoma's young people. Others stand at crossroads they did not see coming.

Grief visits a familiar porch. Long-held land changes hands. Old roots loosen. New families arrive.

When one careless spark in a dry field turns wind into flame, Lawhoma faces the kind of test no town rehearses for.

In Lawhoma Hills, every season writes its mark across the land and the people who love it.

Come sit on the porch awhile:

Lawhoma Hills Website

Ellis McHale is a native Oklahoman, nursing educator, gardener, music lover, and the author of the Lawhoma Hills series. She created the fictional town of Lawhoma Hills; the families, businesses, traditions, and stories woven through its community. When she is not writing, she can usually be found in the garden, with her dogs nearby, or answering to the name Yaya from her twin grandsons. She is also the founder of Pink Door Publishing.